ISBN- 978-1-7384046-2-9

This novel is entirely a work of fiction. The names, characters and incidents portrayed in it are the work of the author's imagination. Any resemblance to actual persons, living or dead, events or localities is entirely coincidental.

Cover Art by Emma Russell
Illustrations by Emma Russell

Other Works by Emma Russell

Welcome to Wonderland

A Witch's Guide to Tipton

Content Warning:
This book contains conversations involving gaslighting and
has multiple descriptions of anxiety and panic attacks.

There are also comments made by characters that hint at
transphobia, swearing and a scene which depicts an assault.

Main Character Pronouns:
Grim- She/Her (later Xe/Xem)
Lukas- He/Him
Cain- He/Him
Remi- They/Them
Finn- He/They
Anna- She/Her
Ms White- She/Her

By Order of Chaos

To my Dad.
Because I'm an idiot, and this book should have been dedicated to you all along.
Thank you for believing in me from the moment I started writing this.

FINAL GRADES

Rosewood Evening School for the Advanced Magus

Class of 2010

Congratulations to all our graduating students! We know you are going to prosper and be wonderful Magus that the Order will be proud to welcome. This is the final standing among the class, which is a public document that is used by the Order and the prestigious Elderwall Boarding College, should you wish to apply there.

Lukas Lightchild- 99

Ahmed Diaz- 92

Caitlin Rahmen- 87

Kaira Glenn- 85

Jason Long- 80

Austin Regan- 76

Lacy Spence- 76

Tillie Moss- 72

Zavier Mays- 65

Raven Mortem- 32

It has been our pleasure to teach you over these last few years. We wish you all the best of luck in your future endeavours.

Bellery College & Sixth Form- Exam Results
Student Name- Raven Alexandra Mortem
Student Number- 238109

Fine Art   A*
History   A
English Literature   B

Bellery College & Sixth Form- Exam Results
Student Name- Lukas Lightchild
Student Number- 195782

Physics   B
History   B
Psychology   D

FAO: Lukas Lightchild

Dear Mr Lightchild,

Thank you for your application to Elderwall Boarding College. Following your exemplary grades and outstanding recommendations, we would be happy to offer you a place for this upcoming academic year.

The Order would never say no to a fine Magus such as yourself, and we have faith that you will thoroughly enjoy growing your abilities and expanding your horizons.

Please fill out the attached form to confirm your acceptance of the offer and keep an eye out in the coming weeks for information regarding your accommodation and plans for the academic year.

Faithfully,
Ms Audrey White.

Dean of Elderwall Boarding College

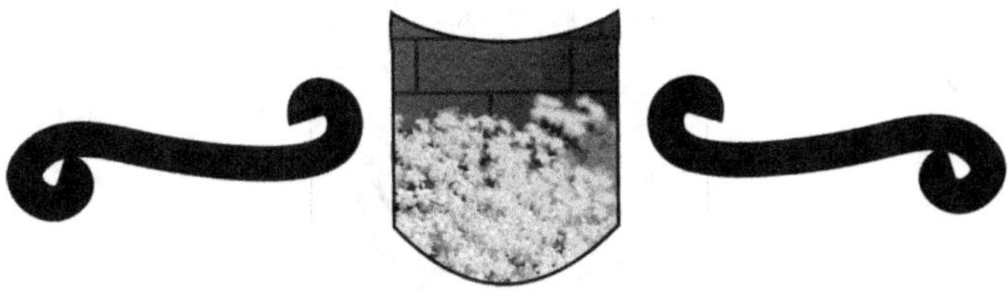

FAO: Raven Alexandra Mortem

Dear Miss Mortem

Thank you for your application to Elderwall Boarding College. After a personal conversation with your parents, who have been dedicated to the Order for many years, we have agreed the best course of action for you is to attend Elderwall.

We believe you have potential, you simply need guidance and encouragement, which this institution can offer you. When I meet you in person, we can discuss what additional classes you can take to improve your abilities.

Please fill out the attached form to confirm your acceptance of the offer and keep an eye out in the coming weeks for information regarding your accommodation and plans for the academic year.

Faithfully,

Ms Audrey White.

Dean of Elderwall Boarding College

My darling Raven,

I never thought I would see the day that my gorgeous girl would go off to Elderwall. It was a difficult path for us to get you here, and I know we hit plenty of obstacles along the way, but your father and I knew with enough determination, that **anything** *was possible.*

I understand that this is not what you wanted, but it's time for you to put aside foolish dreams and start thinking about your future. Your pursuit of art was a pipe dream, and I said that from the outset. It is time to start thinking rationally Ray.

We will no longer be indulging in this pastime of yours. Take a note from Lukas and put your focus on your progress as a Magus, take the extra classes, pass the exams, and do us proud. Our family name has a legacy, Raven. Do not bring it down from the heavens.

All my love,

Mother x

September

There were three things Grim noticed when she walked into the common room of Elderwall Boarding College. The place that would be her home for the next four years.

One.

There was a lot of magus. This shouldn't have been a surprise but surprised she was. There were more young people than she thought. More who wanted to aspire further as Magus and take their place amongst the Order.

Two.

The room was dark. Not dark as in *oh no alas I can no longer see,* but more of *they should invest in better lighting.* Despite the modern phenomena of electricity, this room had a classic approach. A roaring but completely safe fire was nestling in a cobbled fireplace. A far too intricate chandelier hung from the ceiling, lit with humming old bulbs that were fit to burst. The room had that old wallpaper you would find in regency homes. The kind that nobody would dare to replace, for the simplicity of it being history. The red wallpaper had gold leaves. Grim was almost certain it was real gold. The oak floor creaked with every student's step, neat and bound together with no dark gaps. The room was full of sofas, chairs, and armchairs. Chess sets sat on tables. Students, eager to please, gathered around them. They pulled up wooden chairs and challenged their newfound frenemies to a round.

Grim didn't know why she was paying attention to such things. It was a distraction technique.

Where was she?

Ah.

Three.

The students of Elderwall Boarding College were some of the most uptight, pretentious, and *moronic* people she had ever met.

Another surprise that shouldn't surprise her. What was she to expect? These were the people who cast their eyes downward on anybody who didn't pursue a life as a magus. Who used their talents as a party trick to flaunt. Who turned their noses up to the mere suggestion that's all they were; a flair for the dramatic.

Magus didn't do anything. Grim had realised that early on when she shadowed her parents for a day at the Order. She was thirteen and had spent the day listening to gossip and filling out unnecessary forms. The forms often involved the organisation of the Order's next board meeting.

The world didn't know about Magus, because Magus did nothing of note to make the world notice them. They drilled into her head that the Magus had been the frontrunners throughout history. They had encouraged inventors and industrialists

Was there any evidence of it? No.

Did that stop them from bragging about it? Definitely not.

The room was full with the next generation of them. Snobbish aristocrats who overestimate their importance. The whole room was too loud. Too much muffling chatter could numb even the sternest of minds. She had already arrived on edge, her heart racing, and this environment was making it worse.

She glanced across the room to her friend Lukas- well, the back of his blonde head. Steady, smart, and confident Lukas. He would have already made five friends and become a member of some prestigious club. A nice boy with a good heart, according to everyone who talked to him. And a good friend, one who had helped Grim through many trying times in her life. He was milder mannered than she would ever be. He turned around, smiling at her, and bid goodbye to his newfound acquaintances to sit back down next to her.

"It's pretty amazing, isn't it?" He said with a stupid grin on his face.

"Don't make me stab you with a pencil Lukas."

He kept his smile, running a hand through his dirty blonde hair. "Ouch, first day and you're already grumpy."

"I got up at 5 am to get the train here. Forgive my lack of perkiness."

Lukas laughed. Grim heard some girls whispering and giggling as they walked past the two of them. Out of the corner of her eye, she saw them pointing at Lukas. An immediate realisation came to her, and she knew what they were laughing about.

"You've got admirers already." She said to him, gesturing to them as the group walked to the sofa by the fireplace. "It's college all over again."

"Not again." He groaned.

"What do you mean not again?"

He shrugged. "It's…distracting, you know?"

"For god's sake Lukas." Grim punched him in the arm. "You're one of the smartest first-years. Your scores were some of the highest in the country. People are going to know you, it's unavoidable. Get off your high horse about it."

"Sure..." He shrugged at her, distracted by something.

Grim rolled her eyes, nudging him again, encouraging him to smile. "You're going to be the stellar student, who plays sports, has a heart of gold and all that bullshit. Then I will be your sidekick who everyone thinks you took pity on."

"Don't sell yourself short like that."

"It's an inevitability, Lukas. History repeats itself."

"Listen, Grim, you could be a great Magus-,"

Someone came over to the table, interrupting him. Grim recognised him from the welcome talk they had that morning. It was Oscar, a fourth-year student. He had stood in front of a hall full of happy-go-lucky first-years that morning. The light in the room reflected on his round glasses with gold rims and made his dark brown hair shimmer. His dark skin was smooth, and there was a huge smile on his face. "Lukas! Hey!"

"What's up, Oscar? This is a night for the first years." Lukas replied, a joking smile on his face, already speaking full of charm.

"Oh yeah, like you guys have any authority." He rolled his eyes, but the smile never left him. "Listen, I spotted Remi, I want you to talk with them about the student council."

Lukas stood up. "Great idea!" He turned to Grim with a wink. "I'll be back soon."

He left. And Grim sat on the table, alone once more. She flicked a chess piece over with her hand and groaned to herself. But realising that the noise was too loud, she panicked, putting the chess piece back upright. Guess who's stuck quiet again. She looked around the room, dulled to the sensation of excitement.

She decided to end the suffering.

With her chest still messy and her head a blur, Grim kept her head hung low and walked out of the room. She pushed open the heavy double door and walked into the corridor.

Then immediately crashed into something.

"Shit!"

Actually. Crashed into someone.

Grim looked up. He had black hair and dark eyes. They were almost black like Grim's were. He was wearing an old denim jacket over a shirt, with some dark jeans. For a moment, Grim frowned. He and Lukas looked alike, but she could not put her finger on it.

She stepped back and put her hands up. "Sorry, I am so sorry. Really-,"

"Hey, hey, don't worry about it!" He smiled at her. "I wasn't looking where I was going- are you okay?"

Grim shrugged, plastering a fake smile. "Why wouldn't I be? I'm here, aren't I?"

He chuckled. "You don't have to pretend with me you know?"

"I came out of a room of pretenders." Grim rolled her eyes. "If you'll excuse me, I'm going to head back to my room."

She started walking, but he walked with her, adding to the sudden awkwardness of the situation. "Are you sure you're okay?" He asked, with persistence.

"Yeah, of course."

"Can I at least walk you back to your room? This is a big place. It's easy to get lost."

She stopped walking and turned to him. Grim noticed his pale skin, tinged with pink, and the ache in her chest tightened. "I'm fine." She explained, with a firm and adamant tone.

He sighed, rocking backwards on his toes to be dramatic about it. "Okay, can I at least get your name?

"It's Grim."

"Grim? I didn't see that name on the score sheet."

She smirked. "You wouldn't."

He smiled at her. "You have humour. I like that. I'm Cain."

"Cain? I didn't see your name on the score sheet."

Cain let out a bark of laughter, and Grim let her wall come down a little and held back a laugh.

"You wouldn't." He said, with a wink. Grim stumbled on her feet a little bit, holding her head, and Cain noticed. "Hey, come sit down. You look a little out of it."

There was a bench in the hallway, a simple wooden one shoved against the wall. A few more were along the hallway, under the windows, where the moonlight streamed in. He led her to the bench and sat her down. "Can I get you some water?" He asked, his voice soft.

Grim shook her head. "No, no, it's fine."

Cain smiled a little. "Were you also tired of being in a room of pretentious wannabes?"

She rolled her eyes but smiled back. "A little."

"There are some rare gems in that pile of rocks, but I couldn't stand being in there."

"Neither could I, to be honest. I'm not good with people."

"Well, you're doing pretty good with me."

"Thanks, I guess." She rubbed her forehead a little bit. "I don't even know what I'm doing here."

"If you're like me, then this wasn't your first choice of life after college. I don't want to stick my hand into a fire to find out my abilities and whether I'm worthy."

The Baptism of Fire. The Order's way of discerning what their next generation of Magus looked like. New students, after they had settled in and taken their first classes, took part in the ceremony. The fire never hurts, but you feel the magick rushing through you. Then when the flickering flames shift hues, that's when you know what you can specialise in. All your classes shift to that focus. The classes you took growing up helped cover the basics before the Baptism took place.

As somebody with a complete lack of ability, the ceremony terrified Grim.

"I cannot believe it's still a thing."

"Neither can I," Cain said with a shrug. "Seems such a trivial way of determining someone's power. It's limiting."

"I don't want to get burned."

"Why would you-,"

The double doors swung open back towards the common room, and Lukas stood there with one hand on the door. The liveliness of the room was bursting behind him.

"I was looking for you, Grim! What's going on?"

Grim immediately stood up again and stepped away from Cain. "I was heading back to my room."

"Why would you do that? I was going to get you to meet Remi and Oscar." He smiled, proud of himself. "I got into the student council."

She grinned at him. "Congrats, but I still want to head back."

"Are you sure?" Lukas asked, glancing over at Cain, who stood watching the two of them. He had a small smile on his face, for some odd reason.

Grim nodded. "I'm sure. I'll be fine. Have a good night for me."

Lukas raised an arm and mock saluted her as he shut the door. "Yes ma'am!"

Cain looked back at her. Before he could say anything, she turned and walked away, calling back to him from over her shoulder.

"See you around Cain. Was a pleasure."

third floor. lukas is on fourth.
to classroom is down the stairs to first floor. turn left. fifth door on the right. opposite the windows.
the grand hall. can't wait to burn my skin off with a smile on my face.
X marks the spot. I guess!
Startching's classroom. Our first lesson is here
there are multiple common rooms. ugh. for some reason this one is ours.
the dining hall. We cannot eat unless told to...it sucks.
dining hall is on first floor. next to the grand hall.
the common room. apparently they're holding us a party here after orientation

The first day of class would thwart even the mightiest of confidence. The uncertainty of the knowledge gifted upon them. The curiosity of whether one could prove themselves. It all fed into this pit of worry.

Grim had woken up on this first morning of class. She was ready to systematically break everything in sight. Only stopping when she was satisfied there was enough carnage. She never liked the beginning of anything. There was always too much uncertainty with no outlet until the end.

Grim's neighbour was the complete opposite. Minda was a fourth-year student. She had experienced the full force of Elderwall and adored every part of it. Minda now took on the responsibility of being a mentor to the first years, and Grim was on her list of newcomers. The two of them hadn't talked much since Grim arrived. But, Minda had knocked on Grim's door that morning. with a declaration of passion that she should head off to her first class.

"It's the first day of your brand-new adventure Raven!" Minda had explained, as she tucked a hairpin in to hold her rose-pink headscarf into place. "You've got an introductory class with Professor Starching this morning- don't worry he's not as scary as he looks.

"Great."

The conversation hadn't extended beyond that point.

When Grim reached the classroom, the room was already alive with anticipation. Rows of tables and chairs ascended the steps, curving around the front of the room, with an empty teacher's desk. There were only a few empty seats.

Grim's eyes wandered up to the back of the room. She saw Lukas chatting away with a group of people she didn't recognise. New friends, he had made in an instant that morning.

"Hey, do you wanna sit here?"

She looked back to the front of the room at the voice. A young man with thick curly hair, freckled dark skin and chestnut eyes greeted her. He looked like the younger version of Oscar. Next to him was a young woman, with pale skin, dark eyes, and black hair combed into a ponytail. She sat in her wheelchair at the end of the table.

The young man waved a hand at her. "You're Grim, right? Lukas' friend."

"How did you know that?" She asked.

"Oscar's my brother."

That explains his appearance.

He continued. "Although I don't really talk to Oscar much, I still hear things. Anyway, I'm Finn, this is Anna."

The woman, Anna, looked up from her notebook and smiled. "Hi!"

"So, do you want to sit down?"

Grim looked back up at Lukas, who was still chatting away with his new group. She shrugged. "If you don't mind."

"If we had a problem with it, Finn wouldn't have offered," Anna explained, then grinned at Finn. "But then again nothing can stop Finn from being nice."

"Excuse me I can be mean sometimes."

Grim nudged past Finn and Anna to sit down and pulled out her textbook and a notepad. Anna punched Finn in the arm. "You couldn't cast a spell on a bunny rabbit."

"Bitch, I *totally* could." Finn tried to toss his hair back, and the two broke down laughing.

"Sure, keep telling yourself that." Anna leaned forward to face Grim. "So, how did you find last night? I didn't see you around."

"I left early."

"We stayed for what…half an hour? It was boring as hell." Finn explained, reaching down into his bag to grab a pen. "Everyone was…dull."

"That's pretty much how I felt."

"It's how we all felt." Anna chuckled. "They sold Elderwall to be this glossy, beautiful place. I hope it starts to meet expectations.

The door to the classroom swung open. The not-to-worry-about-he's-not-that-scary Professor Starching walked in. He walked with a black cane and had a lack of any silver hair on his head, but he made up for it with a neat, grey-combed beard. He wore a shirt, tie and waistcoat, with suit trousers, all coordinated in a deep ocean blue. He walked with purpose to the front of the classroom, looking up at the faces of the new, and nervous magus recruits.

"Welcome students, to the beginning of your new lives. What you learned as teenagers in your evening classes will expand here. At last, you can use your magickal abilities to their fullest potential. You will become an integral part of the Order. Today we will be refreshing your memory on the main principles. In our next class, I will give you your first assignment. But first-,"

Starching raised his hand, and turned his wrist, summoning a piece of paper into his hand and reading it. "Let's start from the bottom…Raven Mortem?"

Shit. Shit. Shit.

With no haste, she raised her hand, and Randall smiled in her direction.

"Ah, wonderful, you're here. Please explain the principle of sympathy."

Grim tapped her book with her pen, a rhythm of nerves. Then muscle memory kicked in.

"The similarity of two objects can serve as a carrier so that influence may pass between them. The more alike these objects are, the more easily they can and will affect each other. These objects do not have to be similar in the literal sense but can be a representation or a concept. An example of this would be using the power of planetary alignments and lunar cycles to achieve specific goals."

The whole room was brewing in silence, and Grim felt ready to melt back into her seat. The comfort of a skill drilled into her made her speak without thinking. Everyone turned to her.

"*Raven.*" Starching was stern. "I would appreciate it if you did not read aloud out of the textbook."

Grim sighed through her nose, clenching her fists. Finn and Anna looked over at her with worried eyes.

She closed the textbook in front of her. Her hands were shaking, but she held them together to keep them steady. With her voice stern, she started again.

"The similarity of two objects can serve as a carrier so that influence may pass between them. The more alike these objects are, the more easily they can and will affect each other. These objects do not have to be similar in the literal sense but can be a representation or a concept. An example of this would be using the power of planetary alignments and lunar cycles to achieve specific goals."

The room broke out into whispers, and Grim would have preferred not to hear what they were saying.

"Bet she used a spell so she could pass the exam."

"But she *barely* passed. Someone told me she failed all the practical assessments."

Starching, to her surprise, smirked at her. "Please accept my apologies. That was most impressive."

Four basic principles: sympathy, correspondence, contagion, causality

Sympathy- The more alike two things are, the more easily they can and do affect each other- the similarity of the two things serves as a carrier for influence to be passed between them.

Manipulate an aspect of reality by manipulating what is available to you

Example. Attuning to the planets

Elemental principle

Correspondence- "as above, so below", things which exist in one part of existence are represented in all other parts of existence.

Often confused with sympathy. The difference is sympathy is influence, and correspondence is representation.

Big ties to astrology. Even though the Magus thinks astrology doesn't work.

Skulduggery principle

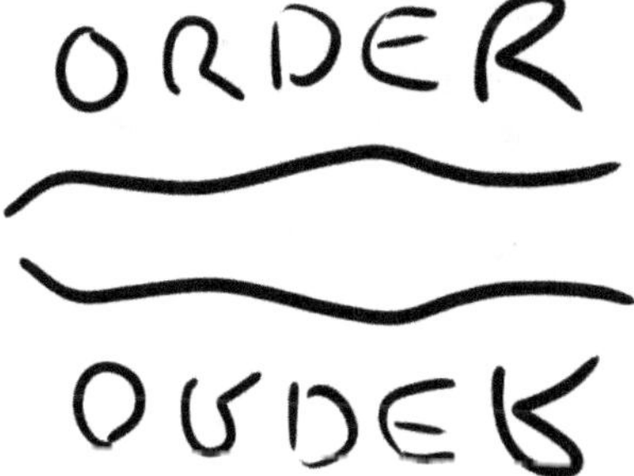

Contagion- Two objects/people that come into contact share a magical link that persists at some level of potency

Summoner principle

Causality- Addresses the relationship between events- an initial event contributes to the production of an event that follows it. Cause and effect

The most basic of Magus principles. but the cause and effect of something is more complex than basic everyday events

Psychic principle

As promised, Starching gave out the first assignment in the next class. A full research paper about one of the focuses of magick. Along with a practical demonstration to the class, which will be due in November. Perfect timing for before the Baptism of Fire. All Magus had evening classes in high school to understand the basics of each focus. Enough knowledge to show off when they got to Elderwall.One part of this task was easy, but the other part was not so much. Grim was already thinking too far ahead. She was churning through the sources she could cite in the paper. Working out what principle she could demonstrate. She tried to ignore the part of her that was saying she would fail miserably during it.

She had read so many books before arriving at Elderwall. Whatever the evening classes would give her, she would read. Whatever books her parents approved, she would read. The information never made sense to her. At least she could memorise it to the extent of reciting it back to anyone who asked.

Finn and Anna thought she was some kind of badass super genius. They kept asking her for tips during class on how to remember the material. Grim hadn't sat with Lukas. He had found a fabulous group of people from class. Either they are on the school council, the football team, the honour society…or all three.

Despite this, they had been catching up at breakfast. Grim liked to let Lukas talk. He always had a conversation topic, enjoying the freedom of being able to talk about his interests. Grim let him talk.

Lukas was waiting for her outside at the end of Starching's class, leaning against one of the walls.

She noticed his dull expression. "What's going on with you?"

"I didn't know you had become friends with Finn." He explained, flicking through the notebook in his hand.

"We have sat together in two classes. I wouldn't exactly call us friends yet." Grim retorted, crossing her arms. "He knew you through Oscar."

Lukas nodded, smiling a little. "Oscar always says Finn doesn't take being here seriously."

She frowned. "Maybe you shouldn't judge Finn without meeting him."

He gave her a small smile and put a hand on his shoulder. "And I want to make sure you're meeting the right people. Rumours fly fast around here, you heard what people were saying after you made a show of reciting that text."

"What are you even-,"

"How long have we been friends Grim?" His tone had changed with urgency, that it made Grim step back, and his hand fell.

"We met when we were four. You gave me a flower; I threw dirt at you." She said, having explained this so many times to everyone who had ever asked.

The smile came back again. Lukas had always liked the story. "Exactly. We've stuck by each other through everything. I don't want either of us to start hanging around with the wrong kind of people."

"And Finn's the wrong kind of person?"

"I'm not saying that-,"

"You are saying that. It's all over your face."

Lukas stopped for a moment, his mouth curving and ready to say something else, but Grim spoke before he could.

"I know you mean well. But not everyone is like you Lukas. Not everyone gets the top grades or wants to work for the Order or is generally…perfect. I'm not, and you don't think I'm the wrong kind of person."

He sighed, dropping his hands. "But it's you. That's different."

She shook her head. "Please get over yourself. You're hanging out with different people, and so am I. It's not going to change anything."

"I know that. I'm not stupid." He rolled his eyes, closing the notebook. "You could be a great magus, Grim. I want to know you're going to stay on the right track."

"Ugh, god Lukas you sound like my parents."

He chuckled, removing all the tension between the two of them himself. Lukas and Grim never argued, only disagreed. He was often the one who decided when the disagreement ended. Grim never had a problem with avoiding an hour-long disagreement with her best friend.

"I'll drop it…" He suddenly paused and called out. "Hey George!"

Lukas leaned out and looked over Grim's shoulder and waved down the corridor. Grim turned around and another student was sprinting toward them. She recognised him immediately from class. He was the one who was sitting next to Lukas, all the way at the back of the room. He looked as if he didn't have a care in the world. Oversized clothing and his brown hair tied in a bun at the top of his head, dark circles under his cocoa eyes. But if Grim knew the company Lukas always desired around him, looks would deceive.

"George, perfect timing. This is Grim."

He said her name with a suspicious amount of emphasis, and George responded to it with perfection. His mouth dropped into a small circle shape, which then morphed into a bright smile.

"Grim!" George thrust his hand out towards her. "Lukas has told me all about you. I can see why he likes you."

She shook his hand, carefully. "What do you mean by that?" She looked at Lukas. "What did you tell him?"

Lukas' cheeks were pink, and he rubbed the back of his neck with his hand. "Uh- I was talking about you, that's all."

George laughed. "All nice things don't worry. Listen, what you did in class-,"

Lukas immediately cut in. "Let's not George-,"

He continued talking to Grim. "How did you know that? I can't even remember the opening to that textbook."

"I…did some extra reading." She replied, shrugging and trying to dismiss the conversation elsewhere.

This was not the time to bring up all the reading Grim's parents made her do outside of school. The very long nights of drowning in magick theory. The constant reciting. No, not the time to talk about that in front of Lukas' new friend.

"Huh." George seemed to have taken the hint and glanced at Lukas. "Has he introduced you to anyone else?"

She shook her head. "No, not yet."

He seemed to know something Grim didn't. His keen smile turned into a big grin. "Lukas here has met all the right people. Everyone is talking about him."

She wanted out of this conversation. She gripped her notebook tight to stop her from fidgeting with her hands.

George nodded again. "If what you did today is anything to go by…you're going to be a great asset to Lukas while you're both here."

"E-e-excuse me-?" She sputtered out, and Lukas took a step forward towards George.

"George, what does that mean?"

"I didn't mean anything by it!" He put his hands up in defence. "Do you know how hard it is to find anyone at this school who knows how to research as she does?"

Grim inhaled, sharp and quick. "You could address me. I'm standing right here."

"Sorry, sorry-." He turned back to Grim. George seemed to realise he had dug himself a hole. "What I'm trying to say is…when you join the Order, you need the right people around you. Grim, you seem like the right person Lukas needs. I'm sorry it came across the wrong way."

Lukas sighed. "It's okay George, I get it. We should head off. I'll see you at football practice?"

George nodded, and the two boys high-fived each other. He strode off, leaving Lukas and Grim together as they were before.

Grim could feel her vision starting to blur. She closed her eyes, for a second.

"What is it?"

She opened her eyes. "He was apologising to you, not to me."

"What? He said that to you."

"But I didn't get to respond."

Lukas sighed. "George is like that. Sometimes he doesn't think before he speaks."

"You've known him for a day why are you justifying his behaviour?"

"Because unlike you I'm trying to give everyone a chance."

That hit hard. The thought hit her that she was the one in the wrong because Lukas always did everything right.

"You know why I struggle with people."

"No- I know the excuse you give though."

"It's not an excuse."

He sighed, lowering his head. When he looked back up, he gave her a soft smile. "Grim, I know you're doing your best, but you can do better. I know you can. I'm not going to have us spend our time at Elderwall arguing. Let's forget about it, okay?"

Lukas was all she had. And all she would ever have. So, she nodded and returned the smile.

A Magus should be strong willed, with high intellect. A Magus should be willing to dedicate their life to the Order, ready to cast all unnecessary elements of their life to do what is right for us, and for the world. A Magus should be calm, cool and collected. Ready for whatever challenges they may face. A shining example to the rest of the world.

This is what we hope happens when our young Order members attend Elderwall Boarding College. These are the values we encourage in our (unique) education system. We encourage our students to study before they turn eighteen, attending the Mortal education system to learn more about the world they will soon impact. *i preferred the mortal education system* When a Magus graduates from Elderwall Boarding College, they are expected to take a role among the Order. Those who help the Order are supported by the Order for the rest of their lives, such is the way we have been operating for centuries.

We welcome our new members in a ceremony, during which they take an oath swearing their loyalty and lifetime devotion to the Order. The oath is as follows:

I (name), herby swear to honour the foundations and laws of the Order. I swear to keep our secret from Mortals, to serve my fellow Magus, and help this world progress with the ability that has been gifted upon me.
I will honour my family name, I will honour my ancestors, and I will claim my birthright. I understand now that greatness has been gifted to me, and I will not waste the opportunity. *greatness appears in every Order book…*
starting to wonder why we are so obsessed
After the oath is sworn, then the Magus in question is able to find their place amongst the Order. There are many positions available suitable for a wide range of skill sets, so do not fear if you do not know which path you wish to take. Such positions can include (Research, Administration, Community Leaders, and many more.

Even if there is not a position for you within the Order, you can still fulfil your duty as a Magus. Many of our members also have jobs among the. Mortals, helping them in areas that can aid the progress of humanity. Many Magus are currently working with scientists, politicians and inventors, helping to shape a future we can all live in.
but heaven forbid a Mortem has a Mortal job

50

"I still think what you did in class was wrong."

Grim stopped in the middle of scanning a bookshelf. Her hand hovered, as a switch of doubt flicked on in her brain. "I thought it was pretty cool…"

"That's not what everyone else thought." He said with a shrug, reaching up to grab a book from a shelf above him. "You need to think about what others think sometimes."

"Why should I care?" She turned to him, frowning.

He stepped forward and put a hand on her shoulder. His thumb brushed her neck, and she shivered, almost wanting to pull away. "Because I don't want it to be like our classes growing up, where you got shunned for being you."

Grim stepped back so his hand dropped. He straightened himself up, and for a moment, Grim saw a flash of disappointment on his face, but it was gone. He turned back to the shelves. "Now…what principle are you going to try and explain?"

She had almost forgotten the reason that they were in the library. They had both agreed to research their presentations together. The principles of magic were a long-unused concept, but Elderwall made them relevant. It was important to understand how you could work with magick before the Baptism. The Magus liked to think of themselves above everyone. But, they still had to obey the laws that magick laid out for them. Understanding the fundamental principles was a key part of that.

"I'm thinking causality. One event leading to another is obvious to show." She traced the spines of the books once more. "Might do that electricity example they taught us back when we were fifteen."

"That's a straightforward one even you can do. I'm thinking correspondence."

She nodded. "You always had a knack for that."

Lukas bundled the books he had grabbed in his arms. "I'm going to go grab us a study table. Do you need anything else?"

Grim looked down at the list she had made on a scrap piece of paper. "I need something from a few shelves down. I'll meet you there."

"Cool, see you in a bit."

He walked off, heading to a different section of the library. This was one of the only things that excited Grim about coming to the college. The Library of Elderwall was world-renowned. A hive of knowledge tracing back centuries, right to the beginning of the Magus. The library took up a large section of the college. It took inspiration from old churches. The kind the Magus used when the Order was first established. The roof pointed upwards. There was a huge stained-glass window that shone rainbow lights across the library. The walls were lit with small oil lamps. There were two floors to the library, the second floor hung over the first, the shelves guarded by rails. She hadn't had time to go up the spiral staircases. Grim desired to see the heavy tomes. The ones bound in old cracked leather. She wanted to feel the crinkled pages with her delicate fingertips. Liking books and libraries was a strange passion, and one Lukas always teased her about. But there was something beautiful about hearing nothing but echoing footsteps and the frantic turning of pages.

She turned a corner, looking down at her list. "242.5…"

"Oh, hey Grim!"

She looked up to see Cain at the other end of the row, a book in his hand. She waved, trying to be polite. "Good to see you again."

"Yeah! I'm trying to navigate the shelves." He thought for a moment. "Looking for…267.2?"

Grim chuckled. "You were at the right end."

She immediately went down to where Cain was and spotted the number he mentioned. Within five seconds, she offered him the book.

"Damn, you're good." He said with a grin, taking the book off her.

Grim shrugged, dismissing the compliment. "I've spent a lot of time in libraries. You learn the system."

She turned back to the shelves and grabbed 242.5. *A Beginner's Guide to Magickal Principles.*

"By the way, random thing, but I never got to tell you. That thing you did in Starching's class-,"

"Please don't mention it." She interrupted him and covered her face with one hand. "I know I screwed up so-,"

"What? I was going to say that was the most *badass* thing I have ever seen!" Cain sounded so enthusiastic; despite the fact, that he was keeping his voice down in the library. "How could you recite that?"

She turned her face away, feeling her face heat up. "Photogenic memory? I don't know, I…remember useless shit."

He started laughing. "Teach me your ways! That's such a skill."

Grim laughed as well. She couldn't help it; Cain had some sort of infectious encouragement.

"It's not."

"I'm coming to you when I need research help, it's official."

She didn't know how to respond to that. "Sure."

"So…" Cain filled the awkward silence that had awakened between them. "How much have you read? About magick and the Order. You seem to have a pretty good grip on things."

"Whatever my parents got a hold of for me. Read all the history books, theory books… a lot of useless information to be honest."

Cain nodded, leaning on one side against the bookshelf and looking at her. "My dad works in the archives at the Order, so he was always good for historical stuff. Have you ever noticed that weird gap in the 1600s?"

"There are weird gaps everywhere if you've read enough. Different stories on the founding of the Order. Different dates, things not matching up." Grim found herself talking with a natural ease. She found comfort in the knowledge that she did not care about. "Even the first Magus wasn't reported until the 1750s…also, what the *fuck* was The Great Bear Hunt of 1492?!"

Cain started laughing and had to cover his mouth. "I thought it was 1493!" He exclaimed, in a hushed whisper.

"No, no. 1492. It was December, so some idiots rounded it up to 1493 because it went a tiny bit into the new year. It started in 1492."

"But wouldn't bears be hibernating in December?"

"Exactly it doesn't make sense!"

They both started laughing between themselves. There was a small, mischievous smile on Cain's face. The two of them had only talked on occasion, but it was like they had been friends for a long time. Grim looked down at her books and remembered where she needed to be.

"I need to go meet Lukas." She explained. "He's helping me with the presentation."

He nodded. "It was nice talking to you. I'd love your help if you'd offer it, even if it's to talk shit on historical inaccuracies."

She rolled her eyes at that last comment, but she was still smiling. "We seem to have a knack for running into each other, so I'm sure you'll know where to find me."

He grinned. "Definitely. Oh…know where 167 is?"

She thought for a moment. "Try three shelves down."

"Got it!"

Cain headed off, and Grim realised the final book on her list was on the top shelf. She raised her hand, trying to feel some shred of energy charge through her veins. She was lacking confidence. Something did click into place. The book next to the one she wanted swished past her ears. With a high-pitched gust of movement, and skidded onto the floor.

Goddammit. Almost had it.

She huffed and bent down to pick up the book. The title read *The Four Principles: And Beyond.*

Not sure what the beyond part meant, but it would do. It was close enough to what she wanted. Grim didn't fancy the stress of having to ask someone where the nearest stepladder was.

She walked into the next section of the library, the study area. It was the second part of the library. A massive room filled with desks and chairs, each with its lamps, and a small book holder. There were smaller rooms that branched off, all available to book out for whatever nefarious thing needed a private study room. Grim spotted Lukas on one of the corner tables, chatting to somebody she didn't recognise.

They were leaning over the desk and ran a hand over their shaved head. Grim heard their conversation as she walked to the table.

"Council meeting is next week. The east wing, okay?"

He nodded. "Yeah Remi, I'll be there."

"Cool."

Their voice was cold. They walked off as she sat down across from Lukas, dropping the books onto the worn table with a loud slam.

"Why is it that whenever I find you, you're always talking with somebody new?"

"I told you, I made a lot of friends." He replied, a smug smile glued to his face.

"Well, good for you."

His smile dropped, and he scoffed. "Come on, don't be like that."

"Like what?"

"Bitter."

She rolled her eyes, and she felt a gnawing desire to counter him, to defend herself in some regard. Lukas knew more about the world and its reflections on personality than she did.

"Sorry…"

"What took you so long anyway? Did you get lost?"

She shook her head. "No, I was helping someone find a book. Cain, I don't know if you've met him."

"Huh. I've seen him around. He seems weird."

"You think everyone seems weird at first. He's nice."

Grim looked up, and Lukas' eyes were hard and serious. "You can never be too careful."

She sighed. "Okay, I get it. I'll be careful, I promise. Anyway, I need to see if I can remember the electricity thing."

The tension shattered again as if it had never happened. "You need to call it something other than the electricity thing," Lukas said with a chuckle.

"Fine." She opened one of the books. A Magus Guide to the Principle of Causality. "In this presentation, I will demonstrate the principle of causality. I will be using the common example of charging electricity. By charging this singular lightbulb with magick, I will cause the lightbulb on the other side of the room to explode."

"Wait a second…" Lukas leaned back in the wooden chair, folding his arms. "You did this presentation a few years ago."

"Yes," She looked down at the pages, triggering the relapse in memory from the time she had read this book before. The paragraphs all came rushing back to her, down to every comma. "It failed then, so might as well fail now."

"I'll help you practice it before Friday. Don't go off reciting book pages again. Nobody would appreciate it, though I find it charming."

Grim smiled at him, not looking up from her book. Everything about it felt familiar. There was hope for this presentation after all. "No promises."

October

Autumn was the time for change. The air grew colder, the night came sooner. The world slowed down to a graceful slowness as the world prepared to stop before the snow came. September had flown by. Soon all the students at Elderwall had settled into the rhythm of their new lives for the next year. The clubs and classes had started. Everyone seemed to be doing well for themselves. They had found might in their newfound academic triumph.

Every student that Grim knew was receiving letters from home. The small wooden boxes outside each dorm room door often had a letter slotted inside it. An eager student always waited to open them. The rest of the world used cell phones, but the school's alumni had declared that the signal was terrible.

Grim had received a letter from her parents. It was as simple as it could be. The main point to draw from it was that her parents were planning to visit her at the Baptism.

She and Lukas had hung out a limited amount of times, though he always insisted they met for breakfast every day. He had made a success for himself, all in as little as four weeks. He had been winning football matches, acing the classes. He even made a wonderful impression on the student council.

"You'll get into it soon, you'll see." He had said to her one morning in the dining hall.

Lukas was a notorious optimist. But in this case, he was wrong. Grim was currently making her way up to see Headmistress White. The specific reason was never made clear to her, but she could think of a fair few on the walk up the stairs.

She was in the east wing of the College, where a lot of the teaching staff resided. She passed a large window, the autumn light piercing in and leaving beams on the wooden floor. Onwards she climbed, before reaching the second floor, turning towards the Headmistress' office. It was the last in a long line of small rooms that served as the other teacher's offices as well. The hallway had dark wooden panels and golden candelabras on the walls. There was no art on the walls, instead, there were bust heads on plinths with no life or character, only a name. She reached the office door and knocked.

"Enter."

Grim opened the door. Headmistress White looked up and smiled at her. It was deceitful in its gentleness. "Ah, Raven. Do sit down."

Ms White was a woman in her early thirties, with golden blonde hair plaited down her left shoulder. She had gentle blue eyes, like the sky, and wore a floral dress with a blazer over the top. Her office didn't seem to match her appearance. It matched the hallways. The only difference was that she had one large window with the ruby curtains open. She sat behind a heavy-looking oak desk, in a large brown leather chair. On her desk lay neat piles of papers, and a singular potted plant. Neat and arranged cabinets were against the walls behind her.

Grim sat down. "Why did you want to see me?"

Ms White put down the paper she was looking at. With a twirl of her wrist, the pen rose into the air, onto the paper, and started writing. "This is me checking in, that's all. I know from your test scores, and from speaking to your parents, that it's looking like you might struggle."

"Not surprised my parents were gossiping about me," Grim said immediately, with a casual shrug.

She chuckled at Grim. "They are both excellent members of the Order, and I know they have your best interests at heart."

"Sure."

"I've been hearing from some of your teachers that you are struggling with the practicalities of magick."

"Okay."

"How well can you tap into your abilities?"

"I can't."

"Have you tried?"

"Yes."

Ms White sighed. The pen stopped moving while she paused. She looked at Grim, her eyes narrowing and her lips thinning.

The pen continued as she leaned forward on the desk. "We are trying to help you, Raven. You cannot keep rejecting your calling to magick."

"No offence Ms White, but magick has already rejected me."

"I think not. There are plenty of opportunities for you with the Order when you leave here. You have to take them."

Grim crossed her arms against her chest. "Neither you nor my parents can decide that for me."

"Maybe not. But we can steer you in the right direction. The Baptism of Fire will help with that." The pen continued scribbling away. "I heard from your mother that you like painting?"

Something dropped in Grim's stomach. She sat upright in her seat. "Why would she tell you that?"

"Because we have a…*wonderful* art club here at the college. I thought you could attend, and keep painting while you study. I'll also arrange some extra sessions outside of the timetable for you to get some extra practice in."

Grim knew she could not say no. She knew exactly what that pen was writing. A full transcript of their conversation is to be sent *directly* to her parents.

"Fine."

"Excellent, I will get it all arranged. Now go and enjoy your evening."

Grim stood up, pushing her chair back with a slow creak and walking to the door.

"Oh, and Raven?"

She stopped at the door and turned her head back.

"If there is ever anything I can do, please tell me. I want you to do well, for yourself."

She smiled a little, wary but still maintaining the conformity of politeness. "I prefer Grim, Ms. White. Not Raven."

"Ah, your father had mentioned your-," She paused again. "*Nickname*. In that case, I will see you soon Grim."

Raven,

I expect that so far you are enjoying your time at Elderwall. From the reports I've been receiving, you have been attending all your classes. I would not have accepted anything else from you.

If I still remember Elderwall's scheduling, you'll be expected to present to the class soon. This presentation has a great bearing on your final grades, and as such I expect you to take it seriously.

I will not tolerate any report of you refusing to participate in the presentation. Your shortcomings are not an excuse for failure.

On a final note, I know you have requested your mother and I use the name Grim from this point onwards. But you are our Raven and will always be our Raven. A Mortem takes pride in who they are from birth. They take pride in everything their family is. You do not get to decide who you are, Raven.

Take care,

Father

The art club was an absolute lie, and any ideas of what it could have been like were completely inaccurate. It wasn't a club, it was an empty classroom that was collecting dust. Discarded but still existing to fill an academic quota. The room had a desk in the corner and an array of stacked chairs. Grim stepped onto the scratched wooden floor, glancing at the scuffed stone walls. The teacher's desk was covered in large sheets of paper and jars filled with different-sized paintbrushes. Easels leaned against the wall, with canvases already scuffed by dirt piled on the floor. The sunlight streaked through the dirty, foggy windows. The dust particles floated without purpose.

Grim stood in the doorway. Ms. White had *greatly* exaggerated the art club. It didn't even have a teacher. She had asked Lukas to come along because she was nervous, but he had football practice. Maybe that was a good thing.

Guess it was time to start painting.

She pulled an easel from the wall and set it up, then somehow managed to dig out the cleanest canvas. There were drawers filled with a messy bundle of art materials, from tubes of paint to crayons and chalk. She opened the chipped drawers, with handprints and thumb marks over every handle. Grim managed to find what she needed, pulled out a stool from under one of the tables, and sat down in front of the easel.

Now came the hard part. To begin was always a struggle. Once you make your mark, the world will never let you forget it. There was no going back and correcting yourself. No smudging the paint and trying again. Now you had a purpose. The intention is to create something true and wonderful.

Grim was always told she was wasting her time.

Well. It was her time to waste.

She closed her eyes and put the brush on the canvas.

An hour had passed. Or was it two? Time becomes irrelevant once you become completely enamoured with what you love. It was after classes, Grim had no schedule to keep now. She could paint well into the evening until the cleaners kicked her out to lock the room.

She had made progress. She thought this canvas was small, but it was always fascinating how little her paint had covered it. But she was calm, and that meant everything to her. Often, all she wanted was for the world to slow down a little. Let time slip away from her, away from all the impending doom the world seemed to thrust on her. Painting allowed her to do that, albeit for a short amount of time.

But then there was a knock at the door.

She snapped out of the peaceful trance and looked over, surprised by who she saw.

"Hey, Grim!"

"I can't believe somebody is finally using this room."

Finn and Anna lingered in the doorway, looking over with gentle smiles on their faces. Grim lowered her paintbrush and rested it against the easel. "Ms. White told me about it. Not much of an art club but-,"

Anna had pushed herself into the room and leaned around to see what Grim was working on. "Holy shit Grim! That's badass! Finn come see this."

Finn walked around. "Goddamn. Who needs test scores when you can paint like that?"

Grim's face flushed, and she covered it with her hands. "Stop it..." She mumbled, embarrassed.

"I will *not,*" Anna said with a grin. "What are you doing in here by yourself? I thought at least Lukas would come with you."

She shrugged. "He had football practice."

Finn walked over to the desk and started looking through all the paper. "You know, I'm pretty good at origami. My dad tried to teach Oscar as well, but Oscar never had the patience."

"Still baffles me that your brother, *head* of the Student Council, lacks patience," Anna explained, still looking over at Grim's painting.

Finn sat on the desk, eyeing the sheet of paper in his hands. "He's got everything else together, I think he's allowed to slip over some paper swans,"

"Lukas and I have been friends since we were little. He has always been someone who would rather look at the picture instead of making it." Grim added, as she put her brush down on the palette.

"I've talked to Lukas a few times now; you guys are very different." He said, looking over at Grim.

"We always have been. We...ended up sticking together."

Anna pushed her wheelchair towards the drawers. "Wow, they even have charcoals, I haven't messed with that stuff in years."

Finn raised an eyebrow. "You, Miss *must be clean*, used to draw with charcoals."

"My mom's into art as well, so she encouraged us to get a little messy. I grew out of it a little once I started studying magick."

Grim turned on her stool towards Anna. "How long have you two known each other?"

Finn and Anna looked at each other at that exact moment and laughed in unison. "I moved about two years ago," Anna explained. "And joined the evening classes Finn was in. We got on well and…that was that."

"I remember how your wheelchair wouldn't fit in the door, and one of our teachers said you were a fire hazard."

Anna laughed, tilting her head back. Grim couldn't help but chuckle a little as well. "I remember that! My mum filed a complaint about the Order and the managers of the building. Next thing I knew the place closed for a week to undergo *essential repairs*."

Finn shook his head, smiling. He had started to fold the paper. "Our teacher was *so* pissed."

Anna pulled out a box of charcoals from the drawers and looked up at Grim. "Do you want some company?" She gave Finn a look that Grim noticed. "We could hang out here until you're done then we can go grab dinner."

Finn seemed to recognise the look. "Yeah! We've still got ages until they stop serving food. It looks a little lonely in this dusty room."

Grim looked down at her hands. "It's okay, I don't want to force you guys-,"

"Um. *Excuse me*? You're not forcing us to do anything." Anna pointed a finger at Grim, but it was very clear it wasn't threatening. "You finish your painting, Finn and I will attempt to tap into our creative roots, and then we will all go eat dinner."

"It's pizza night," Finn added as if the pizza had any bearing on the decision.

Grim rolled her eyes, but she was smiling. "Thanks you two. The company would be lovely."

Elemental

Commands the four basic elements of fire, earth, water, and air. Some Elementals also have control over more specific elements, such as light and dark.

Skulduggery

Manipulates reality by changing perspectives, can cast projections and visions. The depth and scope of these projections depends on the strength of the Magus.

Psychic

Uses the energy of our world to control objects. They can move objects or a certain weight and size, and multiple Magus can work together to move larger objects.

Summoner

Can use and change objects to generate magickal energy. Common objects include candles, incense, crystals and herbs.

Do you remember that show with the bald psychic?

He wasn't a psychic Finn, he was a mutant.

You could be the bald mutant psychic Anna.

Didn't he die?

SPOILERS???

For the next few days, Finn and Anna dragged Grim to dinner with them. They especially did so when she said that Lukas was too busy. The two friends were the most light-hearted of students. They didn't talk about magick at all. Instead, they reminisced about the time Finn ate a pound coin, or when Anna decided to give herself a haircut.

The dining hall was large enough to fit the entire student population of Elderwall. Wooden tables and chairs in lines row after row, with each one being for each school year. A chandelier hung from the ceiling, coiling in golden weaves with flickering candles. The room was somewhat dreary. There were no windows, only several doors that branched out into the other corridors.

But, tonight was different. Tonight, Lukas was free, and Grim had agreed to meet him in the dining hall. He was fifteen minutes late, but Grim never held that against him. He sat down across from her, putting down his tray for food. She noticed his hair had flecks of dirt in it, likely from the fields outside.

"Hey," She said, leaning back in her chair.

He smiled at her. "We keep missing each other."

"You need to stop being so busy." She joked, taking a bite of her food. "How is it going?"

"It's going well!" His face lit up as he continued talking. "Getting ready for the next match, attending all the student council meetings. It's nice being busy."

She nodded. "You always liked it when school was busy, I was the complete opposite."

He chuckled. "You still are."

Grim shrugged and picked up her cup to sip from. "What are you even doing in student council anyway?"

"Right now? It's helping to arrange the Baptism of Fire."

Her blood ran cold, the fear of the flames flickering in her chest for only a second. "You're involved with that?"

Lukas ran a hand through his hair, his tone casual. "We're arranging timeslots for everyone, sending the letters out to the parents. Your parents will tell you they're coming soon."

"Oh joy." Grim frowned, and Lukas shook his head at her.

"Hey, come on. I know you've not always agreed with your parents, but I bet they'll love to see you complete the ceremony."

"I'm going to get *burned*."

Lukas rolled his eyes. "You don't know that. It hasn't happened in *years*."

There was a rustling, and the whole hall fell silent. The chandelier trembled above them, and one by one, the candles went out. Grim looked around, but everything was in darkness. She instinctively reached out, remembering the midnight nightmares she had sometimes. She felt Lukas' hands on hers.

He squeezed them, tight and firm. "It's okay. It's okay. It's a student messing around."

The room came alive with whispers, and then from above them, the ceiling started to *glow*.

A gentle blue. The kind of cloudless skies on a summer day. It began to separate, illuminating the room once more. It skittered across the archways until it set in its formation.

This was not a student messing around.

THE ORDER IS WATCHING.

The whole room erupted.

"The Order? As in the *Order* Order?"

"Did we do something wrong?"

"This has got to be some kind of crazy prank."

Constant chattering ground against Grim's ears. She gripped Lukas' hands tighter without even thinking about it. It felt like all eyes were on her, even though that was irrational.

Then, as if nothing had happened at all, the words disappeared, and the candles flickered back on. The room re-erupted into sheer panic.

"I'm getting a teacher."

"Go find Ms White!"

"What does this mean?"

Half the dining room cleared out, the gossip was humid in the air. Grim realised she was still holding Lukas' hands, and she snatched them away. "Sorry."

She looked up and noticed Lukas' hands were still open, and his cheeks were pink. He put them back in his lap. "Are you alright?"

"Yeah." She nodded but winced at her plate of food. "I've lost my appetite now."

"I have as well."

Grim pushed her chair out and stood up, walking around to Lukas. "I'm going to go back to my room."

"Let me walk you there." He said, rushing to stand up as well.

"No, it's fine, I know you're busy-,"

"*No*." He put a hand on her shoulder. "I know what that was."

"*Lukas!*"

They both turned to the voice, and it was Oscar, running over in a panic. He stopped in front of them and caught his breath, taking off his glasses and wiping them on his shirt. "Emergency meeting. *Now*."

Lukas looked back at Grim, and then to Oscar. "Let me walk Grim back to her room and then I'll be there."

Grim gently took his hand off her shoulder. "Hey, it's fine you need to…"

"*No*." He said again, in that same low tone. He turned back to Oscar. "I want to walk Grim back and then I'll come to meet you all."

Oscar nodded, putting his glasses back on. "Be quick, alright?"

"You got it. Come on Grim."

As they walked back, the college was alive. Bursting at the seams with discussions of magick. Hundreds of theories on what sort of focus could have possibly created that. The corridors to the dorm rooms were quiet though. Lukas and Grim walked along in quiet peace with each other, going past the tall glass windows that shone through the evening light. She noticed Lukas looked as if he kept wanting to say something, and when they reached her door, she decided to get to the bottom of it.

"Something's on your mind, say it."

Lukas chuckled but avoided looking at her. "How could you tell?"

"You always make sure there is *never* silence when we're talking."

"I wanted you to enjoy the walk."

"Or you want to say something, but don't know how to."

He sighed. "I forgot that you still had nightmares."

"Therapy didn't make them go away Lukas. It didn't fix everything. As much as you wanted it to."

"Yeah…" He nodded. "I was so scared for you at that moment. I forgot that you don't like it when things happen without warning and, well…I'm sorry I forgot."

"It's okay, Lukas."

"But it's *not.*" He put his face in his hands. "I should know this, and I should be looking after you. I know how much you need me-,"

"Hey, listen. It's not something for you to worry about. I'm managing it."

"You're not managing it, Grim. What you did in Starching's class-,"

"What did I do in Starching's class?"

"Your weird memory thing. People are going to talk, Grim. You need to get a grip if you want to do well."

She sighed. "I know you want the best for me."

"I do."

"But I need to work things out on my own."

"I want to be there for you though."

"And you are," She knocked his arm, a playful and light smile on her face. "You're being a good friend. That's all I need."

His smile came back. "I do my best." He pulled her in for a hug. She never expected it and he knew that she didn't like them all that much. But she decided to let him have his moment and hold her. When he pulled away, she noticed he had a look in his eyes, a dreamy gaze. She couldn't work out why he would.

"Go get to the meeting." She said, nudging him away from her door.

"Alright, alright. Sleep well."

The Baptism of Fire is a noble ceremony for all Magus in their first year at Elderwall Boarding College. First established in the early 1800s, it became a way for Magus to find their true calling, to find what we now know as a Focus.

This historic event is a key part of a young Magus' journey, and as such it is taken seriously. A week is allocated to the proceedings, allowing all first-year students to participate. The event is concluded with a several celebratory dinners, to praise our young Magus for their courage and bravery.

The ancient flame is not something to take lightly. By committing to the Baptism, the students of Elderwall are committing to the Order, and its sacred rules and structure. A Focus defines you, gives you purpose and allows you to harness your natural ability.

It is true, that the flames burn some. To deny any knowledge of that would be deceiving our young Magus. But the cases are so few and far between, that we should still encourage everyone to take part in this great ceremony.

Really glossing over the risk of burning huh.
I bet my parents will make a speech at this year's ceremony.
It's probably father's turn.

Grim did not sleep well.

Maybe it was the intensity of the evening. The newfound revelation that not everything was as perfect as it appears. Or it was the fact that the conversation with Lukas was repeating in Grim's mind. His worry, his panicked expression, or the expectation he had presented to her.

Or to simplify matters, it was because it was okay to have a bad night's sleep sometimes.

Grim groaned as she turned over in her bed, switching her lamp on. She had fallen asleep for about an hour but had woken up after a nightmare entered her rest. It had faded as soon as she opened her eyes, but the feeling of dread and despair remained. She leaned over to grab her watch and winced, realising it was the early hours of the morning.

The nightmare contained a castle covered in thorns, and a dark and stormy night. She had no idea what it meant.

If she was at home, Grim would have laid in bed in silence. The seconds drained away before the sun rose and she could give herself an excuse to get out of bed. If she even dared move or switch a light on, her parents would know about it in an instant.

One perk of magick, she guessed. Being in tune with the mysterious workings of the universe meant you could sense your child not sleeping.

But Grim *wasn't* at home. Which made the situation better, in a weird way.

She pulled herself out of bed and slipped on a pair of trainers. She reached for the jacket she had left hanging over her chair. For once, she was glad she slept in loose jogging bottoms and oversized t-shirts. She opened the door to the hallway and stepped out into the night.

The lights were all still on. Her parents had told her, that Elderwall was still active during the night-time, to accommodate the student's and teachers' needs. If a student wants to cram some last-minute studying in, the library would be open. If for personal or religious reasons, somebody needed a meal at midnight, then one of the cooks was happy to cover the night shift. Elderwall would cater for all and appreciate all. That's what her mother had said.

Well, Grim thought they didn't like her so much. But that was a matter of opinion. She decided to go to the common room, hoping to at least warm her bones at the fireplace before the day began again. She pushed open the door, being careful not to make it creak too loud into the night. A part of her still thought this was the makings of a troublemaker. She forgot sometimes, while being here, that she was an adult.

"Um…hello?"

The voice coming from near the fireplace startled her, and she took a step back. To her surprise, she saw Cain sitting on the sofa as the fire roared. She hadn't seen him much since that moment in the library. She only spotted him between classes and found him hiding at the back of the room during lessons. They hadn't spoken a word to each other.

Grim took a step back. "Uh-hi, sorry I didn't realise someone was here, I can leave-,"

He immediately interrupted her. "No-no! It's fine, come sit down."

She stepped forward, awkward and nervous. She folded her hands together as she sat on the sofa opposite him. A log split on the fire, crackling open. Cain had a book open in his lap, but she couldn't see the title of it.

"Having trouble sleeping?" He asked. The look on his face suggested he was feeling as awkward as she was.

"I always do." She replied with a sigh. "What are you reading?"

"Oh-this?" He looked a little surprised as he held up the book to her. "It's uh…it's a book about mechanical engineering."

"A Magus reading a book about something *not* to do with magick? Colour me impressed."

"One could say that it's quite easy to combine magick and engineering, especially if you are of the Psychic focus."

"Don't be a smart ass." She mumbled and then realised what she had done. "Sorry."

"It's okay."

"It's not, I'm sorry…I'm tired, as you can tell."

"We wouldn't be here, sitting in front of a fire, if we were not tired." He closed the book and put it down next to him.

"Tired is my constant state of existence." She replied, rubbing her eyes with a groan.

Cain was trying to smile, but it was quick to fall into a frown. "I know we're not close or anything, but…are you okay? Have you had a rough night or something?"

"A nightmare. I'll get over it."

Grim wasn't going to get into the details with Cain, no matter how nice he seemed. She had learned to never open her heart unless she was ready. She refused to bow to any sort of pressure put on her to open up to anyone. Her parents had tried that too many times.

It always ended with a slammed door and a one-sided screaming match that Grim could never fight.

He nodded. "I had nightmares a lot when I was a kid. Night terrors, my father said. Always joked it was my imagination, but he knew the cure was a hot chocolate."

She smiled a little. "Are you going somewhere with this?"

"Yes, actually." He chuckled, standing up. "I was going to offer to make you a hot chocolate."

"No thanks."

He stood up. "Come on, let me at least think that I've helped you sleep better."

"Cain, I don't want one."

She spoke with a degree of finality that made Cain stop. He sat back down. "Okay. Okay. I won't push it, but the offer is there."

Lukas would have insisted, but Grim was too tired to take that thought anywhere. She stood up herself this time. "It's not long until I would get up anyway. I'm going back to my room."

"Are you okay getting back? I can walk you there."

"*No.*" She paused, and took a breath, noticing the anger in her voice. "No, it's fine. I'd prefer to go by myself."

"Grim, no offence but you're barely standing."

"I'm fine."

Cain huffed, letting out a long sigh. Grim could tell he was trying. Everyone was trying. Finn. Anna. And now Cain. The cracks were finally starting to show and the whole world could see them.

She bit her lip, took a second, and turned to him. "Stay here, enjoy your book. I'll see you around, okay?"

He still look worried, but he didn't fight her. "Okay. See you around."

My dear Father,

I hope you have been keeping well, and that the expectations of the Order are not weighing down too heavily on you. Elderwall is as you told me, an institution forcing perfection and entirely built on lies.

Despite my opinions though, I will keep my head down and do what they ask of me. I am worried for the Baptism though, we have both always said my magick does not fit into any traditional focus. I will try and not to cause a fuss, I promise you that. I do not want you to face the consequences at the Order because of me.

I have been trying to make friends, since I know Remi is so busy with their work on the Student Council. I have always found it difficult, but it's especially hard here. I am surrounded by swarms of sheep, and I am reluctant to try and connect with anyone.

There is someone, however. She seems different. Perhaps befriending her will be the silver lining among everything.

Try not to worry, we have it all under control. I will write to you again soon.

With love,
Cain

After her meeting with Ms White, Grim had received a timetable of the extra classes she was taking. To her utter dismay, her first one was today. She had completed her main classes for the day. It involved trailing behind Lukas and George. They spent the day discussing some details of magickal politics that she hadn't grasped yet. Something about a subsection of a section.

She had split off from them, leaving the two to enjoy the conversation and the free time. Grim savoured the silence before she entered the classroom. Her teacher, Mrs Locklin was waiting for her when she opened the door.

According to Mrs Locklin, she was usually the teacher for those who had the Psychic focus. *However*, she was going to give Grim a refresher course in the basics.

"After all, as you learnt in your evening classes, your basic detection magick is the cornerstone for any Magus." She explained as Grim sat behind one of the desks in the small classroom. "If you understand the threads of reality from which this world is built, then you will be able to adapt it to your focus."

"But I don't know what my focus is yet," Grim commented, resting her head in one hand.

"You will soon though. The Baptism is closer than you think. We don't have a lot of time to get you some practice. Now, stand up, shoulders back, let's try detecting the magick."

Grim obeyed, and Mrs. Locklin tied back her long red hair into a ponytail.

"How were you taught to detect magick?" She asked, turning back to face Grim.

"They taught us that it was various threads that you could reach out and touch, and that's what you used. It's external power, not internal."

Mrs Locklin smiled, impressed. At least Grim had gotten one thing right today. "Exactly. We reach out to the power of this world, and we use it as we see fit. That's what we are going to practice. Reach out and utilise."

She frowned at the teacher, a headache already starting to form at her temples. "What am I reaching out for?"

"Lay your palms flat, and you'll feel it."

Grim turned her hands, opening out her palms, and uncurling her fingers over and over. Mrs Locklin leaned against the desk, crossing her arms, and waiting. Her desk had stacks of books and unmarked and unscrutinised papers. A mug left a stained rim on the wood.

The silence hung over them both, overbearing.

She tried to feel the energy in her palms, the current of the world passing through like sand in a storm. Tried to understand how it was possible to connect with everything. How it was possible to become more than yourself. The Magus knew more about the depths of existence than many. That is how they stood on high, enjoying the knowledge of knowing all.

It was so subtle. The magick, at this moment, was subtle. Not like the whole barrel of aristocracy that Grim had become accustomed to. She didn't have the means to grab onto anything. The threads of the world would not weave to her.

"Can you feel anything?" Mrs Locklin asked, breaking Grim out of the dullness of concentration.

Grim shook her head. "I feel like…a buzzing."

"A buzzing?" Mrs Locklin shook her head. "No, no, you're not concentrating hard enough. You should feel a spark, not a buzzing. It needs to be stronger."

Grim tried to hold back a scowl. "I can't help it."

Mrs Locklin let out a sharp breath between her teeth. "This is…the foundation of being a Magus. We cannot progress further until you've mastered this."

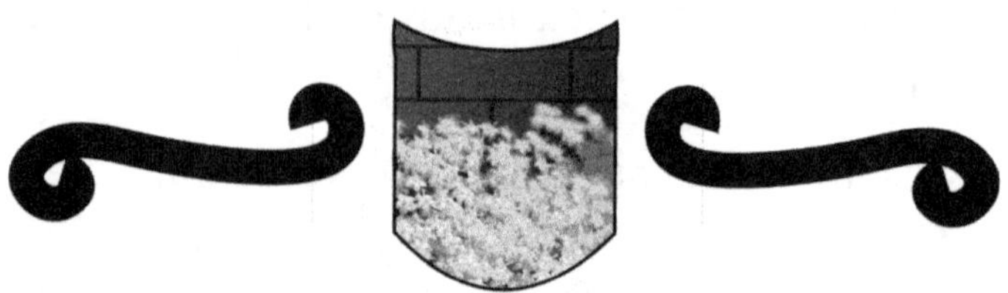

FAO: Ms Audrey White

Ms White,

I present my report on our first-year student Raven Mortem. As you requested, I started the private classes with her in order to help advance her magickal abilities.

Unfortunately, I have to tell you that our first class together did not go as I planned. Raven's ability is significantly below the level we expect from our new students. She struggled to sense any magickal energy, and could not harness any magick when asked to. I admit, I am worried as to how we can help her progress. However I know it is our duty to maximise the potential of every magus that walks through our doors. I would suggest discussing the matter further with her parents, as I know the Mortems will know what to do.

There is one final matter I wish to bring to your attention. Raven seems to be of a temperamental character, and this was revealed to me during one of the exercises. I think it is also important that we quell this anger inside of her, as that might be the issue that is holding her back.

I look forward to discussing the next steps with you. Mrs Scarlet Locklin

"I had to breathe *for thirty fucking minutes.*"

Lukas moved the chess piece up the board, not looking up at Grim while he did so. "It's your move."

"I already told you I didn't want to play." She replied, muttering, and rolling her eyes.

"Your parents didn't spend an entire summer teaching us for nothing, so make your move."

Grim reached over to pick up a pawn. "I never even wanted to learn in the first place."

She glanced around the common room. A few students were hanging around. By the fireplace, a group were cross-referencing spells and summoning materials. She looked through the windows outside. Another group were in the courtyard, trying to get flowers to bloom from the soil. This was despite the fact it was *autumn,* and they were summer flowers. Such is the way of disturbing the natural order.

She moved the pawn one square. Lukas sighed. "Did you allow me to check you on purpose?"

"Yes." She gave him a glance from the side. "Because I don't want to play."

"How come?" Lukas moved his bishop. Avoiding check. On purpose. "I know you're angry that you were stuck with Mrs Locklin, but she's not that bad."

"She loves you, the golden student who can sense the spark, not the buzzing." Grim took his bishop with a pawn.

"I hate being talked down to, and I don't want to play chess. Go for checkmate already."

"Nobody's talking down to you." Lukas moved his piece, preparing to win. "They want what's best for you."

"Oh, sure." Grim tried her best not to groan out loud and made an opening for Lukas on the board. "The condescending tones come from a place of *love*."

"They want to do right by everyone…checkmate."

Grim looked at the board. "Good game."

"If nothing else Grim, you have your wit. Want another game?"

She stood up. "I don't want to play." She said, realising she was repeating herself. "Chess doesn't calm me down; it makes me even more pissed off."

He chuckled. "How can chess get you angry? I know a lot of things get you angry…but chess?"

"My parents *forced* me to learn over the summer, and you joined in. Life becomes suffocating when everything becomes an obligation."

"It's a valuable skill and a fun game."

"We can add it to the list of skills they forced me to learn."

Lukas crossed his arms across his chest. "You're too hard on your parents."

She laughed, words bitter. "You don't know half of it, Lukas."

"Then why don't you tell me?"

Lukas' sentence was more of a demand than a question. He knew more than he let on, Grim was already aware he was more observant than most. There was always the unspoken between them. The harsh realities that they both tried to avoid for the sake of peace. Lukas knew more. He always had.

"You have to let people in at some point Grim." He continued, as he reset the chess pieces. "You can't be angry at the world forever."

She looked at him, and their eyes met for a moment. He put the final pawn back into its starting position, ready for the next player. "Either way, I'm used to the anger, so it's different for me." He concluded with a laugh, and stood up as well, turning to face her. "Come on, I'll walk you to the dining hall. I've got an Honour's meeting."

My dear Momma,

I was so glad to hear from you, and I apologise for not getting back to you sooner. I have been busy since starting at Elderwall, with the Student Council, the football team and my classes. We always talked about how wonderful it would be when I started, but I have to say Elderwall has exceeded my expectations.

I know you had your concerns, as you always do. I understand that your experience of Elderwall was different to mine. But think of what I could achieve here! The professors think highly of me already Momma, and I have been having discussions with them about what I could achieve after I graduate. I couldn't have asked for a better start.

I will admit, though, that I worry for Grim. You expressed concern for her in your previous letter, and I feel the same way. Even though Grim lacks the magickal ability, she could still do something great within the Order. They could use someone with her talent for research. However, she is still rejecting everything about Elderwall and the people within it. It doesn't help that she's caused a rift between herself and her parents over something as silly as her identity.

I worry for her, Momma. I want her to fit in, I want her to be well and not get so stressed all the time. She does it to herself, really. I'm going to do my best to help her graduate, she means a lot to me, after all.

And yes, I will ask her to the ball. I need to find the right moment. But I promise I will.

Plenty of love and light,
Lukas

Grim was in the library finalising her presentation when Lukas charged towards the table with an obscene amount of determination. This could only mean one thing. Lukas had an idea. He was the kind of person who once he had the seed of inspiration, would stop at nothing to see it through to the end. Usually, these ideas involved learning a new piece of magick, acing a test, or getting involved in some new club. Something that meant he could have a purpose.

"I need you to do some research for the Student Council."

It seemed that today, this idea involved her. What a twist.

She looked up from her books after it was clear that neither of them would attempt a greeting. They had reached beyond the point of *needing* a greeting. Sometimes though, Grim appreciated the effort of starting the conversation.

"Research?"

He took a seat next to her, leaning forward to an uncomfortable degree and dropping his voice. "You know that thing that happened in the dining hall?"

"You mean the ominous bioluminescent letters that were probably a not-so-subtle threat from the College to take our education seriously? Yes, I remember them."

He rolled his eyes. "That wasn't from Elderwall, it's to do with something else."

"What does this have to do with me, Lukas?"

Lukas reached into his pocket and pulled out a folded square of paper and slid it across to her. She picked it up, and unfolded it, reading the contents as Lukas continued talking.

"It's the Order of Chaos. They've been causing trouble here for the last few years. There were traces of them in the 80s as well." He pointed to the paper. "These are a few starting points that you can follow. With your knowledge of the libraries here, you have a good chance of finding us something. You can even request extra items from the Order if you need to and-,"

"Whoa, whoa." She dropped the piece of paper back on the table and turned to face him. "L-Lukas, it's a prank. This is…this research is just excessive."

"It's not excessive." He put a firm hand on her arm, almost squeezing it. Grim had never seen Lukas look more serious in his life. "They're dangerous. They were spreading fire back then, and they're spreading fire now. This is only going to cause more problems."

"And how is digging up old history going to help with anything?"

He smiled, the kind of smile he did when he was making a point. "Whoever is behind this, they are a genuine threat to the Order, to everything Elderwall stands for. The more everyone believes their lies, the more we are at risk of losing it all."

"Lukas…get to the point you're so desperate to make."

He let out a laugh, shaking his head. "I told everyone at the Student Council what a good researcher you are. If they've slipped up somewhere along the way, you would be the person to find it. This could be your chance Grim! We always talked about what we would be in the Order, and what we could do. This is how you prove yourself, make everyone proud."

Grim's eyes fell back to the piece of paper. "You know nobody would be proud of me Lukas."

"Well…" He frowned. "I would be proud of you."

She sighed, shrugging her shoulders. "I am your best asset, aren't I?"

"George shouldn't have said that, and I've told him he should have kept his mouth shut. He didn't mean anything by it. Hey, look at me." Their eyes met again, and Lukas immediately smiled. "You could be a great Magus Grim. This is your chance, and I want you to take it."

Ms White said that Grim should take every opportunity presented to her. Regardless of that quiet threat, Grim knew that people would talk. Lukas would tell his mother, who would tell her parents, who would then send another letter of joyful distaste. The pile gathering in her room would grow larger.

"I'll start looking into it after the presentation. Let me get through that and then I'm all yours."

Lukas kept his smile. "I know. I mean I *know* you need to do the presentation first. But as soon as possible, yeah? We're running out of time."

She closed her books with a heaved sigh and stood up. "No need to be so dramatic. You'll handle it. You handle everything."

"But this time I need you."

She nudged him with her free hand. "Sure."

"I mean it."

Grim nodded. "Course you do."

"You know you don't need to doubt if I'm being genuine to you. I mean everything I say."

She gathered her books. "I know…I know. Do you want to join me for lunch?"

He looked away. "I have a meeting with the Student Council. I said I'd stop by to see you before I went."

"You can tell them that they have a researcher."

Lukas grinned. "Thank you, Grim. I mean it. You're going to be a big help."

"Enjoy your meeting." She replied and watched Lukas leave.

November

The lecture room was alive with dangerous electric energy. The conversation was suffocating. People were handing books and notebook pages back and forth, up and down the ascending seats. There was a repetition of concepts and presentation practice. Everything happened in a hive of toxic academic activity.

The nerves had kept Grim from sleeping. Her notes were in her bag, perfect on colour-coded flash cards. Precise recollection would not help her in front of an academic audience. She was nauseous, and everything was blurry since this morning. Lukas had been waiting for her in the common room, eager to pick her brains and get her to quiz him on his presentation. Not that he needed it, his confidence and practical proficiency would see him be successful.

Lukas had already headed up the stairs. She was about to head up the stairs when she spotted Finn on the front row with Anna. He started waving at her, and she walked to the front of their desk.

"Hey! How-." Finn's expression shifted from his sweet smile to concern in the space of a single sentence. "-holy shit you look ill. Are you okay?"

"Appreciate the bluntness, Finn." She replied, rolling her eyes at him. "I'm fine, didn't sleep much, that's all."

This was a lie.

"Do you need to go to the infirmary?" Anna asked. I'm sure Starching won't mind if you skip the presentation when you don't feel well."

"It's fine!" She put on a very obvious fake chipper tone. "I want to get through it, I can handle it."

This was a lie.

Finn nodded. "Okay, well…why don't you sit with us?"

"Grim!"

Lukas called her from the other end of the room, and it was only by some miracle instinct that she heard him. He was beckoning with his hand for her to come over to where he was sitting.

Anna looked across the room. "Seems like that's a no then. Mr. Valedictorian wants you over there."

Finn turned to her; mouth open wide. "Anna!"

"That's what Grim calls him! So, why can't I?"

Grim chuckled, but she felt like she was choking on her false laughter. "She has a point. I'll see you guys after class."

When she reached Lukas, and sat down next to him, laying her hands on the desk, she noticed his dull expression. "What's going on with you?"

He glanced at her as if he was assessing her. "You shouldn't be so nervous."

"We are *not* talking about this-,"

The door swung open, and Starching walked in. The room immediately fell into a scared silence. "Good to see you're all committed your education."

He was making the dramatics of the situation casual. With the flick of his hand, the infamous list appeared once more.

"I would like to remind you all that this is a *graded* presentation. As such, the list I have here will change. This is your chance to prove yourself to me and your fellow Magus."

No pressure. None at all.

Starching read Lukas' name first. He stepped to the front of the class, all suave and dazzling confidence.

He looked down at his cards *only once* and began.

"The principle of sympathy works on the idea that the more alike two things are, the more you can influence them. Some of these connections are physical, some only spiritual…"

Lukas smiled at everyone, taking only a second to remember. "With this idea in mind, due to the planetary alignments, today was the perfect day to grow a plant from a seed."

He pulled out a seed from his pocket. "I will be able to grow this seed thanks to the influence of what is around it."

He had the room enraptured by him. Lukas curled his hands together, and there was a small flash of green glowing light. When Lukas opened his palm again, the seed had sprouted. Everyone applauded, and Grim felt her heart shrivel.

"As you can see, I have managed to influence the seed. I have manipulated its reality using what is available to me."

He bowed his head. "Thank you for listening to my presentation."

There was more applause. Even Starching was applauding. It sounded like thundering drums in Grim's ears, making them ring out and become nothing. The rest of the presentations appeared and disappeared, fumbling together into a blur.

Finn did his presentation on the principle of contagion. He lit two candles, establishing a link between them. When he blew one out, the other went out too. Starching commented on how the example was simple but effective.

Cain did a presentation on the principle of correspondence, and demonstrated the phrase *as above, so below*. He summoned an emerald shard. Starching enjoyed how *clean* the cut on the crystal was.

Then finally, the dreaded moment occurred.

"Raven Mortem?"

Lukas reached over and squeezed her hand, an empty comfort for her at this moment. She stood up, awkward in her movements. She took her lightbulb demonstration with her and made her way down the steps to the front of the class.

As she looked up at the ascending seats, she felt her knees begin to crumble.

"Whenever you're ready Raven." She heard Randall say, but he was echoey to her.

She glanced up and met Finn and Anna's eyes on the front row. Anna gave her a thumbs-up, and Finn mouthed *you've got this*.

Okay.

One.

Two.

And-

"Today I will be discussing the principle of causality. This is similar to the concept of cause and effect, in which an event can contribute to, or sometimes *cause* an event that follows it. This is often seen as quite a basic assumption, something that occurs in our everyday lives. Yet, extensive study of this principle has meant we must re-evaluate the relationships that exist between events."

Grim gestured a hand to the two lightbulbs standing upright in two brass holders and held the wire in her hand. "This is a common example of causality. In Mortal homes, when you flick a light switch, the lights will turn on, simple cause and effect. In magickal terms, I will generate that magick that I will use to send down the wire I am holding to the first lightbulb. The intent of my magick will become the cause, and the effect will be the lights switching on. The after-effects of the magickal energy should cause the second one to light up as well."

The whole lecture hall seemed to be waiting in excitement. Grim couldn't tell if it was from the chance of seeing success or seeing failure. Her eyes glanced over to Randall, who was leaning forward on his desk. Intrigue lit his worn face.

She gripped the wire in her hands. She felt *something* surge, a small buzzing in her wrist. The hum of trying. But then nothing was happening.

This was bound to happen. Failure was always on the horizon she would greet. Past the easy part of the explanation, but the demonstration? That was where her difficulty lies. She always lacked the drive to prove the knowledge she possessed. Always one step behind.

Her breath hitched, losing itself in her throat. Black spots buzzed at the corners of her eyes. But still, nothing happened.

No electricity, no light. No demonstration of pre-existing knowledge. No evidence to explain the bullshit she spoke to the rest of the class.

Was the room spinning? It felt like it was spinning.

Still no light. Oh god.

People were whispering, and Grim felt herself gasping for breath.

What is she doing?

Can she just…not do it?

Huh, be expelled by the end of the year.

Despite Grim's sweaty palms, the wire dropped from her hands.

Her presentation ended with her bolting out of the room.

Presentation Notes: Principle of Causality
by Grim Mortem

open with explaining basics of causality- reevaluating casual
relationships between events. idea of cause and effect etc

practical- two lightbulbs. take energy to charge one which will
light the other

focus the energy down the wire. needs enough magickal energy to
create a ripple effect

HOW AM I GOING TO DO THIS???

Inhale.

Exhale.

Count to seven. Count to eleven.

Inhale.

One. Two. Three. Four. Five. Six. Seven.

Exhale.

One. Two. Three. Four. Five. Six. Seven. Eight. Nine. Ten. Eleven

A rhythm. A dance. A delicate practice to stop dangerous intentions.

She could feel her heart screaming like she was ready to die.

Inhale.

Exhale.

Seven.

Eleven.

Inhale.

Exhale.

Seven.

Eleven.

Grim wiped the tears that she could finally feel on her face. She ignored the fact that she was smudging her dark makeup across her cheek. She had run out of the lecture hall and towards a quiet corner of the building. She could embrace the quiet that came from everyone still being in their morning classes. A hidden blessing it seemed. What would the world of the young magus say if they saw her like this?

"Grim?"

She looked up, blinking away more tears, still focusing on her breathing. Lukas stood there. Steady, calm Lukas. He stepped forward, putting a soft hand on her arm.

"Hey, come on." He pulled her into a hug, whispering sweetly in her ear. "You're being silly."

"Fuck you." She mumbled into his shoulder, knowing full well he was messing with her.

He pulled away, lifting a hand to brush the tears away from her cheeks. "You would have been able to do it, you know that."

Grim pulled her sleeve over her hands and wiped her face again. "Doesn't matter now, does it? Already got the failing grade."

"Well…" Lukas turned his head away from Grim and shrugged. "Starching finished the class. He wants to see you."

"Why?"

"He didn't say, he asked me to go find you. He said I would know where you ran off to."

"I don't want to see Starching." She said, with a sigh. One. Two.

"Grim, you don't have a say in the matter." He said, self-assured and she knew he was right.

And that was that. They walked back to the lecture hall together. Lukas dropped Grim off like a child on their first day of school. He promised to meet her later for dinner, a time agreed on the way. Lukas walked off, and Grim entered the lecture hall once more, knocking on the door as she did so.

Starching was at his desk, looking over some papers. He looked up, smiling with a degree of lightness when he saw her.

"Ah, Miss Mortem. Thank you for coming back." He gestured with a hand for her to enter. "Shut the door, would you?"

She did and stood in front of Starching's desk. Immediately, he passed her a piece of paper.

Presentation Grade: 30/100

Needs assistance in the practical areas of magick. Has potential.

Failing grade. As perfectly predicted.

"Why did you choose to attend this institution Raven?"

The question came as a shock to her, Starching's bluntness was a surprise. "I didn't, sir."

"Well, that explains it." His eyes glanced up at her. "I saw your entrance exam. You completely failed the practical assessment. No spark of magick, no trace of anything to call yourself a magus."

And the bluntness continued, bordering on insulting. Grim stiffened at the harshness, standing up straighter and raising her chin.

"You have potential in other areas though." He continued. "Your ability to grasp concepts is astounding, and so is your attention to detail."

"Thank you?" She replied, hesitantly.

"Raven, I don't know why you came here. Nevertheless, if you can apply yourself to your classes more, what is beyond here will be very exciting for you. The Order could always use someone with a talent for facts."

"What if that someone doesn't want the Order?"

Starching's eyes widened for a second, but he chuckled. "Then they're a fool. I'll see you next class Raven."

Grim turned, and walked to the door, but looked back at Starching. "I prefer the name Grim, sir."

He shook his head, clicking his tongue in thought. "If that is what you wish to be called, I will call you it."

Something in Grim's heart swelled, and she smiled at him. "Thank you." She replied, with genuine kindness.

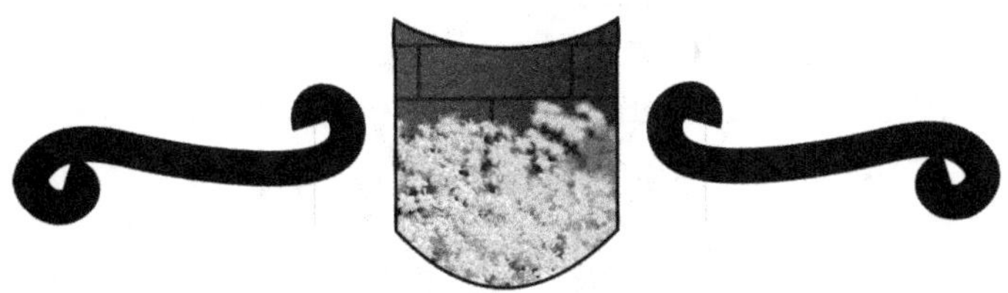

Year One Class- "Basic Fundamentals and Principles of Magick"

Assignment: A presentation and essay on a principle, one of the student's choosing.

Assessed and Graded by Professor Randall Starching

Lukas Lightchild: 80

Khalid Bloggs: 76

Rome Welch: 74

Danni Hutchinson: 74

Tanya Waller: 72

Khushi Liu: 72

Miguel Hansen: 71

Sommer Barry: 69

George Wellman: 68

Cai Heaton: 67

Cain Blackwood: 66

Louise Frye: 64

Stacie Hartley: 61

Neave Neale: 60

Anika Montoya: 59

Finn Becher: 58

Anna Lin: 40

Raven Mortem: 30

Grim walked out of Starching's classroom. The halls still held a smattering of students, even if it was now lunchtime. She leaned against the stone walls, taking a moment to collect her thoughts.

If you can apply yourself to your classes more.

Ugh. What righteous bullshit.

"I'm glad you're doing alright."

She looked up at the voice, and Cain was standing a few feet away from her. He gave her a goofy smile and a cheerful wave. "I got worried when you ran out, Finn and Anna felt the same."

"I'm fine it was just…" She waved a hand at him, dismissing the idea of trying to explain. "Just whatever."

He nodded. "Why did Starching want to see you?"

"Got a firm talking to about how to apply myself better."

He winced. "Ouch…well I think you're applying yourself enough."

He spoke at a quick pace, and Grim could see he was getting flustered. She shook her head, chuckling at his mannerisms. "Thanks, Cain."

Grim felt the floor shake. This time, it wasn't in her head. The College's old wretched floorboards began to tremble. Cain looked down as well, and the students who had been lingering around sounded off their alarms. Grim stumbled a little, and Cain caught her.

It was like in the dining room, but the lettering was more distorted. In the midday light, it sprawled across the floor, curving up the walls and bending over the ceiling. The words still glowed as the floor continued to rumble.

Who said that magick was based on simple principles?

The world is not so simple.

Where does it all truly come from?

The words faded as if crawling back into the surfaces they clung to. The whole hallway fell into a whispered quiet, the gossip stirring once more. Grim looked at Cain, and the two realised he was still holding onto her.

"Sorry! Sorry!" Cain exclaimed in a panicked voice, as he let go of Grim. "I didn't want you to fall."

She straightened herself up and stepped back from him. "It-it's fine." She looked around, down at the floor, trying to follow the trail of the words. She didn't have the power to trace such things. "Things are getting weirder by the second…"

"Yeah…" Cain looked a little lost in thought.

Grim watched the students in the hallway, mumbling in hushed tones. They rushed away, fleeing from the scene of the incident. She looked back at Cain, who was watching the floor as if trying to find the source of the rumbling.

"I-I'm going to head off. Thanks."

Cain seemed to return from his daydreams. He smiled at Grim, watching her without saying anything for a moment. He looked away as she turned down the hallway.

"See you around, Grim."

Grim's bedroom was the standard assignment that the College gave every student. A small box-shaped room with a single round window. A bed in one corner, a desk and chair opposite it, and a single wardrobe. The communal bathrooms were on either end of the dormitory floors, all with individual cubicles. She hadn't had much from home to decorate with, apart from an old red patchwork blanket over the bed and filling the wardrobe with her clothes. On the desk were a couple of stacks of library books, but in a cardboard box on the floor next to it, were Grim's art supplies. She hadn't been able to take everything, but there were sketchbooks, pencils, and charcoals. At least now she knew where she could find paint.

Grim sat on her bed, a book from the library open in front of her. She had started making notes. But, it was hard when you had already memorised the entire passage. The useless knowledge branded into her memory. It was hard to try and condense it for your next assignment without finding yourself accused of cheating. This was how it was going to be for the next four years. Never smart enough to be fully accepted, but smart enough to be accused of plagiarising your intelligence. Grim could hardly contain her despair.

There was a knock at the door. Two light taps. "Come in. It's open." Grim called out, not moving from her cross-legged position on the bed. The door swung open, and Minda walked in, closing the door behind her.

"Hey! Just checking in. No creepy visions or anything like that."

Grim looked up and shrugged. "Well, they wouldn't focus on my room. I'm not important."

"You never know…can I sit down?" She asked, pointing to the desk chair.

"Sure."

Minda turned the chair around to face Grim, who closed the book she was looking at and moved it to one side. "Is there something you need, Minda?" She asked, leaning against the wall.

"As I said, checking in. The teachers wanted us to do a little… *well-being* check."

Grim didn't care. She did not give a damn about any of this. "I am well, and I am a being. Satisfied?"

Minda's reaction suggested that she was surprised at Grim's coldness but didn't act on it through words. Grim was tired. Deeper than the physical exhaustion.

"There was another illusion thing, you know. You must have missed it."

Grim looked up, immediately interested by the spark of rebellion. "What was it?"

"They named themselves."

"Huh?"

"We have a name. They are calling themselves the Order of Chaos." Minda said this with a scowl. "Same people as last year. Just some stupid pranks."

"You think they're pranks?"

She leaned forward, and Minda crossed her arms. "Definitely. You must be stupid to doubt the Order. They're tied to all history. We change the world."

"Actually…our history has a lot of inconsistencies-,"

"Listen, Grim, I've been at this school for a long time now. I know *us*. We are good people. Don't give in to what trouble this…*group* is trying to stir. It's a prank, and they'll give up soon."

Grim was going to say something. Argue the point a little more, even pull out some evidence. Tell her that this world was not so glorious and righteous. That all was not what it seemed, but Grim couldn't do it. Grim was tired. She was at the edge. She wanted Minda to leave so she could rest.

Minda saw Grim's tired eyes. "Go get some rest, Grim. I know the classes are a lot before the Baptism."

"Tell me about it."

Minda chuckled. "You'll do well, don't fret about it." She stood up and headed to the door. "Oh, and if you see anything, tell me, alright?"

"Sure."

"Great! Good luck!"

Minda left, and the door closed once more. Grim managed to drag herself out of bed enough to now lock it behind her. It wouldn't be long until dinner, but she had lost her appetite. A half-written reply to her parent's letter was on the desk. Grim slowly got back onto the bed and lay her head down, pulling the blanket over her. Within ten minutes, she was asleep.

Mother and Father.

~~I don't know how to say this but~~

To Mother and Father.

I hope you are well. Elderwall continues to challenge me. and I hope I am doing enough to not warrant any worry. ~~However I have to tell you that~~

My dearest parents.

I see now why you sent me to Elderwall. Perhaps you were right. perhaps all of my other passions were a waste of time. As Lukas would say. I should be grateful for the opportunities presented to me. ~~I am sorry to be the bearer of bad news but I~~

Mother and Father.

I failed the presentation. I'm sorry.

Grim had managed to sleep through dinner. But, this meant she had to deal with the unfortunate consequence of waking up in the middle of the night…again. She hauled herself out of bed, switching on the bedside lamp and rubbing her eyes. Her stomach growled, and she remembered what her mother had said. In an act of bravery, by Grim's standards at least, she threw on her hoodie and a pair of trainers. With a breath out into the cold air, she headed into the hallway, making her way toward the kitchens.

For once, the school was quiet. There was no buzz of young minds declaring their academic endeavours and achievements. She thought it was because the weeklong triumph of the Baptism began tomorrow. It would seem everybody had declared that they should get an early night. She walked the halls in silence, heading through the common room. The fire was now nothing but ash, and she finally reached the kitchens.

She pushed open the door and entered a classic-looking kitchen. It was complete with old iron stoves, pots and pans hanging from hooks. Several large ovens lined up along the back wall. It was pristine, clean to the touch, not that Grim would expect anything less.

There was one cook in the kitchen, sitting on a stool with a book open on one of the marble counters. She was an older-looking staff member, with greying hair tied back with a hair net. Soft wrinkles revealed themselves as she furrowed her eyebrows in concentration. Her white apron had dark brown stains on it. She looked up as Grim opened the door.

"Ah! Hello, I believe we haven't met." She marked the page of her book and closed it. "I'm Miss Pennygroat, but everybody calls me Taffy. And who might you be young lady?"

Grim winced a little and her eyes fell to the floor. "I'm Grim."

"Grim?" Miss Pennygroat, or, Taffy, chuckled. "What can I do for you?"

"I...I missed dinner." She admitted, rather ashamed of herself. It reminded Grim of being at home and reprimanded for a common mistake. "If it's not too much trouble, could I-,"

"Say no more, say no more!" Taffy stood up and turned towards the cupboards. "I can't make you anything too extravagant, mind you, but how about some toast?"

"Are you sure?" Grim stepped inside a little more, closing the door behind her. "I know how late it is."

Taffy shook her head, smiling as sweet as her name. "No need to worry about it, this is why somebody is always on the night shift. Do you want white bread or wholemeal?"

"W-Wholemeal. Please."

"Sit down on one of the stools my sweet. I'll sort you out." Grim did so, resting her elbows on the counter. She leaned forward a little, her eyes immediately falling on Taffy's book.

"What are you reading?"

Taffy dropped the slices of bread into the toaster and watched it go through. "Oh, some silly book. Nothing like what you read. It's this Mortal romance series I like."

"I don't think that's silly at all."

Taffy smiled again at her. "I'm glad you think so, though only a few people would agree with you." She turned back around, and in several swift moments, buttered the toast, and put it on a plate, turning back to Grim. "Are you a first-year? I know the Baptisms are this week."

Grim nodded, and when Taffy walked towards her with the plate, she took it off her. "Maybe that's why I slept through dinner."

"I was a student here, too." Taffy sat back down on her stool. "I remember my Baptism; it didn't go too well for me."

"What happened? Did you…get burned?"

She shrugged her shoulders with a laugh. "Not really, but it wasn't a painless experience. They said I would be a great Skulduggery but well…it was very hard for me to pass the written tests. I'm not the best writer, though I am getting better with my reading. So now I work here, for the Order, serving kids like you toast at midnight."

Grim had started chewing through the bread while Taffy talked. She swallowed. "Do you like it here at least?"

"I like a lot of the students, but it's clear the Order likes a certain type of person. I don't fit into that. But I love cooking, and I will happily sit here at night with my book whenever it's needed. Do you like reading, Grim?"

Grim picked up the second slice of toast. "I do, actually. I'm so used to reading Order history and theory books but…I like poetry books. I don't get to read them very often."

Taffy nodded. She seemed happy to have company at this hour. "Good. I feel like you young 'uns are often told to read too much of what you don't like." She laughed. "Now, did that fill you up?"

She looked down at the empty plate and smiled back at Taffy, yawning again. "Yes, thank you. I can clean my plate if you want?"

"Don't you worry Grim. I'll sort it out. You get yourself back to bed."

Grim stood up and walked to the door. "Thank you, enjoy your book."

"Thank you, dear. Sleep well."

Taffy went back to her book, and Grim ventured back out into the night, walking back to where the student dorms were. The quiet greeted her once again until she turned into the hallway that led down to the art room.

She heard footsteps. Pounding against the stone floor. Grim felt her stomach knot, and she ran around the corner to hide. She peeked out, trying to see where the footsteps were coming from.

That's when she saw a figure, fleeing into the art room. She only saw the back of their head, but it looked like one of the teachers of Elderwall.

The art room was always abandoned, except by Grim, and sometimes Finn and Anna. Why would a teacher go in there? There was nothing in there of interest that would fascinate the academics of this college. She watched the hallway for a few minutes, trying to steady her erratic breathing. If there was a mystery here, it wasn't hers to solve. The last thing she needed was a stern letter from her parents telling her to bloody behave.

Even though she was ready to walk away, *loud* voices came from the art room door. A conversation between two people.

"Why did *Ms*. White allow anyone into this room?"

"Apparently it was to keep the Mortems happy. Their daughter has started this year."

"Audrey could be putting *everything* at risk by letting students in here!"

"Do you want to tell that to her? Or answer to Will and Delilah?"

"I-*fine*. Tell her to keep an eye on the Mortem daughter, make sure she stays in line."

"You're worrying too much. Have you seen her reports? What her parents have been saying? She's a temperamental girl with no magick ability. She won't find anything."

"Bet the Mortems are disappointed then."

"Disappointed doesn't even describe it."

Grim felt a shiver trickle down her spine, like melting ice. She clenched her fists, trying to hear more of the conversation, but their voices grew quieter, and faded away. With more haste than she would have liked to admit, she ran back to her room.

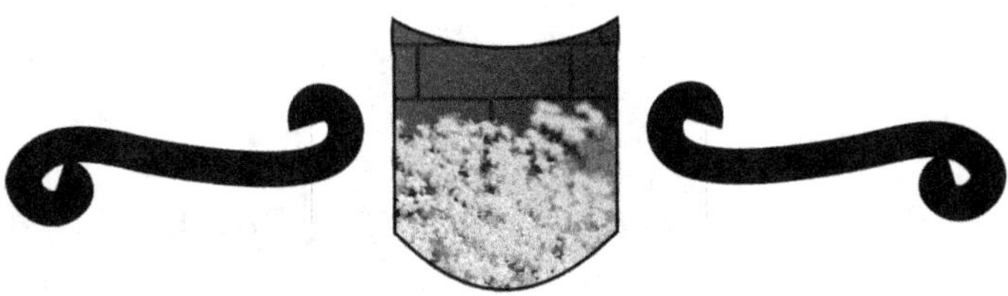

Ms White,

I present my report on our first-year student Raven Mortem. She has continued to attend her sessions with me outside of her scheduled classes. So far, she has had perfect attendance, which is a good sign.

While there has been progress in terms of her attitude to the sessions, I am saddened to report that I see no further progress in her magickal ability. We are still on the basic steps that would have been covered in her evening classes before she started here. I would like to request to see her grades from her evening classes, if that is something you can receive from the Order's Administration department.

My hope is that the Baptism will bring our her Focus, perhaps what she needs is a narrower field of magick to work with. This might help her concentration when practising magick.

I am happy to discuss any further concerns you have.

Mrs Scarlet Locklin

The day had arrived. The time was nigh, and everything had been dawning upon this moment. This week was the Baptism of Fire.

Grim had woken up on Monday morning to an official letter in her letterbox outside the door. Written, in detail, was the schedule for the week, including her exams. On Friday, her parents would arrive and *celebrate* with her after the Baptism.

Lukas had run towards her at breakfast that morning, the letter in his hand and an immaculate smile on his face. He looked overjoyed, going on about how his mother had managed to find a way to get here. And about how excited he was to see what his focus would be. And that he couldn't *wait* until Grim would realise how amazing she could be. She had reacted to this all as she usually would, not managing to match his level of enthusiasm.

Then came the assessments around the core principles they had been learning about. The written exams on the four Focuses they could choose from. They were a breeze for her, a simple case of regurgitating the information she had absorbed.

Now came the true taskmaster, looming over her like a thundercloud, bound to a single flame. They had set the ceremony up in the grand hall. It was for official events, like the Equinox Ball and graduation ceremonies. Grim knew her timeslot, but Lukas had asked her to be waiting outside for when he finished. The wait was daunting as if you were waiting for death. Grim was after him. Maybe Ms. White and her parents thought she would find comfort in his familiarity. The halls were full of other students, all chatting away about the ceremony. In their hands, they held the coloured gemstone that was the symbol of their focus. Some parents were already there, drowning their children in adoration. Expected from any loving family. This was a big day for Magus, even Grim accepted that fact at least. This was the day people her age were reassured that they would receive acceptance and love.

Lukas walked out the door, smiling as he had been at the start of the week. Lukas enjoyed the success of today more than she ever would.

He immediately pulled her in for a hug, holding her for much longer than he usually does. She felt like everyone was watching them, but she lifted her hands and held him back. He was happy, so she let him have his moment.

He pulled away and with an excited grin, pulled out the stone from his pocket. A whirlpool of fiery red, sea blue, forest green, and cloudy grey. He was an Elemental. Grim beamed.

"Congrats Lukas."

She meant it. She knew how much this meant to him.

"Thanks. Oh my god, it was…it's such a thrill, Grim. I can't wait until you come out there yourself. You'll know exactly what I mean." He put his hands on her shoulders. "I'll wait out here for you. Then we can go celebrate with my mother and your parents?"

It hit Grim that her parents were here now. She hadn't seen them. But, there was a note from her mother that morning that they were going to be waiting in the dining hall afterwards.

"Okay."

The door to the hall opened, and Ms White spotted Grim. "Ra-," She stopped herself. "Grim Mortem. Please come in."

Lukas squeezed her shoulder and then nudged her towards the door. "You've got this, good luck."

Grim walked into the room. The grand hall was round, with an elegant, curved roof that had a bright gold chandelier hanging from the centre. The candlelight was dim. She noticed a raised platform on one side, with a grand piano and enough space for a small orchestra. Ms White walked ahead, leading her to the centre of the room, beneath the chandelier. In front of her was a raised stone plinth that had a silver dish on top of it. The bright orange flame danced in the middle, suspended in the air.

Ms. White stood opposite to Starching. She noticed in the shadows of the room there were other figures. The other teachers would find out if this was another student to add to their register.

Starching did his classic move and summoned a sheet of paper from nothing. "Please state your full *legal* name." He read.

"Raven Alexandra Mortem."

"Raven Alexandra Mortem," He continued reading. "Do you understand that this ceremony will determine where your magickal Focus lies? And this will solidify your standing within the ranks of the Order and your fellow Magus?"

"Yes."

"Do you accept that this decision is final?"

"Yes."

"Then, Raven Alexandra Mortem, raise your right hand and place it into the fire."

A leap of faith. A baptism of fire. A cleansing of the mind and soul. Grim felt…*nothing*. No fear, no panic, no worry at all. This wasn't the difficult part; it was what came after. *If* anything came after.

She raised her hand.

Seven.

Eleven.

She felt the heat of the flames.

Inhale.

Exhale.

She plunged her hand in.

And screamed.

FAO: All Elderwall Teaching Staff

PROTOCOL TO FOLLOW DURING THE BAPTISM OF FIRE

During the annual ceremony, students will be allocated a time in which to arrive at the grand hall across the week. Expect parents and guardians of our students to also be in attendance, as they will arrive to bring their children home for the month of December.

When the student arrives, recite the proclamation that will be given to the staff member in charge of the ceremony, and ask the student to agree to the conditions listed. Once they have done so, they may put their hand into the fire.

Please be reassured that the flames will not harm the student. The flames detect the magick within each individual student, and change colour accordingly:

Elemental- Red

Summoner- Yellow

Psychic- Purple

Skulduggery- Grey

Once the flames have changed colour, you may hand over a stone to the student, which reflects the decided Focus:

Elemental: A swirling red, green, blue and grey stone

Summoner: A yellow stone similar to a candle flame

Psychic: A misty purple stone

Skulduggery: A rose pink stone

The student is then allowed to leave and join in the celebrations, and you may call the next student in once the flames have reset themselves.

EMERGENCY PROTOCOL FOR IF A STUDENT IS BURNED DURING THE BAPTISM

In a rare instance, a student can be burned by the flames of the Baptism. The cause of this is not known, but is often related to the amount of magickal ability the student has. If such an event occurs, then the student must be taken to the infirmary immediately, while another staff member takes over the ceremony. If the flame changes colour, a note must be made so that we can assess whether the student can continue into studying that Focus. Once the student is stable in the infirmary, the parents or guardians of the student must be found of notified of the incident. However, no other staff or students should be made aware of the event.

If there are any issues, please bring them up with Ms White before the week of the Baptism begins. We thank you for your co-operation in bringing forth a new generation of Order members and proud Magus.

The teachers took Grim to the college's infirmary. A teacher charged forward and bundled her hand in a bubble of water that they created. Then, they carried her out of the room. Lukas had tried to go with her, but another staff member held him back.

She had heard this all second-hand from the school nurse. She had passed out. From the shock, the nurse said. He used a cooling ointment on her hand and bandaged it up with care. Her parents would arrive any moment, he said, and then she could go to dinner. This hadn't registered in Grim's head. She sat, legs dangling off the infirmary bed, as her parents took some chairs and sat opposite her.

It had already been two months since she saw them, and they hadn't changed. Her parents were the separate parts of her. She had her mother's long wavy hair, even if she cut it all off. Her father's dark eyes, even if she turned them as black as onyx. Their skin tones all matched. They dressed neatly, still representing the Order even outside of work. Her mother wore a dark floral dress and heels. Her father was in a white shirt with the collar button undone, trousers ironed and his best shoes on.

Grim had showed up to the ceremony in a pair of ripped jeans and an old t-shirt with paint on it.

Her mother opened the tension in the air and put a hand on Grim's knee. "Well…this did not go as expected, did it, sweetheart?"

"No." She replied, bluntly.

Her father tried to laugh. *Tried.* "Heh, I thought you would be a Summoner like your old man. Could finally teach you how to make candles."

"Or an Elemental like Lukas. We were speaking to Evelyn. She is *so* proud."

"*So* proud." Her father agreed.

Grim moved her knee, and her mother's hand dropped. She took it back to her lap, folding her hands together once more.

Grim sighed. "So…you're not proud of me?"

"It's not that Ray." Her mother smiled again. "We…*know* you can do better."

"And you're going to do better." Her father said, nodding and turning to Grim's mother. "You won't end up like those silly pranksters we noticed."

She now wanted to pay attention. "The Order of Chaos?"

"Is that their name? Yes, they did a stunt with all the parents. Some nonsense about how we are forcing everyone to become Magus, and we have no right blah, blah, blah." Her mother waved a hand, dismissing the notion. "No ground for it at all."

"Huh…" Grim knew better than to argue with her mother about such things.

"*Anyway.* This is a setback." Her father steered back the conversation, taking her mother's hand. "Ms. White has assured us that we can find your focus and get you into those classes."

"What-,"

"Yes!" Her mother exclaimed. "It's wonderful, we have the holidays to come up with a plan, get you studying, and you'll see this was the right choice for you."

Something roared inside of Grim. And for the first time, she wanted to say something back. "Don't *I* get a say-,"

"Yes-," Her father interrupted, still looking at her mother. "No painting, no distractions, we can get your grades up. Letting you into that art room was a silly idea."

"Don't interrupt me!" Grim protested.

Her parents turned to look at her. "But Raven-," Her mother said, but Grim stood up off the bed.

"No. *No*. Don't Raven me. I am sick of this. All of this. I don't want this."

"Listen…we can get this all sorted out,"

"I don't want it sorted out!" She yelled, her voice echoing in the infirmary. "I never wanted to come here! I never wanted this, but no- *you* wanted this for me! I never got a *fucking* choice!"

"Raven. Do not swear at us."

"I'm an adult!" Grim stepped away from them. "I fucking *can* and I will."

"She's hysterical." Her mother shook her head. "Perfect time to take you home."

"No! NO. You know what? I'm staying here for the holidays."

"Raven we won't let you do that." Her father stood up now.

Grim's eyes bubbled with tears. "You never let me do *anything*. You've never listened. All I am is a disappointment. A temperamental girl with no magic, that's what you've been saying to everyone." She held up her bandaged hand. "And *this*? Is the perfect example of that.

Her mother stood up too. "Raven, you're taking this too far. You don't know what you want."

"I do know what I want. I want to stay here. Go enjoy your fancy dinner with all your friends in this stupid College. I will see you when the year is over."

Grim stormed out of the infirmary, bandages still on her hand. In the distance, she heard the call of her parents demanding that she come back. She started running. Pushing past the flocks of students heading to the celebratory dinner in the dining hall. She didn't know the College as well as she should but managed to find a door leading outside. She followed the courtyard paths and felt the crisp winter air biting her skin. She felt the tears on her cheeks freeze over.

She stopped to catch her breath. She looked up, trying to work out where she was. She had stumbled into a garden. Roses bloomed along the cracked stone walls. The colours were a spectrum, ranging from blood red to luscious purple. Flowers were wild in flowerbeds, a beautiful mess. The snapped flagstone path whirled around the beds and connected back to the courtyard paths she was following. Trees surrounded her. Lanterns hung on poles, swaying in the wind. There was a bench in the centre of this small garden. On that bench, was the last person she expected to see.

Cain waved a hand at her. "Hey, stranger. Want to sit down?"

Grim sat down next to Cain on the bench, folding her hands in her lap. Her eyes drifted to the bandages on his left hand, and she looked up at him, trying to see if he would react. He smiled, knowing what was being said, as he noticed her bandaged hand as well. The two embraced the truth that now connected them.

"They used to call this place the garden of shadows." Cain started explaining, pointing out the flowers. "Because of how secluded it was, and how all the flowers bloomed with dark colours. They said it was because of the magick surrounding the College. I think it's to do with the soil and what plants were grown here over the years."

"It's beautiful." She admitted, leaning back against the wooden bench.

Cain tilted his head to one side, looking toward her. "I come here a lot. It's quiet. I don't have to hear everyone going on about the Order and their focus. Especially today. If I hear *let me see your stone* one more time-,"

She chuckled. "Lukas was so happy about it..." The realisation hit her. "Oh god, it's going to be *hell* when I go back."

"What happened? If you don't mind me asking. You looked a little out of breath when you first got here."

"I passed out after, you know-," She waved her bandaged hand in the air. "My parents came in, and started talking about how they were going to get me back on track, and I could find my focus and-and-,"

"And you couldn't handle someone else choosing for you?"

Her head dropped, and she nodded. "Yeah. I yelled. I swore. I ran off."

"I know that feeling," Cain fidgeted with his thumbs and avoided looking at her. "There's a lot of pressure here, huh?"

She groaned, massaging her forehead with her free hand. "There is."

"The whole thing. It's a lot of pressure. *Find your focus and join the Order ranks.*"

"Everything decided by…what, a fire? It's fucking stupid." She shivered, the winter air hitting her. "It's all stupid."

Cain leaned down, and his hand reached under the bench. He pulled out a blanket and passed it over to Grim. "I always bring one when I read out here."

Grim smiled at Cain and covered her shoulders with it. "Thank you…" She paused. "Why are you being nice to me?"

He chuckled. "I need a reason to stop someone from freezing?"

She rolled her eyes, laughing a little. "No…but we haven't talked all that much."

"To be honest," He sat up a little straighter. "I like our conversations. You are the only one I can talk about anything *normal* with. Everyone else I talk to it's always about the next test, or what incense is best for their spells. We talked about the Great Bear Hunt of 1492.”

“A wonderful moment in history.” She replied with a smirk, tightening the blanket around her.

“You’re nice to talk to. And it seems we are in the same boat in some regards.”

Grim looked at her bandages and his. She frowned a little. “What did your parents think? When they saw this?”

Cain shrugged. “My father was too busy to come. He’s drowning in Order paperwork”

“I’m sorry.”

He smiled, dismissing her concerns. “It’s okay, I know he does his best. It’s easier for him if I’m here. I’m staying here over the holidays.”

She laughed, more to herself than to Cain. “I’m staying here now as well.”

“Wow, how badly did you go off at your parents?” He asked. His tone was light, but she could tell he was curious.

“So bad I said I would see them at the end of the year.” She put her head in her hands. “I couldn’t bear the thought of going home. It would be endless studying. My mother has a wonderful tendency to *misplace* my artwork by the fireplace.”

“Really?.”

“Yep.”

Cain put his hand on her shoulder. His hands were cold, but his touch was gentle. Grim looked up at Cain, and he smiled at her. She smiled back. The truth is left in the air. "Well, do you want to spend Christmas here together? I've heard they do one *hell* of a dinner."

She patted his hand, the one that stayed on her shoulder. "Can't wait to try it."

Elderwall was an hour's drive away from the Tivindade train station. The college, in its infinite amount of funds and resources, offered a minibus service. Grim was still adamant about not going home but agreed to go on the bus journey with Lukas. He was going to meet his mother at the train station to go home. Evelyn had been at the Baptism, of course, but she had left a little earlier to allow Lukas more time to pack.

Lukas' mother had a fondness for her. He had caught her up on everything that had happened that night. Down to the speech Grim's father gave and the extravagant three-course meal. Lukas had told his mother Grim was *too sick* to attend the celebrations.

Grim hadn't cared. She spent the whole time with Cain in the garden of shadows. They had gone back inside after all the visitors had left. Taffy had given them both a plate of leftovers.

The train station was quiet on this particular Sunday morning. No Mortal paid any mind to the bunch of young students who came through the station. As soon as Lukas stepped off the bus, he saw his mother Evelyn waiting by the entrance. Lukas was the spitting image of her. They shared the same sun-kissed hair, blonde with highlights of hazelnut and brown. The same eyes. Evelyn wore her hair loose down her shoulder, wearing a thick coat and a knitted blanket over her knees.

She beamed as soon as she saw them, turning her wheelchair around and moving towards her son.

Immediately, he rushed towards her and bent down, hugging her tight.

So, that is what it meant to be loved like he was.

"Hey, Momma." He was beaming as he pulled away. "How was the trip down here?"

"Not too bad, I forget Psychics can lift a wheelchair sometimes." Evelyn leaned to the side and met Grim's eyes. "Oh my, how you've grown."

"We only saw each other in the summer, Evelyn."

"I know, I know, but *still*, you've got a different look about you Ra- *Grim*." She held her arms out towards Grim, while Lukas turned back to the bus to grab his suitcase. "Come here, give me a hug."

With some reluctance, Grim leaned in Evelyn's embrace. People seemed to forget that Grim wasn't much of a hugger.

"How's your hand?" Evelyn asked, immediately holding Grim's bandaged hand and taking a look.

"The nurse is going to put some new bandages on it when I get back. But he said it's healing well."

"Oh good. I was so worried when Lukas told me what happened."

"I didn't mean to worry you, Evelyn."

"It's my job to worry, you mean a lot to Lukas you know." She explained, letting go of Grim's hand. "But anyway, I know it's not my place to say but…you'll do well, no matter what happens."

"In what sense?" She asked. Grim wondered why Lukas' mother, who was always light-hearted, was trying to give her advice.

"In every sense," Evelyn replied with a smile. "But anyway, about what happened-,"

"You mean about the Baptism?" Lukas called out, as he came back with his suitcase. "You should still be able to do Focus classes, right Grim?"

"I haven't heard anything yet. We'll see in the new year."

"I hope you get classes with me at least. We could learn how to be Elementals together."

"You wouldn't need me in those classes anyway, you'll ace it."

"I know but-,"

"You don't need a focus to get on at Elderwall." Evelyn interrupted, looking at her son with a smirk and folding her hands in her lap. "You'll be fine Grim."

"And I'll be there for you too," Lukas added, with a huge grin on his face. "Anyway, Grim needs to get back up to the school, and we need to get to our train."

"Of course, of course. I'll give my regards to your parents Grim."

Grim felt a stab in her chest. "Thanks."

Lukas pulled Grim into a sudden hug. squeezing her. "I'll see you soon. Be sure to write."

"I will." Grim was the one to break the hug. "Now get going. Bye, Evelyn."

"Bye, dear!"

Lukas held onto his mother's wheelchair with one hand and helped her push herself up the ramp. Grim watched them go inside the station. Lukas turned back to wave one more time before disappearing. She turned, climbed back onto the bus, and braced herself for the coming of winter.

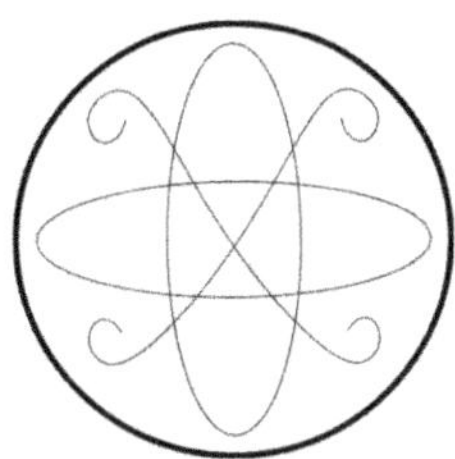

We are proud to say that another successful Baptism of Fire occurred at Elderwall Boarding College. We thank all of our Order members who attended the celebrations in support of their children and their fellow students.

We would also like to thank William Mortem, one of our highest ranking Order members, for giving a speech on behalf of the Order at the celebration dinner. For those who wish to know what was said, the following transcript has been provided:

I would like to say, on behalf of everyone at the Order, that we are proud of everyone here today for completing the Baptism of Fire. The Baptism is a sacred tradition, established to help our young Magus find their path. Today, we saw a new generation, I saw my daughter take her place amongst the Order. I saw all of you take your place as well, and I could not have been prouder. You will remember this day for the rest of your lives, and I hope you continue to make your family proud as you continue your studies here.

However, we have to unfortunately report that two students were burned by the Baptism's flames, an occurrence that has not happened for some years. Both these students received immediate medical attention, and are recovering well. We have informed their families of the situation, and are actively working with them to decide their next steps.

Please join us in congratulating our first-year Elderwall students.

December

Dear Mother and Father.

I don't know what you want me to say. You have already sent me a letter that clearly showed your discontent with the entire situation. Well. put aside your anger. and for once. before leaping to the righteous conclusion you always reach. just listen to your child fill you in on what she's been doing at Elderwall for Christmas. Yes. your *child*. You know exactly why I'm being specific.

I've been sending letters back and forth with Lukas. I sent him a painting as a present. Some kind soul restocked the art club after realising that it was finally being used again. I'm sure you've talked to Evelyn. but Lukas is doing well. He's happy. and I'm happy for him.

The College do surprisingly well during the holidays. There weren't that many of us. a few students from the other years and a couple of professors. Cain. my new friend. taught me how to make what he called *the best hot chocolate*. I'll admit. it was pretty good.

I know there's plenty more we need to say. But until you realise that being at Elderwall is not what I wanted. then we can start moving forward. When I finish the year and come home. I want us to talk about what *I* want. That's all I ask from the two of you.

Sorry. this is so short. I promised Cain I would show him how to find books in the library. Ms White says she will speak to me about my focus once she is back in January.

Grim.

Grim,

Hey stranger! Feels so weird to not be talking face to face. I miss your voice...and your eye rolls. Christmas is going well here. Mother missed me like crazy I think since she's currently *insisting* that we cook together once I've finished this letter to you. I don't know why you decided not to go home yourself honestly. I know you were upset, but your parents had a point.

You're wasting every opportunity handed to you, and I don't want to see you ruin yourself. One day, I want us to stand side by side as proud Magus.

Oh, I hope you got your grades! Mine came through the post, and I think we can both work out what scores I got. I'll be Valedictorian at this rate. Anyway, got to go, see you in the new year!

Lukas.

P.S Thanks for the painting! It was neat.

Grim ripped out the paper from the notebook and scrunched it into a ball. She let her head fall onto the paper, pen in her hand.

"Still struggling?" Cain asked with a chuckle. The two of them were sitting in the empty library. The atmosphere felt different than all the times Grim had been here before. Maybe it was the bliss of the silence or the pleasant company she was keeping. Either way, it somewhat eased her anxiety.

"Why is it so hard to write a letter?" She mumbled into the paper, lifting her head. "You'd think I'd know what to say."

"Nobody ever knows what to say, Grim."

"Says the person who's putting off writing a letter to their father."

Cain put a hand on his chest, faking shock. "I'll have you know I sent it this morning!"

She threw the paper ball at him. "You never told me!"

"I'm telling you now." He said with a laugh. "You'll know what to say soon."

"God I hope so." Grim closed the notebook, forcing herself to not stare at the blank pages ahead of her. She and Cain had come here after receiving their grades from the Baptism of Fire. Cain had insisted they see what "normal" books the library had so they could have a bit of peace from magick. She saw their sheets out of the corner of her eye.

Raven Alexandra Mortem:

Focus: Undetermined.

Written Examinations: 96%

Cain Blackwood:

Focus: Summoner

Written Examinations: 73%

"Can I ask you something, by the way?"

Grim looked up at Cain, who had stopped reading his book on mechanics. "Sure."

"Why do you use the name, Grim?"

She shrugged and rested her head in one hand. "I liked it. It's neutral. It...fits more than Raven."

"Is it something to do with what you said to your parents?"

She had given Cain the letter she wrote to her parents and asked him to read it over. Asked if she was demanding too much, if it was too blunt. Or if it wasn't blunt enough, or if she should be nicer. The anxieties that plagued her head had reached the stage of emotional incapacity. He hadn't asked any questions about the content, until now of course. At the time, he told her that it seemed like she had said what she needed to. That was enough for her.

"It's fine." She sighed, trying to think of how to phrase it. "I don't think I'm- you know- a girl. Ugh, it's weird to explain."

Cain's eyes widened as if something clicked into place. "Oh my god- if I've been referring to you in the wrong way I'm sorry-"

"No, no. It's okay. I don't even know myself. I'm still working it all out."

"You need to meet Remi. They'll understand exactly what you're talking about."

"Remi?"

Grim remembered them. Another person on the Student Council who she had seen talking to Lukas. They didn't seem like the most approachable person.

"Remi is a family friend. I've known them since I was a kid. My father and their father went to Elderwall together." He explained, smiling and laughing. "Anyway, they may be a third-year, but they're cool, and have always looked out for me."

"Has Remi gone home?"

"Only for this week. Like my father, their family is busy." He explained. "When they get back, I'll introduce you."

Grim thought for a moment. "I think I have met them, but we didn't speak. They came to talk to Lukas about something relating to the Student Council."

Cain smirked. "Did they seem like they were going to stab you?"

"Umm…yes?" She replied in a cautious tone, not wanting to insult someone with whom Cain was close.

He laughed. "Yeah, they're only like that with people they hate."

Grim let out a shaky sigh. "They *hate* Lukas?"

"Well…" He hesitated. "I don't know about *hate*. I'm only saying that because I know how Remi interacts with people. Maybe you can get a straight answer when you meet them. But don't worry, they'll love you."

"Oh...good."

To Finn.

I'm not good at Christmas cards. so I'm trying with a painting. Hope you're enjoying the time at home; I'm enjoying the time here more than I thought I would.

I'll make sure your spot in the art club room is there for you when you're back in January.

All the best.

Grim

To Anna.

This is not for Christmas. It's for Hanukkah. I made sure of it. I better not hear any complaints.

Hope you're having a good time. Being here is strangely peaceful. I'll see you in January. The art club got restocked with charcoals. Go annoy Finn for both of us.

All the best.

Grim

Cain did make the best hot chocolate. Grim wasn't sure where he got the experience from to qualify for such things, but it didn't matter. Her frosty veins warmed when Cain pulled out a thermos in the garden of shadows and handed her a plastic cup. As well as in the library, the two had been meeting there when it hadn't snowed. It became an unlikely tradition. An unspoken promise that they would bundle themselves in their coats and head there.

Sometimes Cain would slide a note under her door or catch her as she was leaving the dining hall. As Grim knew, Cain had a knack for always finding her. Maybe she was that predictable.

Cain always came with some books on engineering or inventions. Meanwhile, Grim armed herself with a sketchbook and a pencil. Grim enjoyed the silence that came between the two, there was a certain peace to it. Unlike what she felt around her parents or Lukas. She felt content. It could have been the company, or it was the relief of the pressure. Whatever it was, it calmed Grim's mind and balanced her heart.

She hadn't had a good experience with the holidays. They had never been enjoyable. The constant pressure to smile through tradition often left her burnt out. With Cain, it was calmer. On Christmas Day, the two of them sat on the floor by the fireplace in the common room, unopened parcels in front of them. The fire was already burning, and a sparkling Christmas tree glimmered in the corner of the room.

"So…on the count of three?" Cain suggested, his eyes looking down at his box and placing a hand on it.

Grim pulled hers onto her lap, nervously biting her lip. "You count."

"One. Two. Three!"

The sound of cardboard ripping rippled into Grim's ears. She lifted the box flaps and chuckled the packaging foam aside. Cain pulled the contents of his present out first.

A red multi-tool, a book on botany, and a card, all from his father.

Grim reached into her box and first pulled out a pair of pyjamas. Next, the latest edition of Order protocols and guidelines.

"Damn, they're pushing it, huh?"

"Always have…" Grim leaned forward, peering at the title of the book. "Botany?"

He chuckled, his cheeks going pink from embarrassment. "I mentioned to him in a letter that I wanted to know what flowers were in the garden of shadows."

"I think it's sweet." Grim flicked through the book of Order protocol. The page numbers and references had already been seared into her brain. An irreversible process at this point.

Cain smiled, opening the card. He paused for a moment, and his eyebrows raised as he closed the card back up again.

"What is it?" She asked, dropping the book onto the hard wooden floor.

"My father wants to meet you. He's asking if we could meet up in Tivindade for lunch before classes start again."

"H-he wants to meet me?" Grim sat up straighter, her breath catching in her throat. "Why?"

"I-um, I've talked about you quite a bit to him, and it's because I never talk about anyone else apart from Remi." Cain looked flustered as he put everything back into the box. "You don't have to come, honestly, it's *fine* if you don't want to, my father just likes to know who I'm hanging out with and-,"

"I-I would love to." She interrupted his ramblings. "It's... I'm not sure if he'll like me and I don't want to embarrass you..."

"You've been to one too many dinners, I can tell. I bet someone paraded you around in a cupcake dress and told you to shake a million hands."

"My parents are high-ranking Order officials. Of course, I was to be the model of a perfect young Magus."

"Well, my father isn't like that, he's kind of the black sheep of his office. Never attended a dinner party and never forced me to do anything either. Being here is more of a formality so everyone leaves him alone." Cain looked up at her. The flames crackled in the moments he was thinking. "Can I ask you something?"

"Sure."

"Your life at home sounds like hell. This life the Order has created seems to work against you. How has it not broken you?"

Grim inhaled, the warm air filling her lungs. "Who says I'm not already broken?"

Cain's silence spoke the world.

"I wish I knew how to make it better."

She shrugged. "You cannot fix a world that doesn't believe it's broken."

He paused, taking a moment to think through his next words. When he spoke, he spoke with care. "What if there was a way to fix it?"

She smirked. "Whoever is claiming they can do that; I'd like to see them try."

Cain chuckled, and stood up, picking up his parcel with one hand. He offered a hand to Grim. "Why don't we spend the evening identifying the flowers in the garden of shadows?"

Grim reached up and took his hand, and Cain pulled her to her feet. She reached down for her parcel and looked back at Cain, who was watching her, waiting for an answer.

She smiled back at him. "Sounds perfect."

Dear Lukas,

I've tried to write this reply a load of times, but I keep struggling with how to phrase everything. You know what I'm like when it comes to these things.

I'm glad the holidays are going well for you, and congrats on your grades. They still haven't worked out what they're going to do about my focus. I'm not that bothered honestly, I'll leave them to their discussions, doesn't seem like I'll get a choice in the matter anyway.

I wrote to my parents— but I doubt I will get a reply. Even if I do get one, I bet it'll be a mouthful of excuses and insults. Perhaps it's best if I save myself the trouble of worrying about it.

Things here have been good— Elderwall is so quiet without the constant chatter, it's almost peaceful. I've been spending a lot of time with Cain— he's in Starching's class with us. I'll have to try and introduce you. He's kind, helped me with the letter to my parents. We've been exploring the College and having too many hot chocolates. He's become a good friend and it's nice to have the company here. I think I would be worse off if I had to spend Christmas here alone.

Give my love to Evelyn. Tell her I'll come over for the summer so we can catch up.

See you soon.

Grim

Grim,

Cain? Do you mean Cain Blackwood? I'm surprised you're talking to him. He distances himself from everything to do with the College you know. I also heard from your parents that his father's a bit shady even though he works for the Order.

Be careful around him. I don't trust it. You need to surround yourself with the right people. I'll introduce you to George and my other friends on the football team. You'll see they're exactly the type of people we can get along with.

Also, try to see what's happening with your focus. You say you don't have a choice, but I think you should force yourself to have a say in the matter. I don't want you to get to the point where they might ask you to retake the Baptism. Take some initiative! Practice some magick while you have the place to yourself, especially by yourself. Work out what feels right to you. You can tell me everything when I'm back.

Love,

Lukas

P.S Mother says hi! She would love to see you soon.

Grim had decided to follow Lukas' advice...to an extent. He was correct in the fact that she needed to try and explore where her focus could lie. Yet, Grim decided it was best if she had a little help in the matter. Cain was more than happy to offer his help when Grim asked, he needed to work things out too. He also decided it was the perfect time for Grim and Remi to meet since they had come back to Elderwall a few days ago.

They agreed the three of them would meet in the sports hall that afternoon. To Grim's surprise, this was the only sports hall the College had. But, they did make up for it with the massive fields that the football and athletics teams had at their disposal. Remi and Cain were already there when Grim arrived, the two of them standing in the middle of the hall. The sports hall wasn't glamorous. It was a rectangular room with a high ceiling, lit up by small spotlights. Complete with wooden panelled walls and a scuffed floor. White paint lines mapped out various markings for sports. By all accounts, it was pretty standard. A twist for Elderwall by any means.

"Cain, are you *sure* about this?"

The two of them hadn't noticed that Grim was there. Their voices echoed enough for Grim to hear.

"I have a good feeling Remi. A *really* good feeling. I-," Cain turned and beamed when he saw her at the double doors. "Grim!"

She waved to the two of them. "I'm not early or anything, am I?"

"No." Remi smiled, a stark contrast to Grim's first meeting with them. "You're right on time."

"Sorry," Cain started walking towards her. "We were talking about stuff."

"It's okay." Grim shook her head. "You don't have to explain yourself."

Remi laughed a little. "Come on then you magickal mischief-makers. Let's see what we can do."

"I'm not sure I like the term *mischief-makers*." Cain joked as he followed Remi back to the middle of the room. Grim followed him.

They turned to the first years, their eyes gleaming with wisdom from being at Elderwall for so long. "What would you prefer Cain, *intrepid heroes*? Or better yet-,"

They turned back to the two of them, spinning on their heel. They opened their arms with glamour and dramatics, raising their chin. "Those who have disgraced the Order!"

Cain burst out laughing, but something about Remi's flippant disregard unnerved her. Grim wasn't one for Order propaganda and knew that it wasn't an idea to receive praise, but to Remi, it seemed personal.

"Alright Remi, get off your high horse. You said you wanted to help."

"Fine." They said, and the three of them stopped in the centre of the hall. Remi reached into their jacket pocket and pulled out an apple. They balanced it on the palm of their hand and looked at Grim. "Take a couple of steps back and try to take the apple from my hand."

"Why me first?" She asked.

They replied with a smirk. "I already *know* what Cain can do. I want to see what you can do. It's more exciting."

Grim didn't know how to respond, but she shrugged. Usually, this would be the moment when she would feel the sudden rush of embarrassment. To her surprise, she felt calm. It was unclear why this was so.

She lifted her hand and tried to concentrate all the energy on her fingertips. She felt the slightest spark, not enough to cause a storm. But still, it flickered, like a shiver in a dark room or when a candle was first lit. Grim sent that speckle out, and the apple moved. It flung itself out of Remi's hand and flew to the right, rolling onto the floor with several thumping bumps.

"Goddammit." Grim huffed and picked up the apple. "Sorry Remi, this always happens."

"Why are you apologising?"

Grim looked back at them. "Because I messed up?"

Remi glanced at the apple, and back at Grim. "Despite what this College teaches, you still did magick. Don't be so hard on yourself. Cain, are you ready? Do you have your candles?"

She remembered that Cain was summoner. Perhaps Remi was going to help him practice the principle of contagion.

"Umm…" Cain's eyes dropped to the floor.

"*Cain…*" Remi glared at him.

"About that…"

"Cain Blackwood get your ass to your locker and get your candles."

Like a blur, Cain sped out of the sports hall, and Grim heard his footsteps fade as he barrelled towards the lockers. Remi laughed to themselves. "He's pretty good at tracking things down. Shouldn't take him too long."

"He always seems to track me down." Grim joked. "We had a knack of running into each other before we started hanging out."

"Doesn't surprise me." Remi crossed their arms. "Can I ask you something?"

"Sure."

"You're good friends with Lukas, right?"

She nodded. "Really good friends."

"I know this is overstepping, but I heard about the argument with your parents from him. He was telling people in the student council about it."

Grim looked at Remi in shock. "He- what? Why was he telling people?"

"He was trying to see if we could intervene and get you to go home regardless. Said it was the best thing for you. I replied with what everyone else said-,"

"That I'm an adult and I have the right to make that decision?"

"Exactly."

She felt something burning inside of her. She wasn't sure if it was anger, pain, regret, or something else unknown to her.

Remi shrugged, letting out a long breath. "Cain probably told you, but I do not waste my time being friendly to people I don't like. Lukas seems two-faced. I can never tell if that smile of his is manipulative or genuine."

"It's always been genuine with me; we've been together since we were kids."

"So, your families know each other and everything?"

"Yeah, of course."

"Then why didn't Lukas invite you to come home with him?"

The question hit Grim like an avalanche "I... well it's not my place to ask and..."

"Grim, he insulted your decision. He didn't agree with your choice but refused to offer you an alternative. He..." Remi groaned. "It's not my place, I know."

"It's okay, I appreciate the concern."

"I know what it's like for people to think they have your best interests at heart, and then find out it's a lie." They explained. "I've observed Lukas a lot. He knows how to put on a show. He's been doing it for months."

"Remi...I know Lukas."

"I know you do. And because you know him best, you can see through him. Just…observe." They paused, relieving the tension that was now existing in this conversation. The corners of Remi's mouth lifted into the smallest of smiles. "Then let me know if my hunch is right."

Grim didn't want to doubt Lukas. That was the last thing she wanted. If anything, Lukas was a constant force in her life that always seemed to do something good for her. But even if she hadn't committed to the extraordinary Elderwall experience, she had experienced something. She experienced new people, and new challenges, and realised that people actually…*liked* her. She always hung out with Lukas because it seemed like he was the only one who could tolerate her. Now she knew this was not the case. It would be okay to take a moment to review the situation.

"Deal."

The doors to the sports hall burst open, and Cain stood in the entranceway, a bag of candles in his hand. "I'm ready!"

Cain managed to light five candles. With a little encouragement from Remi, Grim lit one.

Hello Grim,

I know I'm probably the last person you expect a letter from, but Lukas is preparing to pack to come back to Elderwall, so I had a few minutes to myself.

I hope you're doing well sweetheart; Lukas has been filling me in on what you've been up to it all sounds very positive for you. I'm writing to you because Lukas also told me what happened with your parents. I've talked to them myself, and they seem apologetic about what happened, but wanted to wait to speak to you in person about it.

I know it's not my place to dabble in the affairs of a family so close to mine. But I wanted to let you know if you can't heal things with your parents in the summer, our door is always open. Don't worry about Lukas, I'll handle his reservations. You are free to stay with us until you go back to Elderwall.

I've always cared for you like a second child Grim, and I want you to know that. If the situation arises, send me a letter, or simply turn up on the doorstep. I'll handle the fallout.

Take care of yourself Grim. I know from experience the Order is not always kind, and not always considerate. I trust in the hope you will follow the path that feels right to you, even if it is...slightly unconventional.

All my love,

Evelyn Lightchild

January

Tivindade was a small town, with a single train station. The kind people wouldn't visit unless you found it in the article: "Top 5 tourist spots you've missed". It was a pretty kind of small town with cobbled streets and old cottages. Surrounded by farmland and the odd oak tree that had survived a century or two. Perfect, peaceful and quaint, which is why a lot of Magus decided to settle down there. There were mortals there too, and the town of Tivindade lived in a state of coexistence. Completely unaware of the secret right under their nose.

Grim and Cain had gotten the train together that morning, arriving in the town before lunch. They made their way to the café where they were going to meet Cain's father, Marcus. She had woken up with more anxiety than she had anticipated, conscious of everything she was. She fretted about how she was going to dress, what she was going to say, the exact opinion Marcus was going to form of her.

So far, she had been a disappointment to every adult on every front.

When Cain came to her dorm room door, she came out wearing an oversized jumper, jeans and her signature boots. He said she looked great, and there was nothing more to add.

They were meeting Marcus at the Chipped Teacup, a café run by generations of Magus from the same family. It was a place for parents and students to meet up outside of the Baptism. Although, Grim's parents told her they would both be too busy to make the commute throughout the year.

Grim glanced over at Cain as he pushed open the door to the café, the bell clinging as he did so. He had a casual smile on his face, and she could tell that inside he was bursting with excitement.

The café was quiet for a weekday, with quaint round wooden tables and chairs. The walls were lilac with white flowers. Behind the counter, there were rows upon rows of tea sets. Pristine, like all Magus were.

As soon as the door shut behind the two of them, a man stood up from a back table, holding his arms out wide.

"Cainy-boy!"

Marcus Blackwood strode forward and pulled Cain into his arms. He had broad shoulders and was swallowing his son in the embrace.

Cain looked almost exactly like his father, with black hair, and black eyes. They were even roughly the same height. It was strange though, Marcus reminded Grim of Lukas, albeit only by a small amount.

Marcus patted his son's arm. "It's so good to see you."

"It's good to see you too." Cain turned towards Grim. "Oh, this is Grim. The friend I was telling you about."

Grim thrust her hand towards Marcus, her arm stiffening as she forced a shaking smile. "It's a pleasure to meet you."

Marcus returned the smile, taking Grim's hand and shaking it. "Well, come sit down, both of you!" Marcus moved them towards the table at the back of the café, and the three of them sat down.

Cain glanced at Grim, and Grim glanced back. He looked calm, his face projecting comfort and safety.

A waitress came to the table and offered out menus. The words on there were jumbling together, and she had to glare at the page hard to concentrate on it.

"So, how have things been since the Baptism? Any news? I got your letters Cain, but I'll be frank I was less concerned about your Focus and skipped those parts."

"Haven't you already seen the reports?" Cain asked with a chuckle. When he saw that Grim had already detached herself from the conversation, Cain leaned over to her. "My father works in the Orders administration department. Hundreds and thousands of profiles of the students of Elderwall and the Magus."

"Yes, and you think I'm able to find yours in that mess?" Marcus let out a hearty laugh. "My boy tells me that you're also a history nerd. You'll appreciate the fact that the Order records did not start until 1915. And to this day, I and the administrative assistants of present and future are still cleaning up the mess."

Her eyes lit up. "How could we start records during a world war?" Grim noticed she was talking faster by the second. "And if the Order established itself before that then…"

"Exactly. And believe me, those records are-,"

The waitress reappeared, and Marcus stopped his sentence halfway through. She took their orders, and within a matter of seconds, the food appeared in front of them with a *pop*. The plates and cutlery trembled from the impact.

"Huh." Marcus laughed. "I wonder where this came from?"

Grim looked at Cain's father, curious about his comment. "T-the kitchen?"

His eyes changed, and his smile faltered. "Well, that's what we would think, hm?"

Cain started shaking his head. "Stop it, you're doing that thing again."

"What thing?" Marcus asked, raising an eyebrow.

"That thing you do where you try to be mysterious and dramatic, it's dumb."

"Son, I'm offended."

"This isn't some dramatic novel, stop it."

"If it was one, I would at least force us to meet in the forest at night."

"Then you would murder us."

Marcus gasped with theatrical grace. "You think I would murder my son?!" He paused for a moment. "Absolutely. You're a pain in the ass."

Grim covered her mouth as she burst out laughing at the table, trying not to choke on her food. Cain was also sputtering out laughing, turning away from the two of them as he started coughing. It was clear that Marcus was watching the two of them as Cain turned back to the table, and Grim held out a napkin for him.

She wiped her eyes. "Fucking hell I haven't laughed that much in ages." Grim realised her language. "Sorry."

"No, it's quite alright. You should hear me at home, I have a sailor's mouth."

Cain chuckled. "The amount of language you spew out when you break something- god." He turned to Grim. "Also, I've made you laugh before."

"Not like this though."

"Challenge accepted," Cain replied with a smile. "I thought I was pretty funny."

"You are-,"

"He gets it from me," Marcus added, taking a bite of his food. "Just saying."

Grim laughed, and Cain turned to look at her, lowering his voice to whisper. "See, you had nothing to worry about."

She chuckled at his moment of triumph, and Cain immediately brought the conversation back to life, changing the topic entirely. Grim saw Marcus watching them throughout the meal. He had a satisfied smile on his face. It seemed to Grim he was proud of Cain for this newfound friendship.

At the end of the meal, the three of them walked out of the café. They walked to the station together, and right before they were going to split off to go to different platforms, Marcus pulled Cain into a tight embrace.

"Be good Cainy." He said to his son firmly.

Cain held his father for a long time, and Grim watched the two of them. A kind of parental affection she had never fully grasped. Cain whispered something in his father's ear, which made Marcus squeeze him tighter.

When they finally let go, Marcus turned to Grim, offering his hand. "Cain told me you're not much of a hugger."

She smiled, and took Marcus' hand, giving it a firm shake. "It was lovely to meet you."

"Believe me Grim, the pleasure was all mine." He let go of her hand. "You take of my boy, won't you? Stick by him. I think you might be one of the best things that has ever happened to him."

Grim glanced at Cain, who's cheeks were pink. He avoided her gaze. "Dad, please…" He mumbled.

Marcus shook his head. "I mean it. You take care of each other. No matter what comes next."

She didn't want to argue with such sincerity. "I will. You travel safe, Mr Blackwood."

He nodded. "Call me Marcus, Grim. I hope we meet again soon."

Marcus Blackwood turned and headed to the other train platform. Cain turned to Grim, completely flustered and flushed. "I'm sorry for what he said. Half the time I don't know what point he's trying to make."

Grim shook her head. "Cain, it's fine. Your father seems really nice. And it's obvious he cares about you. Don't worry about it."

He smiled, letting out a long sigh of relief. "He worries, I think. There's a lot going on at the moment."

"What do you mean?"

Cain looked as if he was going to explain, but it seemed he decided against it. "I'll tell you about it another time. Come on, let's not miss our train."

Dear Raven,

I am writing to you again as I didn't receive a reply to my last letter. The fact you have decided to not communicate with us is a simple act of immaturity. You need to take charge of your actions, your outburst at the Baptism shows us that you still have a long way to go before we can trust you again.

We have been receiving the reports on your progress, and it is quite clear that we should be concerned. Please continue to attend your classes with Mrs Locklin. Despite what happened at the Baptism, I believe there is still opportunity for you.

Please respond to this.

Father

Lukas sat next to Grim in the library, at the usual table she occupied at the back. He had only gotten home yesterday, mere days before classes were going to start up again. Lukas, in his usual manner, had caught Grim up on *everything* she had missed over the holidays. What he did with his mother and the fact, that he had dinner with Grim's parents.

According to his account, they did nothing but sing Elderwall's praises, "as they should". They also congratulated Lukas and asked whether Grim's focus was set in place.

"Is it?" He asked her, an eagerness in his tone. "Has Ms. White said anything to you?"

"Not yet. But I think she will soon."

"Make sure to write to your parents when she does. They're worried. You haven't returned their letters."

"There's a reason for that…" Grim replied with a grumble. She scowled at the thought of the letters piling up on her desk.

"You can't make excuses for stuff like this, you know."

"I'm aware."

"Someone's grumpy…" Lukas chuckled, reaching over to the books that Grim had in front of her. "How have you been getting on with the research into the Order of Chaos?"

She looked away from him. "If I'm being honest, I haven't found much."

"You haven't found much, or you haven't been looking?"

Grim recoiled away from him on her chair. "What's that supposed to mean?"

Lukas flicked through the top book on the pile in his hand. "You have been spending the last month with Cain Blackwood."

"What the fuck are you implying by that?"

"I've heard rumours, Grim." Lukas slammed the book down, making her jump. "He slacks off in his classes, his father isn't highly regarded in the Order and-,"

"And like me, he was burnt in the Baptism." She snapped back with scorn. "I didn't have you down for a pretentious bastard Lukas."

"I don't want you to mix with the wrong crowd."

"Cain is my friend. Respect that." She stood up, grabbing her books. "When's the next student council meeting?"

"Next month…" Lukas was watching her as she gathered her things. "Grim, I'm sorry I just-,"

"I know. I know what you mean because you always explain it, but you need to fucking check your standards." Grim grabbed her bag. "You'll have some research by the next meeting. Tell me the time and I'll attend. I'm going to the art room."

He turned in his chair as she walked away. "This school has an art room?"

Four elements: Earth, Air, Fire, Water

An Elemental can use and control the four elements, unlike any other Magus.

Magick is a "give and take" which applies especially to Elementals

An Elemental uses physical and visual magick.

Sometimes they can summon an element without needing it nearby, but that is a skill for more advanced Magus. Most of the time an Elemental will need the physical element near them. For example, a jar of water, a fire, soil.

Air is the easiest element to manipulate, as it is all around us.

An Elemental can change the shape of the element, grow and shrink it, and eliminate it entirely.

Elemental is considered the second strongest Focus.

"So, wait…what happened?"

Grim had departed from Lukas at the library. There was not much else she could do now that classes had finished for the day. So, she chose to head back to the dormitories. She had found Finn and Anna at the lockers, a long hallway of metal cases that students could rent out for the year. Finn looked to be distraught, and Anna seemed infuriated.

"Finn lost his locker key, and now needs to get into the said locker," Anna explained, sighing.

This took Grim by surprise, to say the least. Surprised at what she had stumbled into. "You've been back here…not even a week Finn, how in the hell do you lose your locker key?"

"It was in my bag I swear!" He put his hands together. "Grim, you must know what to do, you're smart."

She shook her head. "Have you tried using…you know, *magick*?"

Anna rested her elbows on her wheelchair, rubbing her temples. "I suggested that, but they warded the lockers against that kind of thing."

Perhaps it was a good thing Elderwall Boarding College had thought of using that. The wards were to protect the magus from mortals, but who knew it went down to every single metallic locker?

"Finn…get a new key," Grim suggested.

"I tried." He looked ready to scream. "The office is now closed for the day. I need my objects for my Summoner class tomorrow morning!"

Ah. Finn had the Summoner focus. Good for him.

Anna pointed a finger at him. "Calm down. Don't yell at Grim."

Finn stopped and took a few deep breaths. "Sorry, sorry. I'm stressed-,"

The hallway door opened, and Finn's eyes widened. He started running.

"CAIN! Oh, thank god Cain I need your help!"

Cain, who looked as stunned as Grim did when she walked in, started laughing as Finn hugged him.

"What is it Finn?" He asked as Finn ushered him towards the point of the disaster known as the locker.

"Cain, you're *also* smart, I lost the key to my locker, and I need my objects for Summoner class."

Cain shook his head, but he was still smiling. "I told you Finn; you should have kept this stuff in your room."

"Don't tell me where I should and shouldn't keep my incense, it's none of your business." He gestured with both arms to the locker. "Can you help or not?"

He laughed, taking off his backpack and dropping it in front of the locker, bending down. "Has anyone got a paperclip?"

Anna reached into her jacket pocket and pulled one out. "Always handy to keep one."

Cain took it off her and stretched it out. He lined it up with the keyhole and picked the lock with speed and ease. The locker opened with a satisfying click.

Everyone stared, impressed. Anna clapped his efforts, and Finn looked ready to cry.

"Cain, I fucking love you."

He stood up and patted Finn on the shoulder, picking up his bag. "You're welcome."

"Where did you even learn to do that?" Anna asked.

"Eh." He shrugged. "Not every skill has to be magickal. The key to our house always got jammed, so I picked the lock a lot."

"That sounds unsafe," Finn added, now smiling as he took out his incense bottles and put them into his bag.

"It was only for a few months, could have been worse."

Grim shrugged. "Sorry, I wasn't much help."

Anna waved a hand at her. "Don't worry about it, Finn tends to be dramatic about these things."

Finn stamped his foot. "I am not!"

"Finn, you could have borrowed stuff from me for the class tomorrow. I have some leftover even though I got the Psychic focus."

"But that completely misses the point of bringing my own!"

Anna sighed into her hands. "Cut out the dramatics, I want to go get something to eat." She looked up at Grim. "Hey, you wanna come with us to the dining hall?"

Grim smiled. "I would…" She turned to Cain. "Can Cain come with us? If you want to that is."

Cain grinned. "If you guys don't mind a fourth person, that would be great."

Finn smirked at the group. "You're our friend too Cain, let's go!"

A Summoner's abilities can be tied to the principle of contagion. They use objects to form magickal connections.

Common examples of objects include crystals, incense, candles, and herbs.

Many summoners choose their objects based on the type of magick they are doing.

The power of the magick and the impact is dependent on the object they chose and the power of that object. Summoner's are considered to be a weaker Magus as a result of this.

However, with the right object, a Summoner can have unlimited power.

Cain, Grim, Finn and Anna sat at one of the tables in the dining room. Grim had never been around so many people she could tolerate at once. It was a strange feeling, but one that was growing on her. She felt engaged with the conversation at hand, and for once, the topics varied. The group fluctuated between their favourite restaurants, and everyone's hometowns, moaning about classes. Eventually, things drifted towards the Baptism of Fire.

"Have your hands healed up?" Anna asked Cain and Grim, after swallowing a bite of her food.

Grim waved her hand, now with no bandages. "Got a nasty scar though."

Nasty was one way of putting it. It was deep and dark like a brand. A reminder of her failure.

"Same here," Cain added, showing off his scar, albeit more healed than Grim's was.

Finn nodded. "What have they said about your focus?"

"I'm going to go into Summoner." Cain explained, and Finn beamed as soon as he finished his sentence.

"Summoner buddies!" Finn raised his hand and Cain high-fived it.

"What about you, Grim?" Anna asked, steering the attention away from the Summoner buddies.

Grim looked down at her food, avoiding Anna's gaze. "I'm going to stay in the basic classes and try the Baptism next year. I'm getting some extra lessons to fill in the gaps."

"But wait-," Anna put down her fork. "If you're doing it *again* then-,"

Finn finished her thought. "What happens if you get burnt?"

Cain looked to Grim, putting a hand on her arm. The two of them had already talked about this. Had the discussion. Grim had cried at the thought of the fire. "I'm trying not to think about it."

"There must be a focus that works for you." Anna insisted.

"If there is, then I'm not strong enough in it." Grim looked back up at her and tried to smile at her friend. "I will cross that bridge when I come to it."

"For god's sake." Anna groaned. "If they let me do the *psychic* focus, then they can find the one for you."

"It's whatever."

"But still-,"

The dining hall went dark again. Like before. All the lights went out and the room filled with huddled whispers.

Grim felt herself stop breathing. Seven. Eleven.

"It's them! The Order of Chaos!"

"Oh god, what now?"

"They need to get over themselves."

Same as before. The words crawled up the ceiling and projected down onto them. It illuminated the student's faces.

"Magick was never yours to take. It doesn't belong to us."

Then the room came to life again. The lights came back on, and Grim stared across at Finn and Anna, trembling.

"Well shit," Finn stated, blunt as iron. He noticed Grim as he looked down from the ceiling. "Oh shit, Grim! Are you okay?"

"Sorry, I-" She shivered, shaking her head. "I'm fine."

Cain turned to her, another hand on her arm. "It's okay, you're alright now. It's over."

Anna sighed. "You don't have to be brave for us, Grim. These weird pranks freak out everyone."

Finn looked up at the ceiling again. "What if they're more than pranks?"

Anna shook her head and picked up her fork, ready to continue eating. "If they are, then I wish they would get to the point. I'm not one for metaphors."

Grim smiled a little. "Well, if anything, it's impressive."

Cain smiled back, dropping his hand. His smile seemed full of relief like the world was new. "Yeah, it is."

A Skulduggery's illusions are more complicated than one would think. To create a projection, the Skulduggery must use the *invisible* matter, something the naked eye cannot see.

This is why their abilities are linked with the principle of correspondence— they use what we can't see to make something we can see.

With an illusion, the possibilities are endless. A Skulduggery can make anyone see anything, even Mortals to an extent. Although a Magus is prohibited from revealing themselves to a Mortal, they would still be able to see a Skulduggery's illusion.

A Skulduggery is asked to keep their illusions in check, not to use it to prank, manipulate or scare anyone. A strong skulduggery could change the way someone sees the world.

The Order: A History

Rumblings of Chaos- The Dissolution of Anarchy in Early Order History

How to Master the Skulduggery Focus

A Guide to Common Magickal Practices

The Complete Records of Order Leaders: Condensed Edition

History of Elderwall Boarding College

An Overview of Magick

Magickal Discoveries Through the Centuries

How to Summon and What to Use

Summoning: A Brief Guide

Grim wanted a swift and painful death. Quick and easy.

The stack of books had rotted her brain. The librarian had gotten so fed up with Grim's forced research, that he had given her the trolley to put them back. She had missed dinner the past few nights. She knew at the start of next month Lukas had asked her to present her findings to the Student Council.

She didn't want to let him down. Despite how much he had been bothering her recently, she knew he was as stressed out as she was. He had a lot of expectations to meet, more so than she did sometimes. Lukas always wanted everything to be perfect. She wasn't sure if that was his own enforced standards or the ones that the world had gifted him in toxicity.

He had always been a hard nut to crack, and their consistency to put on a brave face had drawn them to each other. Everyone liked Lukas. Nobody liked Grim.

Lukas liked Grim.

That's where it had started for them, and as disruptive as it was, Grim had needed him. It's not every day that someone could tolerate her for more than five seconds. And yet, here at Elderwall, she had found people who were willing to do that. However now, she hadn't seen them for days due to the inconvenience of becoming a hermit.

Grim stood up, her whole body groaning as she started to pile the books onto the trolley. It was utter madness, a far cry from the intense organisation she usually put into her research. She had lost the energy to try and sort it, but she soldiered on around the shelves.

The librarian was nodding off at his desk, not a night owl. She could see the moon beyond the stained glass window. The light peeked in through the coloured glass. The lamps on the walls and desks were dim, the golden light encouraging students that it was time for some rest. Grim made the floor creak with her footsteps, trying her best not to wake the librarian.

She passed by the very small section of non-magickal books. It was a combination of mortal fiction and non-fiction. The staff of Elderwall must have thought it was an obligation to have a variety of literature. Cain and Grim had already raided the shelves, so she was familiar with its contents.

Yet, sticking out from the rows, was a book she hadn't noticed before.

She had read somewhere that the College was so old, that it had its own sense of magick.

With caution, Grim approached the book, abandoning the almost empty trolley behind her. The spine was dusty and cracked. The book looked ready to fall apart.

She reached out a hand and pulled at it. There was the click of a lock turning, and next to the shelf, a door that had once been part of the wall, opened.

"What the-."

Grim's eyes widened. With a completely blank expression, inside the hidden room of Elderwall's library. She looked around, trying to see if there were witnesses to the secret that had unfolded before her.

She chuckled to herself. "Holy shit."

She stepped forward, crossing the threshold into the room. "Holy shit I'm going inside."

The hidden door shut behind her with another satisfying click. Grim let out a breath, which turned cold in the air. "Seven. Eleven."

She saw a rusted plaque on the wall, reading *The Archives*. The room was small, with a single buzzing light dangling from a precarious chain. There were thick bookcases coated in dust and cobwebs spun into the corners. Grim spotted an oil lamp on a small shelf, and reached for it, flicking it on.

She coughed and moved down the shelves. All the books were the same. Thick, leather-bound cracked spines and wrinkled papers. None of them had titles, and if they did, they were long gone, worn away by the hands of time.

She ran a hand along them, the dust coming off on her fingertips. Letting instinct drive her, she pulled a book off the shelf and opened it to a random page.

We established a connection, though faint, there was a clear presence of magick. I caught a glimpse of two rulers arguing, though it was not clear what it was about.

We're going to continue trying to create a firm link between our world and theirs. There are many more places we can try and connect to. Finally, we can unlock what has been ours to own all this time.

Grim slammed the book shut and stumbled backwards, completely halted by what she had read. She turned around to the shelf behind her and grabbed another book.

We have established Elderwall Boarding College. It has accepted its first round of students. Already we can see the potential. The future of Magus relies on the connections we have made to other realities.

She picked another book.

I hope the girl in the room of white is okay. We seemed to have left her in a dark place.

Her hands were shaking, and the lamp almost dropped out of her hands.

"Fuck." She whispered, her voice unknown to her.

Her hands reached out again to one more book.

The Order is in agreement that we need to have the students focus on different areas of magick. This is to stabilise our connections and not disrupt the portals. We have found the element of a sacred flame from another reality. A Baptism of Fire will serve as the deciding factor for our students.

There were concerns raised over those who were not as strong in their magickal abilities. There is a risk of students being burnt by the flames. The strong will prevail, and the weak will simply exist.

Grim could feel her breath growing unsteady by the minute. There was tightness in her chest. Frantic, she put the books back and switched the oil lamp off. As she ran out of the room, the hidden door closed itself. The old tattered book still stuck out on the shelf.

She leaned against the bookcase and slid down to the floor, and covered her head with her hands.

It took a long time to clear her mind. When she did, one thing was clear.

The Order was hiding something. And Grim was going to find out what it was.

February

Lukas met Grim outside where the Student Council had their regular meetings. Grim walked up to him, a small stack of books and papers in her hand.

"Oh wow," Lukas said as soon as their eyes met. "You went all out with this, huh?"

She raised an eyebrow, scowling at him. "You asked me to trawl through hundreds of years of records and history for this."

"I know, but I didn't think you would make much of an effort." He replied with a casual shrug of his shoulders.

Grim shook her head. She was not in the mood to argue. "How long is this going to take? I made plans to meet Cain after this."

Now it was Lukas' turn to scowl. "I'm sure Cain won't miss you. This will be worth it, I promise."

"What do you have against Cain? Every time I mention him your face looks like a lemon."

This was true, his face would curl up into something akin to disgust or annoyance.

"He's no good."

"You haven't even met him."

"And I don't want to."

Grim's fists clenched. "You should stop believing everyone's thoughts for once."

"I don't want you to get caught up in the wrong crowd." He put his hands on her arms, despite the weight she was carrying. "Imagine the hell-storm that would unleash if your parents found out you were with a bad crowd."

Grim sighed. He had a point. Even though she was reluctant to admit that. "I know."

He smiled. "I appreciate this, by the way. Even though I did doubt you would pull through. It's going to be a massive help."

She thought for a moment about what she had researched. What she had found in the archives. And how she was planning on spilling the news to the Student Council that some things didn't make sense. About how the Order of Chaos might have had a point.

"Grim, I'm serious." Lukas continued, continue to shine his bright smile. "This is a huge thing for you."

She returned it, but her lips trembled. "You don't know the half of it. Let's go."

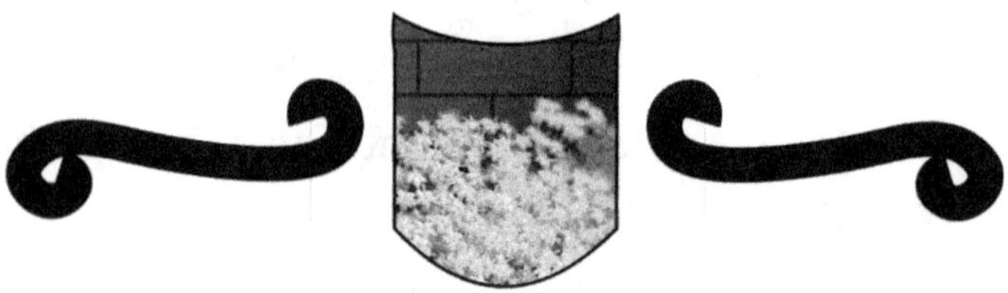

STUDENT COUNCIL PROTOCOL

The Student Council will hold weekly meetings. The members should consist of students from across the four academic years of Elderwall, and should contain students with a variety of Focuses. The students should have a high academic record, and zero behaviour reports.

Once the students have been selected, a list of names should be passed to the Dean, who will then pass the names onto the Order.

At every planned meeting, the head of the Council will arrange an itinerary, and send a report to the Dean on what the discussion points of the meeting will be. This report will be passed onto the Order. After the meeting has taken place, the head of the Council, or an assistant that they assign, will write up detailed notes of the meeting, to pass onto the Dean. These notes will be passed onto the Order.

Failure to provide the correct documentation to the Dean will result in disciplinary action. This may include removal of students from the Council.

Sitting at the table were Oscar, Minda and George. Standing up at the other end of the table was Remi. Lukas walked ahead of Grim and immediately greeted the room.

"Hey guys, sorry we're late."

George waved a hand at him. "Don't worry about it. A couple of the other council members are running late too. Take a seat!"

Oscar chuckled. "Yeah, typical everyone's classes ran over. We're waiting on Adam and Grace."

Lukas sat down next to George and started chatting with him. He tilted his head to the empty chair that was next to him while looking at Grim. Grim, instead, decided to go talk to Remi, her one other familiar face.

She sidestepped next to them and leaned in a little, dropping her research on the table with a soft thud. She lowered her voice to a whisper. "I forgot you were in this thing."

Remi chuckled. "It has its advantages when I need it to." They glanced at Grim. "I thought you were meeting Cain."

Grim shrugged. "I'm meeting him after we've finished, as long as it doesn't take too long."

They looked up, and over at Lukas. He and George were chatting with excitement about football, as one does when one is on opposite teams. Remi then turned back to Grim. "If you want me to make excuses for you so you can get out of here early-,"

"No, no!" Grim protested, holding her hands up. "It's fine. Don't want it getting round to my parents that I skipped out on this."

"That's what you're worried about?"

"Among other things."

"Huh." Remi paused. "Your parents work for the Order?"

She nodded. "High ranking. Super close with Ms. White. According to my mother, our ancestors helped everyone get out of the dark ages."

"But how-,"

"How could they do that when there are no records of magus before the Order established itself in the 1600s? My question too."

"Well, the magus did not come around until after the dark ages. Around the age of enlightenment."

"I've talked about it so much, but our history is *weird*. I take what my mother tells me with a load of salt."

"The best way to go about it."

The sound of approaching footsteps interrupted them.

"Hey guys, glad you could make it!" Oscar called out to the two new arrivals. "Sit down everyone, we can get started."

Grim found out an assortment of information before the Student Council got to the heart of the reason why they had decided to hold the meeting.

George was a second-year student, and before Lukas, he was the youngest member. The two of them were always together now, as Grim felt the gap between her and Lukas widen.

Adam was a third-year, an Elemental like Lukas and was his mentor in some of his classes. He had bright red hair and brown eyes and dressed like he was already a member of the Order. Neat as a pin and in charge. Grace was a fourth-year, a Summoner, with blonde hair and icy blue eyes. She looked at Grim like she was an unwelcome guest at first but grew used to the new company.

Remi and Grim sat next to each other for the meeting. Remi had a notebook open on the desk, scribbling out what everyone was saying. Once the introductions and general housekeeping notices were out of the way, the discussions turned to the Order of Chaos.

"Do we have any ideas about how they're doing this?" Lukas asked. "This has gotta be more than a one-person job."

Oscar looked over to Remi. "Well, they have to be a Skulduggery."

Adam, Grace, George, Minda and Lukas all looked down the table toward Remi. Grim sat there in silence, realising what cogs were turning. Remi remained straight-faced as the group looked at them. After a moment, they scoffed. "For God's sake, *really*?"

"There aren't that many skulduggeries who can do something like that," Adam commented. "They would have to have enough training to handle something of that scale. So, a fourth or even third year."

"You *idiots*," Remi rolled their eyes and groaned, slamming their pen down onto the notepad. "You've seen my magick. It looks nothing like that."

Minda nodded. "I know Remi, but if you know something…"

"I don't know *any* skulduggeries who can do that. I actually can't believe you all."

"It was a suggestion," Lukas added, smiling at the absurdity of the situation. "I'm sure Oscar meant nothing by it."

"Definitely not," Oscar said, nodding in agreement. "It would have been handy if you had some information, though."

Remi picked up the pen again, and Grim noticed their grip was tight. "If I notice anything unusual, you are the first people I tell. That will continue to be the case."

"Of course!" Minda put her hands together, trying to calm the room down. "Let's move on, okay?"

"Yes." Adam looked at the group. "They only strike when they know people are watching, hence why they focus on the dining hall or the hallways. We need to keep an eye on those areas. See if we spot anyone suspicious."

Yes, like that would work. Because this specific group of people could notice in a crowd of students if something was amiss. Magick could be subtle. Somebody capable would only need to turn their wrist to create what they want.

"I'll try talking to Starching and the other professors," Remi added. Their frustration over the accusation was still burning in their eyes. "See if they've noticed anything in the students."

Lukas nodded. "Sounds good." He looked at Grim again. "Grim, it seems like you've found something, right?"

He turned to the rest of the group. "Grim knows the library well, she's been doing some great research. She's been really useful."

She was useful. What a privilege.

Oscar chuckled. "Heard all about your little trick with Starching."

"Who knew we had a human library in our presence," Adam added with a smirk.

"No wonder you managed to pass those exams," Grace concluded.

Grim wanted to shrink into the chair and vanish. Lukas was right, it wasn't impressive. It wasn't cool. Everybody thought it had been a bad idea.

"Hey," Remi announced from the other end of the table. "We asked her to come here. Show some respect."

Oscar shook his head. "We didn't mean any harm Remi."

"I don't care." Remi glanced at Grim and smiled at her. "What have you found?"

Grim stood up, wiping her clammy palms down her top as she reached for the first book on the pile. "Well, not much about the Order of Chaos, but there have been instances of illusions. Not on this scale, though."

"So…would it be the same people? In these instances that you found." Grace asked, leaning forward towards the table.

"It's not possible. There's too large of a gap between them. They might be working for the same *goal* but not the same group."

"Is it the work of a skulduggery?" Oscar asked, his eyes glancing over to Remi.

"I couldn't say. There is no defined focus in what I found." She took a deep breath. "There is something else. That you need to know about."

There was quiet for a moment. Lukas was the first to speak. "What is it?"

"I found records, from Magus in the past. They were speaking about how we…stole magick from different realities. Thousands of first-hand accounts, with names I recognise from the official history books. There are even records about the first Baptisms. I don't know how much to believe but the Order of Chaos may be onto something, even if they don't have all the information."

The silence held Grim in a choke hold. Adam broke it chuckling.

"I…holy shit if that isn't a conspiracy theory or what… alternate realities? Really? What is this, a dumb novel?"

"I have to agree with Adam," Grace added with a smile. "I don't know *what* part of the library you found this, but you need to check your sources."

"I can show you-,"

"Look Grim, we're the Student Council, we fall under the Order. I'm not going to entertain this." Adam stood up. "I appreciate the *official* research you found for us. But I'm not wasting time chasing dead ends."

Oscar nodded. "I agree, we need to be following the facts. Grim, do you have a summary of your findings from the *proper* sources?"

Grim pulled out a bundle of papers stapled together and handed it to Oscar. She looked at Lukas as she walked back to where she had been standing, he looked mortified. Remi's face showed no signs of expression, they watched the room without reacting to anything.

"Thank you. I hope you'll come back to us with more information Grim, anything will be helpful. If you need any extra documents, I can help you submit a request to the Order."

She slumped back into her chair. "Much appreciated."

Oscar put the report into the folder in front of him. "Alright, I call this meeting adjourned. Thank you, everyone."

Everyone got up out of their chairs and started to make their way out of the classroom. Grim stood up, picking up her books again and trying to avoid the tears threatening to burn her cheeks. Remi stood next to her with their arms folded. "You said you could verify those first-hand accounts?"

Grim turned to them, startled. She wiped her face. "Yes, if I have the official Order profiles, I'm sure the same names will pop up."

"Give me a list of names. Marcus can check them."

"You…you believe me?"

Remi let out a deep sigh. "I do. But you need to prove it."

"Why?"

"Well-,"

Lukas walked over. He had that look in his eyes like he did when he talked about Cain. He looked at Remi with a small level of disgust.

"You need to get some sleep, Grim, you must have been pretty sleep-deprived to start talking in riddles."

Grim pushed her chair out and stood up. "Lukas believe me it's…" She saw Remi out of the corner of her eye, shaking their head. "You know what, never mind. I need to go and meet Cain."

"I can walk you there if you want." Lukas offered, gesturing to the doors.

"No, it's fine. I know the way to the art room better than you do."

"Come on-,"

"Grim." Remi stood up, and picked up their notebook, tucking it under their arm. "I'll see you later, okay? Say hi to Cain for me."

Grim gave them a wild smile, trying to act natural. It was clear Remi knew more than they liked to share. "I will."

Remi walked off, not even bothering to say anything to Lukas. Grim remembered what Cain had said. They're only cold to the people they don't like. It was odd to think about because everyone liked Lukas…right?

Lukas looked back at Grim. "They're friends with Cain too?"

"They're family friends like we are. Anyway, I need to go."

Grim started walking off, as everyone else was leaving the library as well. Lukas grabbed her arm to stop her, spinning her back around.

"Hey, listen to me."

"Don't hold my arm like that." Her demand was polite, and Lukas loosened his grip enough that she could move her arm out.

"Sorry. Look, I need you to be careful. You seem to be going down a dangerous rabbit hole."

"For once in your life Lukas, trust that I have a good sense of judgement."

"I do, I wanted you to come here so-,"

"So I could get laughed at? This was unnecessary, I knew they weren't going to listen."

"It wasn't to me," Lukas replied with gritted teeth. "I have told them all about you. I wanted them to meet you, and then you can *show* me how talented you are."

"I would much rather shove a report in their hands than have to sit there and pretend."

"Nobody was pretending." His hand was still lingering like he wanted to grab her again.

Grim took a step back. "Yes, you were. I need to go. I'll speak to you later, alright?"

He sighed. "Yeah. Can we meet for breakfast tomorrow?"

She smiled, finding comfort in the familiarity of that question. "7:30 sharp. Don't leave me hanging."

"Save me a seat, I'll be there."

Grim headed towards the library doors, not looking back. She heard Lukas and Oscar talking, their voices muffled and absorbed by the books around her. She stepped out into the hallway and was about to turn the corner. But, she saw Minda heading towards her, waving.

"Hey! I don't mean to keep you long." She said as she stood next to Grim.

"It's fine. What is it?"

"First off, I realise that everyone made some unnecessary comments. I'm meant to be looking after you, and I'm sorry if I let them upset you. I speak for everyone in the Council when I say that the intention wasn't to make fun of you."

"It's *fine*. Thank you."

"Great! Great, that's good." Minda's smile was warm. Grim wanted to believe she meant everything, even if her apology sounded so distant and formal. "Also…how do you know Remi? You two seemed to be chatting before the meeting started."

"I met them over Christmas. We have a mutual friend. Cain Blackwood?"

"Oh, Cain! Yes, my friend Alisha is his mentor. Nice person, from what I've heard."

"Yeah." The corners of Grim's mouth turned into a smile thinking about him. "He's become a good friend."

"I'm so happy for you. It's good you're making more friends." Minda put her hands in her jacket pockets. "When Lukas said about you coming to submit your research, he said he was your only friend. He wanted to introduce you to more people."

Her smile dropped. "What."

Minda looked at her, biting her lip, an awkward look on her face. "Is that, not the case?"

She shook her head. "No, it's not the case at all. I'm friends with Finn for crying out loud!"

"Are you?" Minda asked, her face shifting to excitement. "Oscar and Finn don't talk much when they're at school, so maybe that's how it got missed. Well, regardless, I'm glad you've made some friends. Lukas is so busy with everything he does, that he must have gotten worried."

"He does that a lot. I'm running late to something. Sorry, Minda, I have to go."

"Don't let me keep you!" She said with a laugh. "I wanted to make sure I had my facts right."

"No…it's okay. I appreciate you asking me. I'll see you soon."

"I'll come by tomorrow so I can see your new schedule, is that okay?"

"Yeah. Fine. See you then."

Grim waved and walked off, quickening her pace back to her bedroom to dump her books. That conversation had her mind churning. What the *heck* was Lukas thinking by telling everyone in the Student Council that? Did he think, after everything she had told him, that he was still her only friend? She knew that he seemed to dislike every person she had met so far. But they were still people she could trust, and that had to count for something.

It had to count for something, right?

She reached the art room and opened the door. Cain was sitting on one of the tables, looking at his watch. All that pressure she felt building up eased a little.

"What time do you call this?" He said, his tone all jokes and no seriousness.

She let out a breath. "It's a long story."

He noticed something. Maybe it was how out of breath she was, or he could tell she had spaced out after the conversations she had.

"Are you okay?" He asked.

Grim didn't answer. Cain looked around the room. They both heard the chatter of students walking down the hallways.

He slid off the table and took a step towards her. "Do you want to talk about it?"

"No, not really. Can I just show you my paintings?"

He nodded, and that was all the reassurance she needed.

I cannot believe the time has come for us to begin
something such as this. For centuries there has been a
divide between humanity, a call for the right individuals
to rise up and help steer the future. I am a humble man,
but I know I am one of the lucky ones who get to have
a part in this story. This is the start of progress, of
revolution. We are the ones who are strong enough to
handle what these other worlds have to offer. We are
the ones who can take on the magick. Think of what we
could do with this power. We could shape the world
without anyone even noticing.

There are others in the group who are uncertain, but
we will silence their concerns. Opportunities like this
will never be recurring, and the time is now. We decided
that it would be best to establish a governing body to
watch over all our followers who are about to awaken
to their new ability. A group to keep an eye on the
future descendents, to steer them on the path to
truth. Help them find ways to keep the world moving
forward.

This world is full to the brim with chaos. As such, it
needs order. We will be the order.

Cain and Grim continued to meet in the garden, especially when the liveliness of Elderwall resumed. It seems that nobody knew the Garden of Shadows existed. But somehow there was a diligent gardener who kept it maintained. There were eyes and ears everywhere, even if you were in an empty room or a shaded corner. Everyone would hear your discordant whispers. The two of them preferred to talk here since they shared a lot of the same opinions. They would rather those opinions not reach the mass student populous.

It helped that the weather was starting to turn in their favour. There was less rain and more chilling winds, which they could combat. Sometimes Grim brought her sketchbook. There was a comfort in knowing she could keep every single drawing she made.

She had her sketchbook in her lap, sitting on the bench with her knees tucked in and a blanket draped over her shoulders. Cain was next to her, with a blanket of his own, their shoulders touching. He was peering over at what she was drawing, not paying attention to his book.

"You're not even bothered about how dirty your hands are." He commented, chuckling.

Grim lifted her hand off the paper. There were black pencil streaks that were running down the sides and on her fingertips. "Never have been."

"I think your work is amazing."

She smiled. "Thanks. I tried to get into art school, you know. Convinced my parents to let me apply to both there and Elderwall. I got rejected."

Cain's eyes widened in surprise. "Really?"

"I didn't have much work to show because of the fireplace. So, I ended up here."

"Bet that made your parents happy."

"They were *over the moon*." She replied, grinning. "They're going to be *thrilled* when they find out I haven't got a focus."

"Haven't you told them yet?"

"Ms. White said to leave it with her. I bet she doesn't want another screaming match over this." She looked up at Cain, and she met his dark eyes. "What about you? How did your father react?"

"He didn't care about the Focus, but I think he was glad I was being put in the Summoner classes." He sighed, lacing his hands together and looking back out over the garden. "People talk in the Order, from what he's told me. I think everything is a little easier when you can say your kid is doing fine."

Her eyes fell to her drawing, and she ran a thumb over the corner of the paper. She remembered seeing the flames. "Doesn't excuse anything though."

"No, it doesn't. I hope your parents start listening to you when you see them again."

"We'll see."

Cain leaned back against the bench. They were still close to each other. Grim never felt any awkwardness when they were like this. There was a feeling of safety when they were together. Never any judgement or worry, no unspoken bitter words or panic.

"Listen…" He started speaking but stopped himself for a moment. He took a breath and continued. "If things don't work out, I can talk to my father. You're more than welcome to stay with me. He already loves you."

Grim chuckled, remembering Marcus' words to her at the train station. "Thank you. Funnily enough, Lukas' mother Evelyn made me the same offer."

Cain's eyebrows lifted at the mention of the name Evelyn, but he quickly changed his expression and smirked at her. "Doesn't surprise me, but I'm not sure I could handle Lukas for a whole summer, judging by what you've told me."

She burst out laughing. "Come on, he's alright once you get to know him."

"You've known him your whole life, you've had all the time in the world."

The two laughed together. She thought about what Remi said, and what she had told Cain about from the council meeting. Her laughter faded.

He noticed her frowning. "What is it? I'm sorry if I upset you-,"

"No, you didn't…I've been thinking a lot about Lukas."

"In what way?"

"Remi said that Lukas can put on a show. I'm wondering if that's what our friendship was, one big show."

"I think he does care for you."

"I know he does. He makes that part very clear." She bit her lip, thinking. She glanced at Cain. "I hope I'm not right in thinking he cares when it suits him."

He paused for a moment before speaking. "Remi has a lot of bad experiences under their belt with people being dishonest. It was a lot with their family when they first came out. They're looking out for you, in their way."

Grim nodded, closing her sketchbook. "I'm trying not to be a pessimist about it all. Lukas says I need to stop seeing the world like it's my enemy."

Cain chuckled a little at that. "Our experiences shape us. There's nothing wrong with being afraid. Admitting that we are vulnerable makes us stronger than we think."

Grim didn't know what to say at that moment. Her expression shifted as she tried to make sense of everything. A part of her didn't want to lose Lukas, but then again, maybe Lukas was a part of the problem. She had no way of justifying this idea though.

"You have people you can trust, Grim. It may be a small number, but you have people who care for you." He continued. "*I* care for you, and I hope that's obvious."

She giggled. "It is. I mean it."

"I'm glad."

Their eyes met at that moment, and Cain's smile was warm and welcoming. Truth was always hard to acknowledge, even when spoken with such openness. It was often the unspoken that validated the honesty presented. Grim knew he meant it, and Cain knew she meant it, and they sealed the unspoken promise.

Grim broke off looking at him with a laugh. "I feel like we should hug but I'm not that good with hugs-,"

"You know I only do that kind of thing when you're comfortable with it-,"

She laughed again. "I mean, the moment seems to warrant a hug."

He started laughing too. "Yeah okay, we can hug-,"

"Not too tight, okay?"

"Got it."

Cain led the way by putting his arm around her and pulling her in from the side. Her sketchbook squashed between them, but she didn't mind. When they pulled away, Cain had a whimsical smile on his face.

"We should head back for dinner," Grim said, standing up and folding the blanket.

"Are you meeting Finn and Anna? Or Lukas?"

"I usually meet Lukas for breakfast. He's always eating with his other friends."

"Gotcha." Cain stood up as well. "Should we head there together?"

"Fine with me, I'm starving."

"So, it wasn't because of the awkward hug?" He joked.

She couldn't stop smiling at him. "No. I want food."

Hi Remi.

Thanks again for this. Here's the names. If Marcus can get me any information. I would be grateful.

Chang Schroeder

Raul Becher

Hank Morrow

Edwin Mortem

Darron Sutton

Rosario Hansen

Victoria Lightchild

Amie Jensen

Darren Joyce

Bennie Blackwood

Today's feature presentation: the most boastful excuse for an assessment Grim would have to suffer through.

For some idiotic reason, Elderwall decided to host an event where students could show their Focus. The day took place in the grand hall, and first-year students presented in front of everyone in a magnificent display of showmanship.

They divided the hall into four classes: Summoner, Elemental, Skulduggery and Psychic. The question looming was this: what about the Mages who did not have a focus?

Grim was quick to find out the answer. It was a single table, with only a few chairs around it.

She slumped into the chair, watching everybody else pour into the room. The excitement was intense She must have missed Cain and Anna, but she did spot Finn walking in with Oscar. When they stood side by side, it was obvious they were siblings, even if they were very different people.

Finn caught Grim's eye, as everyone else found their seat, and walked over.

"Grim? What the hell are you doing here by yourself?"

"I think this is the table for the undesirables." She explained with a frown.

"That's bullshit." Finn looked around and saw Professor Starching. He started waving the professor over. "Professor Starching, sir!"

Oscar put a hand on his brother's arm. "Finn, what are you doing?"

Starching made his way over. Grim noticed he was muttering something under his breath. "What is it, Mr Becher?"

"Why is Grim here by herself?" Finn asked, turning back and gesturing to Grim.

"This is the table for those without a focus Finn. Miss Mortem is the only one of our current first-years that doesn't have a focus.

"Professor, can't Grim sit at the Summoner's table with me? This isn't fair for her."

Grim stood up, ready to interfere with the conversation. "Finn, it's okay I-,"

"*No*," Finn stopped her immediately. "It's not fair. You shouldn't be embarrassed like this. There's no harm in her being able to sit with a friend Professor."

"The decision is not yours to make, Mr Becher. Please go sit with your classmates at your assigned table."

Oscar reached for Finn's arm again and tried pulling him away. "You're making a scene, *leave it.*"

Finn turned to his brother with a striking glare. "She's my *friend.*"

He pushed away from his brother and sat in the chair that was next to Grim. He leaned back and crossed his arms.

"Finn, get up," Oscar demanded; his teeth gritted. "Don't embarrass yourself."

"No, I'm sitting next to my classmate."

Grim turned to Finn. "Seriously, it's okay."

Professor Starching looked annoyed; his brow furrowed. "Mr Becher I will ask you to leave this event if you don't comply."

"Then let Grim sit with everyone else. We're *all* classmates."

Oscar turned to Starching. "Sir, perhaps this once…"

Starching groaned. "This has been the way we have run this event for years. It's not my fault Miss Mortem is in this situation. I am not giving her permission to move seats."

"Then give me permission to sit here."

Oscar had clenched fists. "Finn *stop this-*,"

At the moment it seemed like Oscar was going to explode. Cain walked up behind them, standing behind him and Starching. "What's going on? Finn, Grim, is everything okay?"

"Everything's fine Mr Blackwood, please join your classmates at the Summoner-,"

"Grim's sat here by herself because she doesn't have a focus. Starching refuses to let her come sit with us, and vice versa."

Cain raised an eyebrow, and his eyes met Grim's. "Is this true?"

"It's okay Finn, go sit down."

"No! You shouldn't have to accept this. It isn't fair. None of this is fair, you let her get herself *burned* and then blame her for it!"

Grim turned to Finn and put her hands out. "Please-,"

He looked at her and saw the panic on her face. Grim could feel the rush in her stomach and everything became fuzzy. Cain stepped towards her, putting a gentle hand on her arm.

"Grim, take a deep breath."

In. Out. Seven. Eleven.

Cain looked at Finn and continued speaking in a low voice, his hand still on Grim's arm. "I know you're angry, I am too. But this is not the place to have this discussion."

Finn stood up. "Let Grim sit with us. If not with her classmates, with her friends."

The double doors to the grand hall opened, and Ms. White walked in. Starching's eyebrow twitched with untapped fury as she turned to look at them. Her expression suggested she was wondering what the interruption to the start of proceedings was about.

Starching sighed. "Get over there. Now. Not another word."

Finn smiled, victorious, and beckoned Grim and Cain over to the other side of the room with him. The three of them sat at the back of the group, their chairs scraping against the wall.

Grim sat back, the nerves leaving her body as she relaxed between her two friends. Finn leaned over to her, talking with a whisper as Ms. White began her speech. "I'm sorry. I didn't know."

"I didn't either." She whispered back.

Cain shook his head. "You were saying all the right things, Finn, it wasn't the right time."

She heard Finn sigh and mutter under his breath. "It's never the right time."

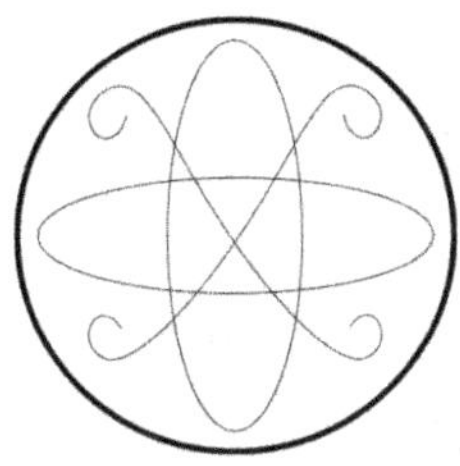

To all our members, you may have already heard from your students attending Elderwall that they have an important event on their horizon. The Focus Presentations are significant step for our students after they have found their Focus. It provides the opportunity to demonstrate what they have learned to their classmates, and to broaden their horizons on what they can achieve.

As always, we encourage friendly competition between our students. We have found that asking them to perform their abilities before each other is a great motivator.

Therefore, we ask that the parents of our future Magus encourage our students to perform to the best of their ability. We wish everyone at Elderwall the best of luck on presentation day.

"That was bullshit!"

Finn kicked his foot against the wall, then turned around and slumped against it. Grim stood across from him, biting her lip and crossing her arms. Cain was next to her. Anna had joined them, catching wind of the rumour that flew around after the presentation.

"Don't break your foot," Anna stated. She flicked her wrist, purple mist appearing at her fingertips. The zip to her bag opened, and as she moved her fingers, she lifted out a bottle of water and took a sip.

"Disciplinary action?!" Finn huffed, clenching his fists and pacing. "They seriously want me to go to Ms. White's office right now and explain myself."

"Finn, you need to tell them what they want to hear," Cain explained. "Apologise, be calm and there won't be any major consequences."

"But this isn't right! They're in the wrong here."

Grim was feeling the guilt gnaw at her that she put Finn in this situation. "I'm sorry, this is all my fault-,"

"*Why are you apologising!?*" Finn shouted, whipping around to turn to her. Grim visibly flinched and froze, and he noticed. His shoulders slumped. "I didn't mean to shout."

Anna pointed to the window ledge that she was next to. "Finn, sit there and calm down. You can't walk into Ms. White's office like this."

Finn dropped down in an almost dramatic fashion, putting his head in his hands. Anna lifted another bottle of water out of her bag and moved her hand, sending it floating towards him. He let it drop into his open palm.

"They're going to want you to show remorse Finn," Cain added solemnly. "Elderwall has a record for perfect student behaviour. You just need to play the part while you're there."

"I can come with you," Grim said. Her voice was shaking. "I'll explain you were trying to be nice; they'll understand."

"You're missing the point, Grim." Finn chugged down a quarter of the water bottle and looked back up at her. "What they did isn't right. They tried to justify publicly shaming you."

"And no matter what you say, they will be right, and you will be wrong," Cain concluded. "There's nothing you can do Finn. They're not going to change a tradition that has lasted since the birth of Elderwall."

Anna sighed. "They spew out their shitty speeches about tolerance and this is how they treat people without a Focus. How come we never heard about this?"

"I think they like to forget the Baptism can burn you," Grim explained, finding the courage to speak again. "Plus, I was the only student this year who failed. There may have been larger groups in the past."

"Stop justifying their behaviour," Finn muttered.

"Regardless, it's wrong, but you need to go see Ms. White." Anna knocked Finn's arm, encouraging him to stand up. "If you don't Oscar's going to get himself involved."

"He can keep his nose out of it." Finn stood up. "Alright, wish me luck. I'll find you guys later."

Psychics can move objects around by manipulating the particles and matter found in the air and in objects. According to the science discovered by Mortals, every material is made up of particles, and this is what Psychics use to make their abilities work.

Of course, we would never dare to admit that a Mortal discovery helped us understand our magick...

Much like how an Elemental uses the air, a Psychic uses the atoms in the air to help move objects. Several Psychics can combine their efforts to move something larger.

It is important to note that it's very difficult for a Psychic to move a person. Although it has been tried, Magus have found it is better not to use magick to manipulate people. Physically or otherwise.

Cain, Anna and Grim couldn't help but worry. That's why they were waiting at the end of the hallway from Ms. White's office for him to come out. Grim was fidgeting with her hands. Cain was walking back and forth. Anna was resting her head on one hand against the armrests of her wheelchair.

Thirty minutes ticked by, and the office door at the end of the hallway opened, and Finn walked down. He looked surprised to see them all, but Anna interrupted before he could say anything.

"Well? What did she say?"

Finn cracked a light smile. "It's a warning this time."

Cain sighed in relief. "Thank god."

"Yeah, I was expecting worse. But she said it was the first time so I need to mind my manners next time and so on… did you guys seriously wait for me?"

"Of course we did!" Anna exclaimed. "You could have been fucking expelled you dipshit."

"God Anna it's like you would have missed me or something," Finn smirked at her, and she punched his arm. It seemed like Finn's anger had dissipated.

Grim stepped towards him. "I know you said it's not my fault, but it was because of me that you got into trouble. You didn't have to do that for me."

Finn frowned and put a hand on Grim's shoulder. Soft but reassuring. "I meant what I said. You're my friend…" He looked to Anna and Cain, then back to Grim. "You're all my friends. I'm not going to stand by and let you get treated as dirt. I'm not my brother."

"Is your relationship with Oscar that bad?" Cain asked, cautious not to upset him.

Finn cut in. "Oscar and I are very different people. He's a very talented Magus compared to the rest of my family. He thrives on it, and I couldn't care less. Makes him a right asshole."

"Reminds me of my parents," Grim mumbled.

He nodded, understanding her. "We've all got our static. Ms. White said she wouldn't tell my parents this time."

"Did she say anything about changing the tradition of separating the classes?" Cain asked as the four of them started heading out of the hallway and turned a corner.

"She said she would discuss it with the other professors, but I don't know if we'll see a change while we're still here."

"Doesn't seem likely," Cain added with a sigh. "Knowing Elderwall, we'll keep being stuck in our ways."

"Yeah…" Finn shook his head, and his smile came back. It was as if he jolted himself out of his sadness. "Anyway, let's all go get something to eat. I'm starving."

They reached the stairs, and Anna groaned. "You're going to need to be patient with me. You'd think Elderwall would build a lift, but no. Heaven forbid they make accommodations for people."

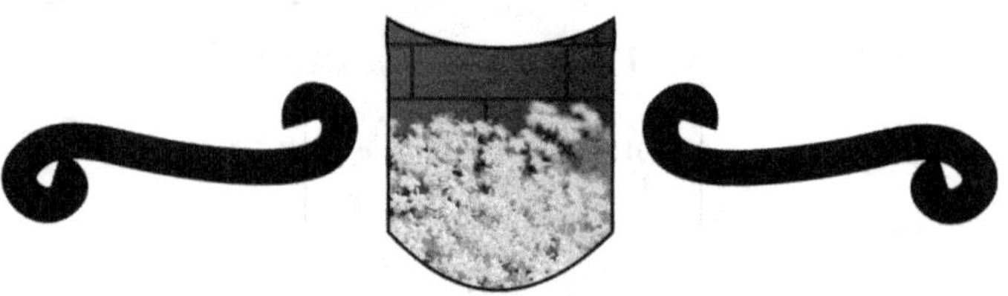

Behaviour Report for: Finn Becher

During today's Focus Presentation, Finn argued with Professor Starching over the seating arrangements for his friend, Raven Mortem. It was explained to Finn that due to his friend not having a Focus, she could not sit with her former classmates. Finn turned aggressive, and to avoid causing a scene in the presence of the rest of the students, Professor Starching agreed to let Raven sit with Finn and their other friends.

I have had a discussion with Finn and have given him a verbal warning for his attitude and reaction to the situation. However, I believe there is no need to involve his parents over this incident. Finn made some excellent points about the way we run the Focus Presentation, and about his friends situation. I believe at our next meeting we should discuss these points further.

Signed,

Audrey White.

Lukas met Grim for breakfast at 7:30 a.m. sharp. He wasn't late, for once. But, instead of saying good morning to her, with that same sleepy tone, he started the morning by presenting her with a bouquet of bright, red roses.

Grim looked up at him, stunned, as he looked right back at her with a foolish and large grin. She noticed the entire dining hall was watching. George was standing behind Lukas, with an equally stupid grin on his face.

She did some mental calculations. Then it clicked.

It was Valentine's Day.

It was *Valentine's Day.*

Fuck.

She stood up and took the flowers off him, her hands shaking. She could feel her face burning with embarrassment as she heard everyone comment on the situation.

"Aw, isn't Lukas sweet?"

"He's such a good friend to her."

"I heard he helps her out since she doesn't have a focus."

"Really? That's adorable."

"She needs all the help she can get. She won't make it here without the right person beside her."

Lukas was waiting for her response. He was putting his hands together and rubbing them together, nervous. He was *never* nervous. George was bouncing on his feet, it was clear he was also brewing in anticipation.

"Umm…" Grim's ears started ringing as she tried to form a sentence. "What…why-,"

"To answer all your questions-," Lukas held her by the arms and guided her back to her seat. She awkwardly flopped back into her chair, still disorientated. She put the flowers down and he sat opposite her. "George helped me grow them. I know it's not a thing I do but I thought this year I would. And…"

His voice went quiet, and George barrelled to the table and stood at the end. "AND they're just friendship flowers. That's what you told me, *right Lukas*?"

"Yeah!" Lukas sprung to life again and sat up straight. His cheeks were bright pink. "Thanks, George, they're friendship flowers."

Grim heard more students talking.

"Oh my god, I want what they have."

"Bless her, she's in shock."

"I would be too if a guy like Lukas gave me flowers."

She couldn't breathe. She couldn't breathe. Oh, fuck she couldn't breathe.

"Grim?" Lukas put a hand over hers, and she wanted to move it away, but she froze.

Seven. Eleven. Inhale. Exhale.

"Grim." He squeezed her hand, and she started shaking her head.

"Grim, come on, it's okay."

They were still talking. *They were still talking.*

"Raven."

She yanked her hand away from Lukas and stood up, her chair crashing to the floor. Without another thought or voice rattling inside her head, she ran out of the dining room.

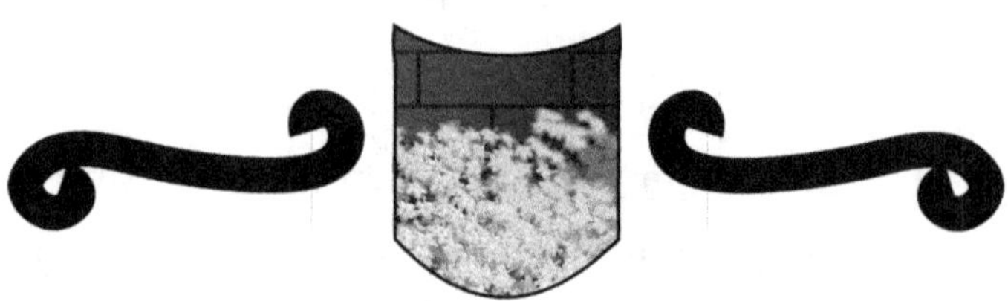

FAO: Ms Audrey White

Ms White,

I present my report on our first-year student Raven Mortem. She has continued to have perfect attendance to these sessions.

I must be frank with you, Audrey. Despite all my attempts to move Raven past the basic magick principles, it seems as though she cannot progress any further. The Baptism did not provide a Focus, an outcome I was not hoping for. I am running out of ideas on what to do. If possible, could you have a discussion with Raven on her thoughts? Perhaps she can provide a perspective on what she would like to concentrate on.

It seems unfortunate to admit, but Grim does not have the same magickal ability as everyone else. Looking at her grades from her evening classes, it seems she has continuously struggled with the same issues. I leave what we should do next in your capable hands. I am open to having a further discussion.

Mrs Scarlet Locklin

"Grim?"

She was on the floor against a wall, under a window, crouched down with her knees against her chest. She opened her eyes and looked up. Cain was kneeling in front of her. He looked worried.

"I've been looking for you. I came into the dining hall and everyone said you bolted out."

She put her head in her hands. "Panic attack."

"Oh, Grim." His voice was gentle. "Can I do anything?"

At first, she was going to refuse his help, but she gave him a small nod. "Help me stand up, please. I'm a little shaky."

Grim lifted her head again, and Cain stood up, offering both hands to her. She took them and he pulled her to her feet. She stumbled a little but held on until she was stable.

"What happened?" He asked, letting go of her hands.

"Lukas gave me some roses for Valentine's." She explained, wrapping her cardigan around herself. "In front of everyone, I freaked out."

"Why would he do that?"

"It's not his fault-,"

"Grim!"

They both turned to the voice, and Lukas was jogging towards her. He stopped and immediately turned his attention to Grim. Cain stepped away and leaned against the wall.

"Are you okay?" He asked, but it sounded more like a demand than a question. "It wasn't meant to go like that-,"

She nodded. Her chest was tight, but she took a deep breath. "I know, but you *know* I don't like that attention."

"For God's sake Grim it was flowers."

"That's not the point!"

"Then what is the point!?" He asked through gritted teeth.

"The *point*," Cain spoke from behind Grim. "Is that you shouldn't have put her in that position."

Lukas turned to Cain with a glare that could spark a fire. "This doesn't involve you. This is between me and my friend."

"Cain is my friend too." Grim snapped back, stepping between them. "No matter what you think of my choices in friends beside you, I would like you to treat him with the respect he deserves. I won't ask you again."

Lukas looked at Grim like she had stabbed him. "The only person I respect is you-,"

Her mouth dropped. What the hell had happened to the Lukas she knew? She turned round to Cain. "Cain, can you let us talk in private please?"

He pushed himself off the wall. "Of course."

He waved to her and walked off down the hallway. Once she was certain he was gone, as sharp as a stone, she turned back to Lukas. "What in the actual *fuck* is going on with you?"

"What's going on with ME?! What about you?"

"We are *not* talking about me right now; I want to know what the hell happened to my friend." She let out a heavy sigh. "Why did you get me flowers when you have *never* got me flowers? And gave them to me in front of everyone, no less?"

"I…" He sighed. "I thought it would be nice, George helped me plan it."

"Oh my god…" She clenched her fists. "You put the whole thing in front of an audience!"

"As I said, I thought it would be nice-,"

"Nice? *Nice*?" She barked out an exasperated laugh. "It was nice for you, it always is! Did you *hear* what they were saying about me? While you were having a wonderful time parading the bouquet, they talked about how pathetic I am WITHOUT YOU."

He didn't reply for a moment and looked at her as if a bomb had gone off between them. It had, in a way. Pent-up frustrations had exploded.

"I didn't…I didn't think of it like that."

"Fucking hell Lukas. Yes, to your surprise, not everyone has been having a fabulous time here. Not everyone can be perfect like you!" She screamed, so much so she felt her voice crack.

Tears were forming in her eyes, and she noticed they were forming in Lukas' eyes too.

"You are so, so perfect. To the school, to your family, to *my* parents." She inhaled. "I am useless baggage compared to you."

"Grim, that's not true." He rushed forward and hugged her. She stiffened, but he still pulled her in close. "You are everything to me."

"Please don't touch me."

He pulled away, not letting go. "I'm sorry. I shouldn't have let George talk me into it. But he had some solid reasoning and-,"

"Oh, so I'm expected to respect George's opinion but asking you to respect Cain's is too much?" She shoved herself out of his grip.

"It's different."

"It's *not*." She crossed her arms. "You've changed."

"So have you."

That was something they agreed on, at least.

"What are we going to do about it?" She asked, demanding. Two could play at that game.

"I don't know." He frowned. "I don't like fighting with you."

She sighed. "Neither do I."

"Can we stop fighting?" He laughed, trying to defuse the situation. Grim still felt the anger, but she knew there was no use in continuing a shouting match with Lukas. He was always above that. "I am sorry. I'll try to…be more aware of things. But you shouldn't let these silly anxiety fits get in the way of things."

"They're not silly."

"Sure." Lukas shook his head. "Let's leave it, okay?"

Grim crossed her arms. "Fine. We can go back and have breakfast."

"You're still coming to my match next week, right?"

"I did promise." She replied, as the two walked back into the dining hall. "And I wouldn't break my promise to you."

He nodded, smiling like he had won an epic battle. "I know."

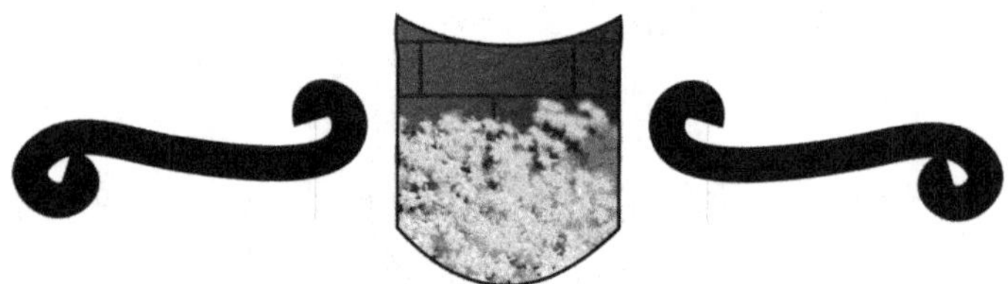

We cordially invite you to the Equniox Ball, taking place in the Grand Hall on the first Saturday in June. We will begin at 7pm.

We expect students to follow a formal dress code. If you have any issues with finding suitable attire, then please speak to a teacher, and we will be happy to assist you.

We look forward to seeing you there.

Grim slipped back into the Archives on the next quiet night. It was still there, it still existed. It wasn't a dream, or a vision, or some glimmer of mystery that she made up.

There were secrets at Elderwall. The Order had secrets.

Something which, all things considered, didn't surprise her.

She shut the door behind her and turned on the lantern again. It seemed that somebody was keeping the oil topped up, which worried Grim. That meant somebody was aware of what had happened.

She decided to see tonight how far the room went. How many records were hidden beneath the deep layer of dust that had settled over history? Grim finally reached it, a tall bookcase that stretched to the ceiling. There was a ladder attached to the shelves. With a deep breath, she put the oil lamp on the ground, its light streaking across the walls, and climbed up the ladder. She grabbed a book from the very top shelf and came back down.

"Fucking dust." She whispered, realising that patches of it covered her clothes. Accepting that she was only going to get more dust on her, she sat down on the floor and opened the book to a random page.

We have found a way to source magick from the portals. It's only a matter of time before this dull and lifeless world is reborn again. We are aware of the consequence of stealing power from these other worlds, but that doesn't matter. Don't we have a right to snatch greatness? To be bigger than the gods and have a monopoly on the wonders we would never see otherwise.

Grim sighed through her nose, a rage beginning to burn
inside of her. From her jacket pocket, she pulled out a
small notebook and a pen. She crossed her legs on the floor
and began transcribing the journal.

We have now given ourselves the title of Magus. It is imperative that we start to understand how our magick works, and how we can make the best use of the gifts granted to us by a higher power.

The geodes we found in the earth contain great crystals, which we can use to stabilise the power we have taken from the other worlds. We have hidden them around the world, in places nobody will expect to find them. These crystals draw the energy from the world and distribute it, and we, the special ones, can harness the power and release it in the four different principles that we have established.

Magick is a give and take, a constant flow that is never ending. What we release returns back to us, as we continue to take from the worlds that do not deserve it. If magick ever becomes a finite source, then there are always more worlds that we can find. This is our birthright, and we will claim it.

We "funnel" the magick so we have more control. What if Magus can use all four principals? But we've been conditioned not to?

Has it always been about control?

Grim found Cain after class in the garden of shadows, as she should have expected. He was lying across the bench, his eyes darting across the pages of an open book.

Spring was coming, but the chills of winter hadn't lightened too much. It was still a cloudy day with very little daytime left, and the sun was ready to set above them. The wind was picking up, and Grim wrapped her jacket tighter around her chest as she walked up to him. Her stomach was somersaulting.

He lifted his eyes from the book to meet hers. "Haven't seen you in a while."

In one fluid movement, Cain swung his legs off the bench and sat up, leaving her an empty seat. She sat down next to him, and he frowned. "You look tired." He continued, closing the book with a defined *thud*, and putting it down on his lap.

She avoided his gaze for a moment, her eyes dropping to her feet. "I've been studying late."

He raised an eyebrow when Grim lifted her head back up. "Burning the midnight oil? I thought you were past that."

"Burning the midnight oil?" She chuckled. "What are you, fifty?"

"My father always said I was an old soul," Cain replied with a smile, crossing his arms and looking back at her. "Are you sure you're okay? Have you got extra work or something?"

"It's hard to explain."

Grim wanted to tell him about the Archives. Wanted to confide in someone about what she had uncovered. But she knew she couldn't…yet. There was too much she didn't understand; unsolved variables that needed unravelling. The mystery of the Order of Chaos still loomed across Elderwall. Even though she trusted Cain, she knew there were secrets they hadn't shared yet.

She would tell him soon. But not yet…not yet.

"I'm here if you want to talk about it." He said after a moment of silence had passed.

Grim shook her head. "Another time. I came to find you for a reason."

He smirked. "And here I thought it was because you missed my company."

"I have missed hanging out!" She replied with a huff as her shoulders slumped. "It's about the other day, with Lukas."

"Oh…" Cain's tone hardened to something more serious. "You mean about what happened on Valentine's Day?"

She nodded. "I wanted to say sorry for how he snapped at you-,"

"Why are you apologising?"

"Because you're my friend and he insulted you and-,"

"Grim, you don't owe me an apology…he does."

Grim could feel her words picking up quicker and quicker as she continued to speak. "But I value you as a friend and I don't want what Lukas said to affect that. I know he's not going to think he did anything wrong so I wanted to clear the air and-,"

Her chest tightened, and she felt a sudden need to inhale a sharp breath. She instinctively put a hand there, feeling her breath shallow like waves on the shore. Cain leaned towards her, putting a hand on her arm. "Hey, *hey*. Inhale. Exhale. Seven. Eleven."

Inhale. Exhale. Seven. Eleven.

She heard the buzzing in her ears settle. Her breath was still shaking, but she kept going, following Cain's voice.

"You're doing great."

Five more minutes of this passed. Until Grim was calm enough to speak without feeling like the world was crushing her. Cain stayed close to her, a hand remaining on her arm.

"I had what I was going to say planned out in my head." She explained between breaths. "I knew exactly how I wanted this to go."

"Well sometimes things don't go as we planned it, and that's okay." He moved away from her, seeing that she was now calm, and continued talking. "Sometimes…we can make mistakes."

"I am sorry about Lukas. I told him-,"

He interrupted her again. "Listen to me Grim, you don't owe me any kind of apology for Lukas. He should respect your boundaries, and you shouldn't have to justify his behaviour, okay?"

"I owe him though. He's done a lot for me."

"You can be grateful for someone, but that doesn't mean you have to paint them in a good light all the time. People change, they come and go, you can't stop it, but at least you know at some point in your life, they cared."

"He's changed, you know. Lukas. He's changed."

"And that's okay. You both have. You're very different from the person who left the common room on her first night here."

She glanced at him, her lip shaking. "You think so?"

"You are an abomination of greatness Grim, and you don't even know it's the most amazing thing about you."

Grim smiled, the tension in her body remaining. Cain offered a hand, and he helped her stand up. When he let her hand go, he grabbed his book off the ground.

"Now," He turned back to her. "Taffy has a stock of herbal tea in Elderwall's kitchens, and I owe you a drink."

March

This was the final football match of the academic year. As such, the camaraderie that came with uniting over the common interest of sport made this day a popular one. Having the last match in March meant the students could have the time to focus on their final exams and enjoy the Equinox Ball before going home.

Grim had made a promise to Lukas that she would come to the last game. Despite their disagreement a couple of weeks ago, their friendship had grown back to the point it was at. Lukas was still himself, busy and still kept smiling. Somehow, everyone else in their year, and beyond, admired Lukas even more since Valentine's Day. The reason why was incomprehensible to Grim, but who was she to start evaluating the politics of popularity?

Now it was back to the present. Bundled in her coat, she sat on the bleachers that the College had built around the outdoor football field. She sat down in the front with Anna. Finn was playing, a surprise to Grim, but he was on the opposite team to Lukas. She had invited Cain and Remi to sit with them, but Remi was helping referee the game and Cain had offered to help them.

"So...I'm going to sound stupid, but how does this work again?" Grim asked, leaning towards Anna.

"Football. It's football."

"Really? Not even magickal football?"

"Nope. Just football."

"That's pointless, and a wasted opportunity."

Anna laughed and handed Grim two little flags. One with Lukas' team colours, and one with Finn's. "There. Now you can support both."

Grim waved them, giggling. "Sports are stupid."

"Yeah, but Finn's excited, and he gets to play against Oscar. So we can let him have this."

"Alright deal."

The field was alive with energy as the stands filled up with students and the players walked onto the pitch. They started warming up while Remi and the professors finalised refereeing the game.

She spotted Lukas across the field. "You came!" He shouted, jogging over.

"I promised, didn't I?" She said, rolling her eyes and waving a flag at him.

"I'm glad. It means a lot."

"Yeah, yeah, now go kick the ball."

He made a sudden reach for her hand, closing his fingers around the fist that was holding his team's flag. "I need you to wish me luck."

She felt her stomach tighten and heard the crowd turn their attention towards her and Lukas.

They were watching.

They were watching Lukas.

She let out a trembling breath. "Good luck." She replied, trying to smile.

He pulled her in and hugged her, before running back to the field. She slumped a little on the bench, regaining her composure.

She felt a light touch on her arm. "Take a deep breath, Grim."

It was Anna, leaning in a little to talk in a low voice. Grim could hear everyone talking again. Again. Again. Again. Again.

"We can leave if you need to."

She shook her head and sat up again. "No, we're here for Finn and Lukas."

"Are you sure? Finn would understand."

"I'm okay. Thank you, Anna."

She smiled and moved her hand away. "Alright, let's watch some dumb sports."

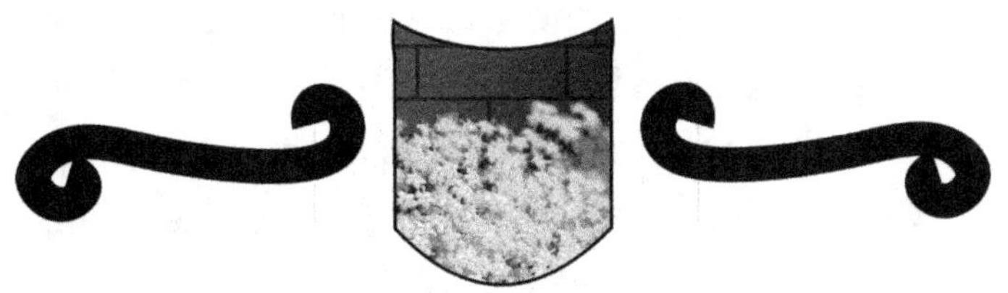

A NOTICE TO ALL STUDENTS

As you know, students who are members of the two school football teams have been training hard throughout the year and playing several matches in order to be crowned champions.

The final match of their season will be taking place on the first Friday of May, starting at 3pm.

The Order Might and the Order Knights are very close in terms of points, and this match is the decider.

Therefore, we request that all students, where possible, be able to attend.

We look forward to seeing you there.

89 minutes later, the score was one goal to each team. Grim hadn't been paying too much attention to the actual goings on within the game. Anna had kindly prompted her when was the right time to clap and wave her flags around.

Remi was standing at the opposite edge of the pitch, ready to blow the final whistle. As they were about to, the ground started shaking. The game came to a standstill, as the pitch trembled. Grim tried to get a better look, but Remi was shouting at all the players to get off the pitch now. As everyone evacuated, the ground started to glow.

The words *SOON* appeared in bright blue letters.

The Order of Chaos.

The words disappeared as soon as the school had registered them.

Remi blew the final whistle.

Lukas was sitting next to Grim on the stands, hunched over, out of breath and exhausted. Anna had gone over to Finn, who was celebrating the fact he managed to not injure himself.

"I can't believe it," Lukas said between sharp breaths.

Grim folded her hands together, turning to him. "Got to give them credit for flair."

"They ruined it. The whole thing."

He sounded...*angry*. Grim would understand if the inconvenience of the game ending early annoyed him. But this was anger, this was different."

"It was just a game, Lukas, calm down."

"That's not the point!" He yelled, making Grim jump. He seemed to have drawn some attention to him, and when he realised there were eyes on him, he softened his voice. "This is getting out of control. What the hell are these people thinking?"

"I don't know, but nobody knew this would happen. You're doing your best-"

"Don't talk like you know what's going on because you don't." He snapped. "You're not like the rest of us."

"What do you mean by that?"

"I mean, you've not been a part of this. You're not a part of any of this."

"What the hell is wrong with you?" She demanded, her heart sinking. "You said I could be. You said I could be a great magus."

"I say a lot of things."

She stood up, ignoring the people who were now looking at them. "Forget this, I'm not talking to you right now. Come find me when you've calmed down."

"No, *Grim*." He reached out and grabbed her hand, stopping her from leaving. He pulled on her hand and forced her to turn back around. He stood up, still holding her hand. "Wait, I…I'm sorry."

"Oh?"

"It's…we didn't win, and we haven't stopped the Order of Chaos. I lashed out."

Grim looked around and realised Lukas' teammates, and their classmates had overheard the entire conversation. Lukas was never one to give a true apology, often allowing his actions to speak for him instead of meagre words.

He was apologising because everyone was watching him.

She let his hand fall and stepped away. "Go calm down, get your head on straight. We'll talk later."

"Please believe me, Grim, I didn't mean it."

People started whispering. She walked away.

What makes a perfect Magus? It is a discussion we have all been having recently. Now that we have grown our ranks, it is important that we whittle out the weak, or at least shame them enough so that they begin to comply.

This is what we have agreed on. We need a Magus to be intelligent, with a high academic calibre. They must also be dedicated to the cause, to the Order, and never stray from the path we have laid for them.

We have clear evidence that intelligence and insight links to magickal ability. If we have the smartest and healthiest people as Magus, then we are already one step above the Mortals.

Ew ew ew ew ew ew ew ew!!!

Of course, it would be wonderful if a Magus' physical attributes matched their mental attributes as well. We must be selective to craft the perfect Magus. It is an art form, one that will take generations to perfect. We cannot stop now, we will have perfection. We will see to it that those who do not fit our image will feel the shame of it.

What the hell??

Perfection and greatness have always been a
factor in our education. I didn't
know it reached this level.

It had been a few days since the football match. Grim and Lukas hadn't spoken much since that day. Everybody else had spoken on their behalf, however. Rumours flew fast through the halls of Elderwall. More than once people had asked Grim about the truth behind them. Some were saying their fallout stemmed from Grim's meltdown on Valentine's Day. Others said that Lukas upset Grim *by accident* after the final football match.

Either way, Lukas was the victim here. Every time someone asked Grim about her perspective, they brushed her off with a lack of grace.

She sat in the library, in her usual seat of comfort and security. She tried to avoid the glances and stares of the people around her. In front of her, she opened a spare journal she had. Stuffed inside were scraps of paper, annotations, and sketches.

Every night. Every night she snuck into the Archives for an hour. At this point, no professor or student questioned anything when they saw Grim walking the halls under the moonlight. To everyone else, Grim must have been trying hard to catch up on her classes, ready to retake the Baptism next year.

Grim had been compiling her facts, obsessed with aligning new information with old. Everything seemed to make sense. Certain historical events appeared in Archive entries, albeit with truth instead of victory. She didn't know *who* she would take this information to. Going straight to the Order seemed like a fool's errand. There wasn't exactly anywhere, or *anyone* who would listen to her. She had a feeling they knew *exactly* what had happened.

She reached for the stack of books next to her. The classic history anthologies she had grown up studying under her parent's watchful eye. Then, she heard a voice exclaim beside her.

"Grim! Good to see you!"

George's booming voice gave her the fright of her life, so much so that she dropped the book out of her hands. It landed with a thud and covered her journal.

"George…" She took a deep breath, the shock leaving her system. "If you're looking for Lukas he's not here."

"Oh, I know, I wanted to speak to you."

Grim stood up, moving the books to cover up her work, forcing George to focus his attention elsewhere. She nodded towards him. "Okay…what is it?"

George looked very sheepish. "I know it might not be my place, but did you and Lukas fight?"

She frowned. In her mind, she congratulated George for stating the obvious. "Not that it's any of your business, but what makes you think that?"

"We were talking a while ago, and I brought you up. He got all quiet and left pretty sharpish."

"Oh…" She paused, a hand resting on the book at the top of the pile. From the sounds of it, Lukas had felt the effects of their disagreement.

George continued. "As I said, ain't my place but…"

Grim turned around and leaned against the desk. She didn't want anyone to bother her with this anymore. "Say what you want to say,"

He took a breath. "Whatever you two argued about…Lukas always thinks about you. And I know that's not justification for whatever he said or did. But…he's a good friend of mine and even when he messes up, he has a good reason."

She shook her head. "I know he does George…but being good isn't enough when you're wrong."

"Yeah, I know, I know." He grinned at her. "I like Lukas. He's chill, and nice to hang out with. We get the work done. Talk it out with him, okay?"

Grim shrugged, not wanting to give him a reaction. "I'll try, but it's nothing to do with you."

George put his hands up in defence. "I know that, but Lukas is my friend too and I hate seeing him like this."

"Is that because I'm useful to him?"

He stared at her in shock, and for a moment, Grim regretted not holding her tongue. George shook his head. "I apologised for that."

"Lukas made you apologise for that."

"Look you misunderstood-,"

"George I don't have time for this. I have work to do, and I have a lesson with Mrs. Locklin I can't-,"

"But I'm not wrong though!" George smirked at her, and it made Grim's blood boil. "Lukas is going to be this generation's best Magus. He has so much potential. And, amazingly, he's got someone as smart as you, who knows the Order inside and out, by his side. He needs you…as much as you need him."

Grim moved the books again, grabbing her journal and slamming it shut. She reached for her bag and shoved everything inside. "What happened between myself and Lukas is exactly that, it's *between* us. Everything to do with our friendship is between us."

George's voice lowered. "Oh…so it's a friendship?"

"Yes! It always has been. And I get it, you want to help him, and make him feel better, avoid all the conflict. But friendships are tricky, and most importantly, *private*." She hauled her bag onto her shoulder. "We will talk when we're damn well ready to."

"He's ready now, you should talk to him."

She had already moved away from the table, aware that she had an audience. "Then tell him to make the first move."

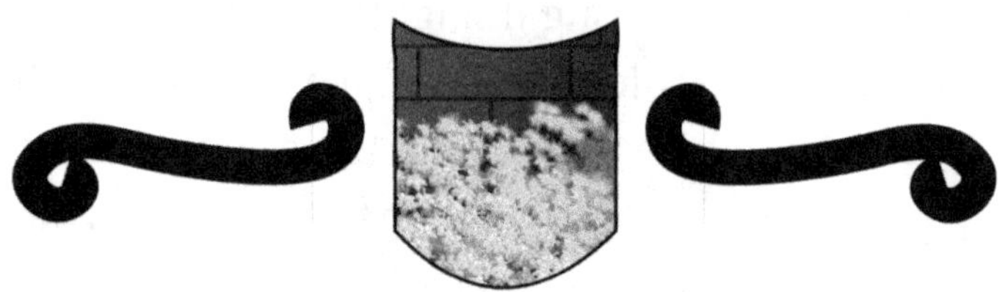

FAO: Ms Audrey White

Ms White,

I am saddened to report that Raven Mortem has once again failed the practical exam, the one that she had failed previously in November.

I gave Raven the opportunity to retry the presentation, as I found her written work to be excellent. However, she once again failed to demonstrate her chosen principle of Magick. I offered her a chance to show a different principle. However, even when given the materials, she could not perform the task.

I am also saddened to say she exploded one of my plant pots, leaving a mess on the classroom floor. If you could please have a word with Raven, as I am unsure what to do. I do not want my time wasted by having her repeat an exam she cannot pass.

Professor Randall Starching.

Grim once again found herself in Ms. White's office. The room hadn't changed, even though the seasons had. Outside the window, the spring sky was blooming. The sunlight was finally returning to the world. She sat in the same chair as before, and Ms. White sat behind her desk, as before.

"No scribbling pen taking notes?" Grim asked, trying to sit like her parents had taught her.

Ms. White chuckled. "No, not this time. It's not necessary."

"Then how are you going to give a perfect and accurate report to my parents?"

"I'm not."

Well. That was a surprising twist.

She folded her hands together over the desk. "They told me what happened after the Baptism, and I told them they were out of line…for once."

Grim rolled her eyes. "If you called me here so we could talk about my feelings-,"

"I can assure you that is not the case." She replied with a laugh. "No, this is actually about your schoolwork."

Shit.

Ms. White flicked her wrist outwards, and a cabinet on the other side of the room opened, and the drawers slid open. A single piece of paper flew across the room and into her hand. "You failed another exam a few days ago."

Grim sighed, ready to explain. "It was a retake of the principles of magick demonstration from the start of the year. I still can't do it, I tried, and Starching knows it."

"You're not in trouble Grim."

She paused. "I'm…not?"

"It's time we accept that you are not going to be able to pass the practical exams this year." Ms. White nodded. "Your written examinations are exemplary. But, I understand that we are forcing you into a position that is not healthy."

Grim blinked a few times, stunned by what she was hearing. "What are you saying?"

Ms. White smiled in response, her white teeth showing. "I know you don't want to be here Grim, and I am not expecting you to come back next year. I want you to finish the year, and then I want to help you work out your next steps."

"Why?" She asked, her voice quieter than she thought it would be.

Ms. White sighed. "I know what it's like to feel like you don't belong there. When I started here, it was after I transitioned, and I had to fire half the staff. I have observed you for a long time. I saw those flames burn you, and it's made me rethink how we take care of our students."

The piece of paper, showing Grim's failures, dropped on the desk like a feather falling. "Also…" Ms. White continued. "Finn and I had an interesting conversation after the Focus Presentation."

"This is a prank or something isn't it?" Grim crossed her arms, getting ready to stand up. She could her blood heating as the endless scenarios ran through her head. "Elderwall has a perfect graduation record. No student has ever dropped out unless they've died or something!."

The headmistress' smile fell. "The reason for that is, as Finn put it, is because we shame and embarrass them to no end. Times are changing Grim, and the Order won't change with them, but at least here I have a chance to change things."

Grim noticed her hand was trembling, and she clenched them together to stop it. She knew that Ms. White could see she was on edge. "I don't think it's wise to send you home now, because I would have to count it as expelling you. Continue to go to your classes, take part in the Equinox Ball, and then we can do all the necessary paperwork."

"Neither of us will hear the end of this, so why are you doing it? The real reason."

Ms White stood up, moved around the desk, and faced Grim. The headmistress looked neat in her emerald green blazer and trousers, but her tired eyes showed weakness.

"Have you seen the messages from the Order of Chaos?"

"Everyone has Ms. White."

"I remember the messages when I was studying at Elderwall. The Order of Chaos has been around for decades now, and I have my theories that there is some truth in it."

Grim tried to mask her shock. The last person she expected to be suspicious of the Order would be the headmistress of Elderwall Boarding College. But it was clear Ms White wasn't joking.

"Do you think it's true then? That the magick isn't ours. That the Magus…"

"I will be taking my claims to the Order when you all have gone home. Along with my proposal to change the Baptism to be a *choice* for every student." She crossed her arms across her chest. "What do you think? About the Order of Chaos?"

Grim didn't want to show her hand, but her mind immediately cast back to her journal full of secret notes. She wanted to trust Ms. White but knew she was planning to go to the Order regardless of what happened. The Order that had stolen magick and ruined lives.

"I think they're right. In what way I don't know." Grim explained, and when Ms. White's eyes started to widen, she was quick to change the subject. "Do you want to write to my parents about my upcoming dismissal or would you like to do the honours?"

Ms. White smirked. "I will handle it. You enjoy your final months here, Grim."

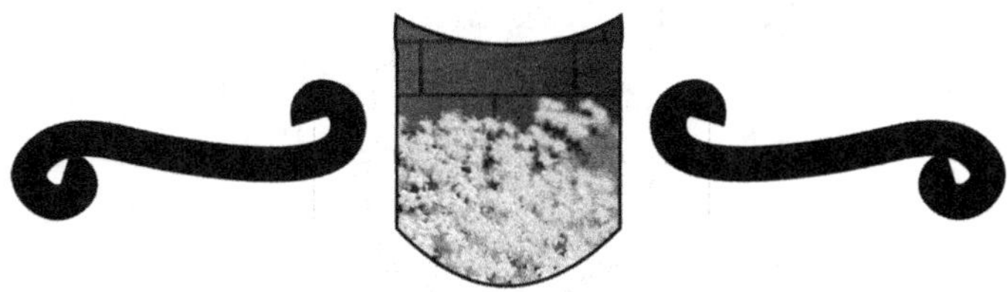

To Will and Delilah,

I hope you will forgive the informality of this letter. I would hope as old friends we would be able to talk without the need for ceremony.

I know you have been receiving the reports on Grim's progress in her classes, and how her lack of magickal ability is still a persistent problem. To give your daughter credit, she has attended all the extra sessions given to her, attended the specific Focus classes, and kept up with her written assignments. Mrs Locklin and I have agreed that Grim is not making the progress we would normally see for a student here. She has still not grasped the basic concepts for controlling her magick.

I understand it means a lot for you to have her graduate from Elderwall. I know your family name is important to you, my friends, but I must implore you to think of this from Grim's perspective. She has been struggling. I am ashamed to admit Elderwall has produced a toxic environment for an individual like her. Grim and I have discussed the situation, and have both agreed it is best for her not to continue at Elderwall. She will stay with us until the end of the year, and then we can meet and discuss what steps need to be taken to ensure she has a bright and happy future.

Please understand this is the best thing for her. I look forward to speaking with you both soon.

All the best,

Audrey

There was a knock at Grim's door one afternoon. She closed the journal she used for her research and knelt next to her bed, stuffing it inside a pillowcase.

The door knocked again, this time more frantic. Grim huffed. "Give me a second!"

After making sure the biggest secret she had ever kept was well hidden, Grim got to her feet and opened the door.

Lukas stood there. He had ironed his blue shirt and even his jeans. That was a new jacket he was wearing. She realised immediately that he had made an effort.

"George said I needed to be the one to talk to you first."

She raised an eyebrow, surprised he had taken George's advice. "Would you like to come in or are we going to make this another public event?"

He shook his head. "I would like to come in, please."

Grim stepped aside, holding the door open for Lukas. He stepped in, and she shut the door behind him, leaning against the door. They stared at each other for a second too long.

"I know you want an apology, and you're going to get one."

She gestured with a hand for him to continue as she kept her expression stoic.

He obliged her and started to pace back and forth. "What I said was out of line…I got upset that the Order of Chaos interrupted the game. I'm sorry for lashing out."

"I don't want an apology for that." She said, her words harsh. "You admitted that I shouldn't pretend I'm part of any of this. That you *lied* about me becoming a great magus."

"I say a lot of things when I'm angry Grim you can't hold me to that."

She stepped towards him, and Lukas held his hands out, almost as if he was getting ready to embrace her. But she kept her arms at her sides, hands clenched tight behind her back. "I thought you better than them, Lukas."

He took the plunge, placing his hands on her arms, keeping his calm composure. She stiffened and shivered. Lukas' hazel eyes were gentle, almost deceiving in their grace. "What can I do to make this right?"

Grim stepped away from him. "I-I don't know. I don't know what I want from you but I am sick and tired of everyone having an opinion about us."

"I've been trying to stop people from doing that-,"

"No! You've been encouraging it, you love the attention!"

"And there's something wrong with that?" Lukas looked her dead in the eye when he said that. No tone of remorse in his voice. He continued his hands in his pockets. "I am sorry for what I said. I am, but because you get so angry at the attention doesn't mean I have to as well."

She didn't know what to say and turned her eyes away from him. Lukas remained still in the middle of her room and decided to carry on talking. "I still want my friend around, but you have to stop letting everyone else be the reason we argue."

Grim sighed. "You know I don't mean to get angry…"

A small smile curled on his thin lips. "I know you don't. Can we put this behind us, please? I need you with me."

Lukas always said he needed Grim, ever since they were young it was always that he *needed* her. In some foolish way, she needed him, for a time. Despite what a small part of her mind was telling her, she still did.

"Okay. I'm sorry too." She tried to return the smile to him. "I'll meet you at breakfast tomorrow."

He nodded. "I'm going to a student council meeting now anyway."

So, she was a stopping point on his way to his true destination. Interesting.

Grim turned around and opened the door back up. She heard voices down the end of the corridor. What they were saying, she didn't know, but they had been waiting for something. Lukas must have heard it too because his smile grew wider. The attention he liked so much was ready for him.

"See you tomorrow!" He flashed his winning smile and left. Grim pretty much slammed the door behind him, conflicted on a major level.

She got her apology. But beneath all that was the uneasy feeling that nothing would be the same. And that it would only be downhill from here.

Raven,

Well I hope you're happy. You finally got what you wanted. Your father and I are disappointed in you, to a degree I cannot explain with words.

*Couldn't you do what you're told for once? Why do you have to be so inconsiderate to your family, to your legacy, to your **birthright**? You have ruined your future, Raven. You have no hopeful prospects.*

What's worse is that you have managed to convince everyone to call you by that ridiculous name. You are Raven Alexandra Mortem. A Mortem does not bring such shame as this.

*You are a Magus, whether you like it or not. You **will** do what you are told. I do not care that you are an adult. You have disrespected and shamed us for the last time Raven. When you come home, we will have a long chat with Ms. White about what to do with you.*

*You, my daughter, are **this** close to being disowned and thrown out onto the street. Sort it out. Fix it. Do not disappoint us.*

Mother

April

This is our final
message to you.

Since everything seems to have fallen into
place.

This magick is not ours.

It was never ours.
What the Order didn't tell you is that our
magick doesn't come from us. We have been
stealing it from other worlds.

And now these worlds are dying.
Their true magick is being taken
away from them because of us.

Because you want to feel
important.
To feel powerful.
To be above it all.

This will end.
Be prepared.

The final message, as dubbed by the student body, appeared in the dining hall. Everyone saw it, read it, and was now in a state of panic. Ms. White assembled the students in the dining hall the next day and told everyone there was no reason to worry.

But, Grim thought there was a reason to worry because she thought the Order of Chaos were onto something. Lukas completely disagreed.

"Grim, they're stupid pranks. You did the research." Lukas said as they wandered the library shelves. "There's nothing concrete about this."

She turned back around to him with a scowl. She still felt on edge with him and was ready to snap back at him more than usual. But they had tried to make peace, and Grim wanted to maintain it. She still cared. Somehow, she still cared.

"But the foundations of magick are still-," She started to explain, but Lukas cut her off.

"Grim, it's all nonsense. I know you've read more than me, but history doesn't matter, what's important is being here now."

"History should mean something here though. It should make some sense."

"Listen," He took her hand, and squeezed it. "Don't get yourself worked up. Somebody is taking this too far. The important thing is…we're good, and we're going to be great magus."

She'd heard that before.

She blinked and moved her hand away. "I didn't tell you, did I?"

"Tell me what?" He asked, concerned.

Grim sighed, turning away from him to slot a book back on the shelf. "I had a meeting with Ms. White. I'm not going to be coming back next year."

His tone shifted, an annoyance in his voice. "What do you mean you're not coming back?"

"I mean," She met his eyes. He looked solemn but seemed to be thinking about something else as well. "She agrees that the Baptism showed I'm not meant to work for the Order. We have agreed I will finish the year, and then work out what I do next."

"But…" He frowned. "I need you here."

"No, you don't!" She replied with a laugh. "You'll be fine. Mr. Valedictorian and all that."

"I want you here. It won't be the same without you."

Grim walked a bit further down the library shelves. She kept her eyes focused on the spines dancing across her vision. Lukas followed behind her. "I can't imagine graduating without you." He continued.

She pulled another book from the shelf, checking the cover. Not what she needed. She looked up to Lukas. "I'm not disappearing, Lukas. We can still write to each other and I'll see you every summer."

"It won't be the same."

She slotted the book back. "This is the best news I've had all year. This is *good*. Finally, I'm able to do what I want to do."

"I know but, I'll miss you." He mumbled, loud enough for her to hear, smiling as he did it. Always smiling.

She waved a hand at him, chuckling. "Don't be so dramatic, it won't be that bad."

Grim heard footsteps coming toward them, and she noticed Remi out of the corner of her eye. They smiled when they saw Grim, but the smile dropped when they spotted Lukas.

"Hey, Remi!"

"I saw you over here and thought I should say hello." They glanced at Lukas. "Lukas."

"Remi." He replied with a wave.

"How are you?" She asked, ignoring the mutual disdain between Remi and Lukas.

They nodded. "I'm not too bad, I haven't seen you in a while."

"I…got wrapped up in some research."

Remi smiled. "Why am I not surprised?"

Lukas cleared his throat. "Are you looking for anything in the library Remi? I'm sure Grim could help you find it."

Remi smirked. "*Actually*, I have found what I was looking for. I thought Grim might want to read it."

"So, this…*wasn't* politeness?"

Remi shrugged, pleased with themselves. *"I found you a book* is a weird conversation starter. Anyway," Remi held up the book. The cover was old leather, cracked. It looked like it had been collecting dust for a long time. "I was looking into whether what the Order of Chaos said was true."

"So am I!" Grim exclaimed, her excitement obvious. "Something about it makes sense."

"Ugh, Remi don't get her started." Lukas groaned. "And aren't we supposed to be *against* proving it?"

Remi stared hard at Lukas. "If what they're saying is true, we have a duty, as the student council, to verify that and be honest with the students. *Wouldn't you agree*?"

"As I said to Grim, history doesn't-,"

"Fucking hell you two, leave the political debate to your meetings." Grim interrupted. Lukas looked ready to explode, but Remi started laughing. She held out her hands. "Can I borrow the book?"

Remi dropped it into her hands. "Of course. Chapter three, about two pages in."

She turned the book over in her hands, the dust getting on her fingers. "I haven't seen this before."

"Found it tucked in a corner. I knew it was here though, just took me a while to find it."

"Well, thanks Remi, it means a lot."

"No worries. I'll see you around." Remi turned and walked away. Before they turned the corner, they tilted their head back to Grim and called out. "And try to get your head out of your books!"

Grim laughed at that and turned her attention back to Lukas. His face looked like a lemon had slapped it. "What is it?" She asked.

"I don't think you should read that book."

"I'm going to." She replied, rolling her eyes. "Even if it's nothing, it's worth a try."

"It's going to cause more trouble…" He huffed. "I'm going off to meet George, you want to come?"

"No, I'm reading this, then going to check on Cain. Have fun."

"Yeah…and think about what I said, okay? I'm worried you'll miss out if you leave."

"I've made up my mind, so unless you want to talk to Ms. White about it, this is my first and last year at Elderwall."

"You're coming to the ball though, right?" He asked as he was about to turn and leave.

"Yeah, of course. It's not my style but at least the room will look pretty."

He chuckled. "Good. Good. Okay, see you for breakfast? If I don't see you later, I mean.

"7:30 sharp."

Lukas smiled, satisfied. He picked up his bag and walked. Grim watched him go. As soon as she saw him disappear around the corner, she walked with haste towards the tables. She sat down, and opened the book to the chapter Remi suggested.

She skimmed the pages. The writer discussed a lot about the principles and the four focuses, trying to discuss their origins and where such power could come from. Then she saw it, right in the middle of the page, mushed together with all the other words. So subtle, but it would mean everything.

They say that our abilities do not come from this world but from others.

Grim almost dropped the book. Remi knew something about this. About the Order, about the magick. They had given Grim this book for a reason. And she had a feeling she knew what that reason was.

When the four focuses were established within our system, concerns were raised about the stability of separating our abilities in such a way. If we were to tell our future Magus what they could and could not be, would that sow the seeds of rebellion, or dissatisfaction?

For our students to go through a great trial such as the Baptism of Fire, then it must mean we have certainty in where a person's magick is contained. They say that our abilities do not come from this world, but others.

By allowing a Magus to narrow down their power into one strain of magick, it amplifies their abilities. A jack of all trades is the master of none, after all. *Not the full phrase but fine*

 If we can contain the magick, we can allow it to prosper for years to come. Generation after generation will be able to grasp the abilities we fought so hard to use.

As we narrow down magick into an individual focus, the Magus in question will have access to more power. If, for example, we allowed a Magus to be both a Skulduggery and Summoner, their powers in both areas would be lesser than if they had only one focus. A summoner would use magickal items to create illusions instead of their mind, and how would their illusions turn out? It would be as if *Is this possible? Would Caio or Finn know?* you crossed two different coloured pieces of string and tried to knot them together. Yes, you would have a longer piece of string, but it would not be as strong as a complete one of the same colour.

Order is maintained for a reason. Regardless of where our abilities and power take their origin, we must remain vigilant in the pursuit of a bright future.

What would happen if fewer and fewer people burned themselves on the Baptism? Would the Order finally have the perfect Magus?

At the end of Starching's lesson, he rounded off his final class of the year with one worrying sentence. Well, several worrying sentences.

"That's it for today. Ah, Miss Mortem. Do stay here. We need to have words."

If someone could aesthetically be frozen over, Grim would be in this moment. The classroom emptied, and she struggled to walk down the steps as the nerves took over her mind and body. Lukas touched her arm as he left with George, offering her a winning smile. If it was to reassure her, Lukas had failed.

A moment later, it was Grim and Starching, alone in the classroom. He remained standing at his desk for a moment. His fingers coiled as magick flowed around the books and papers scattered around the room, organising them back into unique piles. As he did this, one book vanished out of the room. He had returned it to a student who didn't realise they had lost it.

"What did you want to talk about, sir?"

Starching didn't reply at first, making careful movements with his cane to stand in front of Grim. Despite his hunched back, he still towered over her. "Have you enjoyed your first year at Elderwall?"

Grim spoke with caution. "For the most part."

"Elderwall has many things to enjoy does it not? The library particularly has *many* activities for night owls such as yourself."

Her heart stopped. "Yes, I like to go and read in the common room when I can't sleep."

"Hm…" Starching looked back at his desk, and picked up a framed photo, passing it to Grim. "Did you know I taught your father?"

She looked down at the photo. It was her father, in his Elderwall graduation robes, that shimmering deep purple. He stood next to Starching, who looked a little younger than he does now. A woman was in the photo too, in the same robes. Grim recognised her mother immediately. "No, I didn't."

"Your mother too. They were both wonderful students. I remember hearing about their marriage after they had graduated. I kept in touch with your father, and he told me all about you after you were born. How he and your mother were going to send you to Elderwall, destined to be a great magus."

There was that word again. *Great.*

Starching continued after Grim put the photo back on the desk. "Imagine my surprise when I saw your test scores." He said with a chuckle. "That's why I tested you on that first day of class. I had to see what my best students had offered this generation. You impressed me, for a time."

"For a time?"

His eyes met hers, and she felt them burning into her. He frowned. "What I was quick to realise Miss Mortem, is that you were not your parents. You were not Will and Delilah, which was disappointing, to say the least. Instead of a great magus, Elderwall found themselves with an angry, bitter girl, who swears too much and doesn't even have a speckle of her family's ability."

Grim tightened her grip on the straps of her bag. Starching continued to speak, and the next words he said chilled her to the bone.

"Then I find out this angry, bitter girl has been poking her nose in places she's not welcome."

She stepped back in surprise. Starching tapped his cane on the floor. "There are some secrets we don't share, *Raven*. I will let you have your fun. But, if you spout a single word about what you know, you will be responsible for collapsing an entire society. A society founded upon centuries of hard work, all on your wretched little shoulders."

Grim was silent, the air felt like a hand around her throat. Starching's words had made everything feel heavy. Perhaps it was his magick, or perhaps it was his dominating presence.

"Your parents are *great* people, Miss Mortem, it would do you well to respect that."

Finally finding courage, she spoke. "My parents have lost my respect Mr. Starching."

"Then you were never worthy enough to earn it. Now go, and I hope when I see you next year you will heed my words."

"You won't see me next year."

Starching looked surprised and raised an inquisitive eyebrow. "Oh?"

"I'm leaving Elderwall. Ms. White has approved it."

He seemed satisfied with the arrangement. "Then remember what we have discussed. And think what would happen if everyone found out where you had been sneaking off to."

She knew what he was trying to do. She swallowed the lump in her throat. "The truth is a powerful thing."

"A dangerous weapon-,"

Grim stopped him. "Even so, who would believe the angry, bitter girl with *no magick*?"

Starching smiled at her, an empty grin. "Who would indeed? You are dismissed, Miss Mortem."

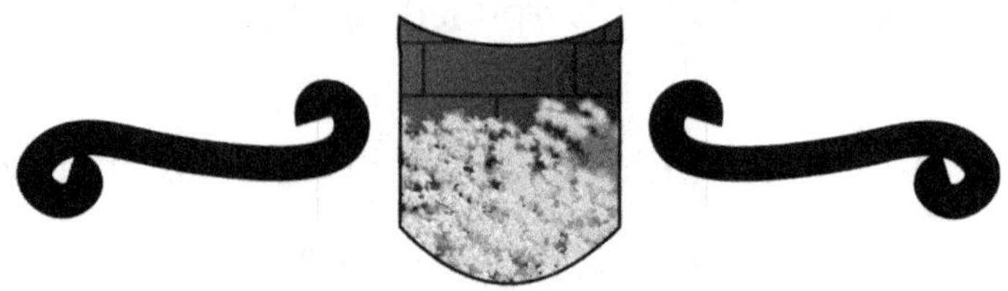

Ms White,

I have recently discovered that Raven Mortem has been leaving her room at night, and going into restricted areas of the college, specifically an area of the library that is only for certain members of the Order.

I have confronted Raven about this issue, and she has denied it. However I have clear evidence to suggest she has been tampering with Order property. I would hate to have to bring this to the Order's attention, so see to it that Raven is properly punished.

Professor Randall Starching.

Grim was frantic as she knocked on Cain's bedroom door, as loud as the night would allow it. After about ten minutes the door opened. Cain stood there, dishevelled in an oversized t-shirt, and chequered pyjama trousers. He rubbed his eyes. When he realised it was Grim, he was awake.

"Grim, are you okay? Do you know what time it is?" He asked, in a low, sharp whisper.

"I need to show you something."

"Can't it wait until the morning?"

Grim clenched and unclenched her hands. "Please."

Cain saw the desperation in her eyes. Tears were forming in them as she tried to keep it together in front of him.

His half-asleep expression softened. "Okay…okay. Wait here. Let me throw some clothes on."

I see the worlds in my dreams sometimes. I see the destruction we caused. The chaos we left behind so we could bring about order to our world. Devastation, ruin, people left cold, lonely and abandoned.

I see many people in my dreams. Often, I see returning characters whose stories are left shattered. Other times, I see brief glimpses of fantastic places. I see dragons and mermaids, fairies and monsters. Sometimes I see a world much like ours, but a little bit darker.

The returning characters are the ones I remember most. Last night, I dreamed of two people falling in love while the danced the danse macabre. They looked into each other's eyes, a feeling neither of them had experienced before. Then it all went black, and I woke up.

What does this mean?

Did some people feel remorse over what the Order did? Why didn't they do something sooner? What stopped them?

As soon as Cain came back out of his room, Grim led him into the library, clutching her bag. They arrived at the secret door to the Archives. The two stopped to catch their breath while Grim found the book to open the door.

"Grim, you're scaring me," Cain said between harsh breaths in and out. "What's going on?"

"I found this place at the start of the year, and the deeper I looked into everything, the more scared I was. I tried to tell the student council but they laughed in my face. Even Lukas didn't believe me…so…" She found the book and pulled it off the shelf, and the door slid open. "I'm trusting you."

Cain stared in pure shock, his mouth dropping open. "What the hell is this?"

"Quick, inside." She pulled Cain in by his arm and shut the door behind them. He saw the oil lamp and snapped his fingers over the wick inside, igniting it. Cain held it up over the dusty bookshelves and saw the sign on the wall.

"The Archives?"

Grim pulled out her journal and handed it to Cain, taking the lamp off him and placing it back on the empty surface. He flicked through the pages; his eyes wide with fury.

"The Order found portals to other worlds containing magick and used crystals to channel that magick into our world. These worlds suffered when they took it. That's why there's such a difference in ability with magick. They've been doing this for centuries, Cain. The Order of Chaos? They were *right*."

She was speaking so fast, her words sounding foreign to her. Cain said nothing, his eyes still on her journal, of the countless entries she had copied. "Please say something…" She said, begging him to understand.

Cain looked up, closing the journal. His expression was unreadable. "I'm going to show you something…and you have to *promise* me that you keep it a secret."

Grim nodded, and Cain opened his palms. Bright, speckled blue light covered the room. Flowers bloomed from the ceiling, trailing down onto the floor. Vines swirled over Grim's feet.

She recognised it immediately.

The flowers from the garden of shadows.

The magick that the Order of Chaos used to send their messages.

She gripped the side of the bookcase as Cain looked at her, trying to read her expression. Her knees shook, and she fell to the floor. Immediately, the illusion dropped. Cain rushed to his knees next to her, helping her sit on the floor. The flickering light of the oil lamp was the only thing illuminating their faces.

She met his eyes. "You're in the Order of Chaos."

Lies do not exist amongst the Order. If history is written by the winners, then surely we can write history according to our desires.   What desires?

If we must keep our fellow magus in the dark about the origins of our power, then so be it. Let them live believing we have won, that compared to the mortals, we are victorious.

Even if we were to tell everyone the truth, they would not care. They would see what the magus before us did, they would see the potential our future can hold. But still, we cannot sow the seeds of chaos. Such ideas would spark revolution.   This is the second time this is mentioned. How scared were they?

Now, we must establish the rules of our race. We must enforce strict regulations in magick to keep ourselves thriving. The future of the Order is bright, and we must not let our light be extinguished.

Wait Wait Wait Wait. So did the Order lie about our history? Did we actually do everything we said we did to help the world progress?

I have said for years that there were inconsistencies in the history books. But my worries were dismissed. In my mother's own words. "but look at what we did Ray!"

How deep do the lies go?

Cain and Grim were on the floor, leaning against the bookshelves. The oil lamp sat on the floor, spreading light across them. Cain sat with his knees against his chest, and Grim had her legs crossed, her journal open on her lap.

"So…you, Marcus and Remi?" She asked, processing everything he had told her.

"Yes. My father started it when he was back in school with an old friend of his. When he started working at the Order, he was digging up all the info we needed, every mention of other worlds. He had heard stories of the Archives, but could never find it."

"But why all the spectacle?" She asked, turning a page. "If you knew about the portals, you could have closed them."

Cain shrugged. "It took over twenty years for us to locate every portal, might as well be a bit dramatic while we bided our time. Fear causes people to slip up. In the rush to cover any leads, the Order would always leave something behind."

"You've found all the portals?" Grim sat up, curling her legs in, and turning her head to him. "You're going to close them, right?"

"That's the plan." He replied, with a determined nod. "Does anyone else know about this place? Any of the faculty?"

Grim hesitated. "As I said, the student council didn't believe me but…Starching knows. He threatened me, told me not to say anything because it would be the end of the Order."

"What did you tell him?" He asked, watching her for her reply.

"I told him nobody would believe me..." She muttered, shaking her head. "I've got nothing to lose by telling you, Cain. My parents have threatened to disown me because I'm leaving Elderwall."

"Oh, Grim..."

She shook her head, dismissing his pity for her. "I have so many questions...how did you do that? The illusion, you're a Summoner."

Cain opened his palm again, forming a single flower. "Remi is a better Skulduggery than I am, but they would have been an easy suspect. This entire plan hinged on the Baptism recognising my Summoner power instead."

"You tricked the Baptism?"

"We tricked the Order," Cain said with a smile. "To everyone, Marcus Blackwood is a dedicated Order member and an absent father. I was his son, acceptable in my way. Remi is a low-ability Skulduggery on the Student Council. We're all people the Order ignores."

"But you got burned at the Baptism as I did."

"Because the flames couldn't work out what I was. That flame is from another world as well. If you think hard enough, it'll believe anything it hears." Cain explained, resting his arms on his knees. "The flames couldn't work you out. It's that simple."

Grim had read about this and continued Cain's train of thought. "Since the magick and the flame are from another world, they connect. As above…so below?"

"The principle of Correspondence. Starching's lessons had some foundation, except it was a theory from somewhere else."

She remembered what she had read in the book Remi had given her. "Can you use magickal objects to create illusions? Is that how you did it?"

Cain hesitated. "Kind of? The objects helped…amplify it."

She nodded. "That's the opposite of what I read. The Order doesn't want the magick to cross because it makes it harder to control."

He looked satisfied at Grim's research. "Nothing gets past you. Yes, we believe choosing a Focus meant the Order could maintain the connections for longer."

"How are you going to do it? Close the portals, I mean."

"Destroy the crystal. If you put enough magick into them, you can override it. Once they're all gone, the magick will linger here for a while, but then it disappears because it has nothing to anchor itself to." Cain looked around the room. The dusty room, the one full of secrets. "Listen, I need to tell Remi that you know."

Grim blinked, registering what he had said. "I think Remi might have already caught on…"

He thought for a moment, a loose smile on his lips. "Not surprising but I need to tell my father as well, and then go from there…we're almost ready to do what we need to do."

She paused, thinking about the diaries they had read, the stories they had heard from the magus of the past. "Cain...do you think we should tell people? The truth, I mean."

Cain looked up at her, his eyes like the night sky against the candlelight. "We've tried. For decades. My father tried, with his friend Evelyn-,"

Grim drew in a sharp breath, almost gasping. It couldn't be the same Evelyn she knew. There was no chance...or was there?

"Evelyn?" Grim whispered, almost in silence.

He nodded. "They lost touch after they graduated. I don't know what happened to her. He tried, we tried, and my grandfather tried as well, from what I know. This has been the Blackwood's burden to bear, and nobody has listened to us. You saw people's reactions, you saw them deny it, call us pranksters-,"

"Ms. White believes you. She could do something." Grim replied, leaning closer with her hands on her knees."

"Ms White has no power in the Order, Grim. My father told me they haven't bothered to change her name on her official documents. She's still *Mr.* White." Cain huffed, shuffling around to lean back against the bookcase. "We've tried to be truthful, Grim. We did it the nice way, now we need to do it the hard way."

"There's no other way?"

He shook his head. "Think of it like this, Grim. Beyond this world, there are a million others who are dealing with the consequences of our actions. You've read the journals, you know exactly what kind of people are in the Order. You know how they've treated you."

Grim closed her eyes, thinking back to what Starching told her. "Who would believe the angry, bitter girl with no magick…"

"Exactly." When Grim opened her eyes again, Cain had folded his hands together. "My father told me about someone from another world. A witch, an *actual* witch, not like us. She's on the run from a demon prince who wants to marry her. *We* did that to her. What of the people whose lives are in chaos because of us? Where's their say on this? They didn't get a choice, Grim. We did. The Order did. The truth has nothing to do with this, it's about doing what's right."

Grim was silent, feeling a soft ache in her chest. Cain sounded like he was choking back tears. "I need to know...are you with us?"

She opened her mouth to speak, but the moment was consuming her. Grim had never seen Cain so vulnerable, so close to breaking. She felt the pain, the burden he had carried, that his family and friends had carried all this time. Then her mind thought of her parents. They must know, right? If they were so high and mighty in the Order, they would know. No wonder they had treated her in that way, and why being a powerful magus was so important to them. She thought of Finn and Anna, and how Finn had stood up for her, how both of them saw the flaws in an ancient system. She thought of her parents, who were ready to say she was no longer their daughter if she wasn't a Magus.

Grim thought of the people whose stories were now ruined by the Order. Those who, as she sat on the floor of a dusty library section, were facing death, despair and chaos.

Who was she to decide that they should suffer because she's a coward? Because she was bitter and angry at a world that she complied with. Now was the time she stopped saying she would do something, and do it.

She had nothing left to lose.

She placed a hand on Cain's shoulder, and his breath haltered for a moment. In the dim light of the room, in that singular second, they signed a silent contract.

"I'm with you."

Cain smiled, wiping his face with a free hand. "Okay, I need time. I need to speak to my father, and Remi."

"What can I do? Is there *anything* I can do?"

"I need you to stay quiet, and keep your head down."

"Don't I do that anyway?" She replied, rolling her eyes.

"*Grim.*" He put a hand on her arm, and she kept her hand on his shoulder. "I'm serious. We can't let anything jeopardise this. Pretend that everything is normal. Don't come back here. Promise me that until I tell you everything is ready. *Promise me.*"

I-I promise." She whispered the serious edge to Cain's voice throwing her out of the loop. He looked so determined.

"Can I take your journal to Remi? They'll know what to do. I'll make sure you get it back."

She nodded, passing it to him. He took off his jacket and bundled the journal up into it. "Thank you. I mean it, you cracked the case…"

"I'm sorry I didn't tell you sooner."

"Hey." He smiled at her. "You're an abomination of greatness, remember? You brilliant, *brilliant* person."

The two of them stood up. Cain went to the door. "I'll go first. Wait five minutes, and lock the door behind me. I'm going to Remi now."

"Okay, be careful."

He gave her a firm nod. They held each other's gaze for the longest time. "You too."

Our meetings continue to go well. Already we have agreed on the founding principles that a Magus will follow, basing it off some information we found from another reality, where magick is more commonplace. We have also identified the four focuses, and how we will make the Baptism of Fire work in our favour.

Everything is falling into place. We have Magus in powerful places, and can now begin established ourselves in various locations, and set up Elderwall Boarding College.

The crystals that are maintaining our connection to the other worlds have been hidden in secret locations, the information of which will be kept as a guarded secret. Only trusted Order members will receive it.

Our time is coming.

How could they keep a giant crystal secret?

The Order, and the Magus are everywhere. These crystals must be in places they have influence over.

May

"You're going to run over your dress."

"No, I'm not!"

Finn, Anna and Grim were eating dinner together. Cain couldn't join them, as his final practical exam was running over by the time the three of them sat to eat. Finn and Anna were proud to celebrate the fact they had finished and wanted to include Grim in that. Grim had special permission to skip the practical exams. She made sure to thank Ms. White for that. The main topic of conversation was the Equinox Ball, the event to end the year at Elderwall. It was everything everyone was talking about. Grim overheard the students discussing their outfits, or what their parents were sending. Also among the chatter was who they were going to ask to go with them. As of this moment, Finn and Anna were arguing about the length of Anna's dress.

"You've done it before!" Finn replied, waving his fork at her.

"Stop dodging the issue."

"What issue?" Grim asked, curious.

Anna smirked and leaned toward Grim. "Finn's too scared to ask Callum to the Ball."

"Anna! Shut up!" He protested, throwing down his fork.

Anna whipped around to face him and started laughing. "I managed to suss out that he was gay, *just for you* and now you won't go ask him out!"

Grim giggled. "You should go for it. What have you got to lose?"

"My dignity Grim, my *dignity*."

"You never had any dignity," Anna muttered, but loud enough for Finn to hear, causing him to smack her arm with a light tap. She laughed again. "Ask Callum."

Grim nodded in agreement. "Ask Callum."

Finn rolled his eyes at them both. "I'll *think* about it."

The trio laughed with each other, thriving in the company of similar minds. As the laughter died down, Remi approached their table. They looked almost upset.

"Sorry to interrupt. Grim, can we speak outside?"

"Is everything okay?"

Remi's face gave nothing away. "Can we talk outside?"

In a hurry, she got out of her chair. Finn and Anna looked worried as Grim followed Remi outside. They walked with Grim until they were in a quiet hallway, out of earshot from any other students.

"You're scaring me Remi, what is it?" She asked as soon as they stopped. Grim thought that this was it, that Remi was going to blow up over the Archives.

"I want to give you a warning. Lukas is going to ask you to the ball in front of everyone."

She took a step back, amazed. She wasn't expecting *this*, out of everything that was going on. "*What.*"

Remi sighed, ready to explain this bombshell. "He's been telling everyone in the student council. He goes on about how he feels like he's messed up and wants to prove he cares about you. So, he's going to ask you to the ball. I tried to tell him it wasn't a good idea, *especially* after what happened at Valentine's, but he was insistent."

"Oh my god." Grim put her head in her hands. "I've been trying to get through to him about this."

"I know, I know. That's why I'm warning you. He's going to do it tomorrow, so just in case, be prepared."

"For god's sake..."

Remi put a hand on her shoulder. "I'm going to head off. Got another meeting about the Equinox Ball." They explained, with an eye roll.

"Thanks for letting me know."

"It's okay. We'll speak soon." They said that last sentence with a keen amount of emphasis.

Grim replied with a nod.

The two of them went their separate ways. Grim re-entered the dining hall with a rage that was only described as hellfire incarnate. She sat back down across from Finn and Anna.

Finn looked at the door, trying to spot Remi. He faced Grim, lowering his voice. "Is everything okay?"

She shook her head. "I don't want to talk about it right now."

He nodded, and thankfully, didn't push Grim further.

Times have changed since we first discovered these other worlds. History has become the present, the present soon becoming the future. Mortals are asking more questions, wondering how the world ended up progressing the way it did.

We could tell them. We could stand in front of every world leader and declare it was us. We did this, you're welcome. Your world is better for it, and you should kneel before us in thanks.

> Was conquest always the plan?

But we cannot. An Order meeting was held, and a notion was carried. The Mortals will know nothing, and neither will the new Magus joining our ranks. Every record of the other worlds, every journal entry, every ounce of research carried out will be sealed away in the walls of Elderwall. Every Order member who knows of what we found, and what we did for the world have sworn an oath of secrecy.

> An oath? Would my parents have taken in?

Young minds are so fickle, so quick to rebel. If they knew what we had done, they would find something wrong with it. We must encourage everyone to discipline and educate their children on the way the Order has changed the world.

> Was this the plan with Elderwall?

One day, one day when we know we are once again perfection, then we will claim what is rightfully ours. This world will bow before the Magus. It must.

> What are we waiting for?

What is the perfect Magus? Why are they so desperate for control? Who started this??

> It was always about control. Grim was the only student this year without a Focus. Their plan to control the magick is working. We're running out of time.

Grim walked into the common room on a quieter afternoon than normal. To her surprise, she spotted Cain sitting on one of the sofas next to a fire, fiddling with a bent key on a chain.

She made a careful approach, sitting down opposite him. He beamed at her. "Fancy seeing you here." He said, before going back to inspecting the bent key.

"I'm surprised to see you emerging from the depth of exams. Are you finished now?" She asked, dropping her bag next to her. It felt strange to not have to feel the weight of her journal with her. Now her bag had the necessities she had obtained before, a small sketchbook and a few random pencils.

"One more to go, then I'm done." Cain reached into his backpack, pulling out a pair of small pair of pliers. Pocket-sized tools…typical for him.

"What are you doing with that key?"

He smirked, holding back a laugh as he explained. "It's Finn's locker key. He bent it."

"He broke *another* key?!" Grim's mouth dropped open in surprise. "How does he keep doing this?"

"I don't know." He replied, chuckling, and shaking his head. "But he needs his incense, and being a Summoner ain't cheap."

On the other side of the room, the door to the common room opened, and George, alongside a few other students, walked in. He whispered something to the group, and they all broke into aggressive nodding. They took a seat around the chess table, with one of them pulling out a deck of cards. George didn't follow his friends. With confidence, he strode over to the fireplace where Grim and Cain were sitting.

"Just the person I was looking for!" He announced, looking at Grim.

"What, do you have a bent key too?" Cain interjected, giving the key a gentle tug with the pliers around it.

"Huh? No, I was talking to Grim!" He gestured to the empty seat next to her. "Can I sit down?"

"It's the common room, George, I can't stop you." She replied. Her eyes tried to meet Cain's, and when they did, he had the same confused expression she did. He went back to working on the key.

"Lukas told me you guys talked it out! I'm glad you could."

She crossed her arms as George relaxed on the sofa, caution in her stance. "We did."

"He was so relieved when he came to tell me at football practice-,"

"You guys are still practising?" Cain interrupted again, which made George furrow his brow. He continued talking, not looking up from the key. "I thought you guys had played the final match."

"We still practice though, especially since we're all going home in the summer. Going to be fighting fit for next year!"

"But you play against each other. Not exactly a competition when Elderwall will always win." Cain spoke with a monotone drawl in his voice, making Grim cover her mouth to hide a giggle.

George rolled his eyes. Cain satisfied that he was being a nuisance, once again went back to fix the key.

"You wouldn't get it," George continued. "Anyway, I'm happy you heard him out. Lukas is a great guy you know; I can tell he looks out for you."

Now she was suspicious. "Uh-huh."

"Everyone else feels the same you know. He's a *great guy*, a good friend, and a killer Magus. I bet you've told him loads of times how he's going to be successful."

"He doesn't need me to tell him." She answered. "He knows that anyway."

George was making several vigorous nods, his façade obvious. "So…must be weird he's got all his exams and you haven't, huh? He told me you're not coming back next year."

This made Grim sit up straight on the sofa, and Cain stopped what he was doing, listening. "He told you that?"

"He was *really* bummed out about it," George explained, leaning forward towards Grim. "He's going to *really* miss you. This is going to be your first and last year at Elderwall. He's worried about how much you'll miss out."

"Well, that was a private thing. I don't know why he told you." Grim fidgeted with her hands, rubbing her pointer finger and thumb together. A pit of stress was beginning to form.

"He didn't mean to, *obviously* but he needed some advice."

"Advice? Why would he need advice? It doesn't involve him, *or you* for that matter."

"He was upset!" He exclaimed, alerting the entire room to what was going on. "Look, he's a nice guy and I know he wants to make your time left at Elderwall special. So… were you thinking of going to the Equinox Ball?"

Through all that meandering, George had finally gotten to the point. It was as Remi had said, Lukas had plans, and he sent George in to make sure Grim wouldn't cause a scene.

"Why do you ask?" She said, trying to stop her nerves from showing.

"If you were going…Lukas would be a great date, considering that you two are such close friends."

Cain put the pliers down, the key straightened up. He raised his eyebrows at George. "Sounds like you should be his date George, not Grim."

The entire room was silent until people started snickering. Grim was too stunned by what Cain said and covered her mouth in surprise. George looked flustered and frantic at first but maintained his composure.

"Just think about it." He said, reaching out to put a hand on Grim's arm. She immediately pushed it back.

"Don't touch me, please." She asked with a firmness in her voice. George got up from the sofa, trying to look like he had succeeded in his plans.

"I'll see you around, and think about what I said about Lukas!"

He walked back over to the table where his other friends were. They all started whispering amongst themselves. Once the noise died down, they dealt out cards and shuffled chess pieces down the board. So sophisticated and wise on the exterior. But inside, the students of Elderwall were as bratty as your stereotypical college student.

Cain put his pliers back in his bag, along with the key while Grim slouched into the sofa, her arms crossed. Wicked thoughts were stewing in her mind, and her stomach was bubbling like a cauldron.

"Are you…" Cain paused. "What was that about?"

"I'm going to raise hell with Lukas tomorrow." She muttered, sitting back up and grabbing her bag.

"Whoa, calm down, what was he going on about?"

Grim's eyes glanced over to the group of happy students. "We can't talk about it here."

He stood up, putting his backpack on. Cain stepped towards her, tilting his head towards one of the doors. "Then let's go talk about it in the hallway."

She nodded in agreement, and the two of them left the common room, stepping into the long hallway. It was the same one where they had first spoken, with the same bench Cain had been reading on. Grim started to pace up and down of her own volition, and Cain watched her with a careful eye.

"Now explain to me what's going on." He asked his eyes following her move back and forth.

She stopped in front of him, clenching her hands together. "Remi warned me Lukas was planning to ask me to the ball in front of everyone. I didn't think he would be inconsiderate enough to go through with it but sending George to talk to me proved it."

He thought for a moment. "So even though after what happened during Valentine's Day…he's still going to do it?"

"Yep. That's the kind of person he is." She let out a long, long sigh. "I am *this* close to fucking screaming my head off at him tomorrow."

"Grim you can't-,"

"Don't go off telling me I can't be angry at him, do not defend him!"

"I'm not!" Cain argued, holding his hands out. "But remember what we agreed."

Stay quiet. Keep your head down.

She lowered her voice. "What am I meant to do Cain? Say yes?"

"I'm not asking you to say yes. Scream your head off at him all you want, but do it in private. Don't make a scene, or you'll draw more attention. If you start something, Starching may have grounds to reveal what you've been up to."

"No matter what I say or do Cain, this school gossips like everything's their fucking business. It'll get out no matter what. I will *always* be the bad guy."

"Regardless, you need to be smart about this, we haven't got long until we can do something. Hold on a little more."

Grim's voice rose to a shout, echoing towards the ceiling. She didn't even realise how much her rage was burning. "Ah yes, have the masses gawk at me for letting someone like Lukas go. My parents will hear about this Cain! I will never stop getting shit over this. It's okay for you, you said it yourself. To the Order, you are not worth any note. For me, every fuck up, every mistake, every word I say is under scrutiny and it is *so much fucking pressure*. And every time I lash out and get angry at this world for being the way it is, *I'm the one who's wrong.*"

Cain was silent, his arms crossed. "Grim, I can't have this conversation with you while you're shouting."

She froze in place, her arms slumping to her sides. She breathed in, and out.

One.

Two.

Three.

Four.

Five.

Six.

Seven.

Eight.

Nine.

Ten.

Eleven.

Seven. Eleven. Inhale. Exhale.

There was a long moment of quiet between them, until Grim spoke, with the most genuine honesty she had in her. "I'm sorry."

Cain smiled. "You're right to be angry, but you need to use your anger in the right way."

She bit her lip, then sighed again. "I would like to scream at him."

"I know you would."

"And no matter what I do, I will be the bad guy Cain. That won't change."

He shrugged, knowing the position she was in. "Then put him in his place. And I'll help you deal with the aftermath…you have one more month. Deal with this shit for one more month."

She smiled a little. "Sounds to me like you know what's going to happen."

He gave her a playful shrug. "Maybe I do, maybe I don't. Who can say?"

"You can, idiot." She said with sarcasm, making Cain chuckle. "Can we not go back to the common room?"

"Sure, do you want to come with me to be Finn's knight in shining armour again?"

"I wouldn't miss it for the world."

This is an early draft of the Magus oath, which I wrote today.

I (name), herby swear to honour the foundations and laws of the Order. I swear to keep our secret from Mortals, to serve my fellow Magus, and help this world progress with the ability that has been gifted upon me.

I will honour my family name, I will honour my ancestors, and I will claim my birthright. I understand now that greatness has been gifted to me, and I will not waste the opportunity.   This oath hasn't changed at all.

Only I know the true meaning. The meaning of greatness. I believe we may adjust this as time goes on.

We have found that if we make the oath a blood oath, then this strengthens the magick, and our connections through the crystals. This, of course, will be kept a guarded secret until the ceremony. We cannot have any Magus running in fear at the sight of a little blood.

There's a blood pact????

    YOU'D THINK MY FATHER WOULD MENTION A BLOOD PACT???

Holy shit We are a cult.

The next day arrived, and Grim sat in the dining hall for breakfast, waiting for Lukas, at 7:30 sharp. Her stomach was tight, her breathing was uneven, and she hadn't touched her plate of food. Every time the door opened, she looked up, expecting him to appear.

Five minutes later, he walked in. George was behind him. When he did walk in, the whole room exploded with excited chatter. Her heart dropped into a pit. George was talking to him, grinning, almost as if hyping him up for what he was about to do. Grim knew what he was about to do.

He stopped in front of the table, and all eyes were on them.

"Good morning!" His greeting was full of joy, and Grim once again couldn't breathe. "Listen, I knew it's early but-,"

He pulled out a single pink rose from behind his back and dropped to one knee.

He's doing it. He's actually doing it. The prick.

"Will you go to the ball with me?"

The whole room was silent. Someone squealed in the corner. The whispers came back louder than ever. Talking about how cute and wonderful this was, how he was *such a nice guy*, and how *lucky she was*.

Grim didn't know how to reply at that moment. She thought back about what Cain had said, about keeping her head down.

She stood up, took the rose from his hand, and offered him a hand to his feet.

"Is that a yes?" He asked, pleading. The whole room was waiting for the response.

"Can we talk about this outside please?"

The look on his face was soul-crushing.

She walked towards the door, and Lukas ran after her. "Grim, hang on! Slow down!"

She led them both outside, where the spring air hit Grim's arms. The sun was out. It was a peaceful morning, that Grim and Lukas were now going to disrupt.

"What the hell is wrong with you, Grim?" He demanded as soon as they stopped walking. "Why couldn't you say yes there and then?"

"What's wrong with me? *What's wrong with me?* Oh, that's rich, coming from you."

He stepped towards her. "You *embarrassed* me in front of everyone. I was trying to do a nice thing for you."

"That was you being nice?" She laughed in utter dismay. "Making me feel like shit in front of everyone is YOU being nice?"

"I didn't make you feel like shit, you do that to yourself." He snapped back, running a hand through his hair. "You don't understand any of this, you don't understand why I do what I do for you."

"And I stopped trying to understand you months ago." She replied, stepping away from him, trying to keep her distance. "This place has changed you. Cain was right, we've both become different people."

Lukas' face contorted into a rage at the mention of Cain. "Really? We're going down that route. You're going to try and say that this place hasn't been good for me?" He opened his arms out to her like she was going to fill the space with an explanation. "I have tried *so* hard to get you to fit in here, I have tried to get you involved-,"

"The only thing you did is make YOU look like the hero!" She screamed back. "Every time the opportunity came up, you made yourself look like the dashing superstar."

His arms dropped. "No, you don't get it."

"No, I do! I finally get it! It took me long enough but it's finally fallen into place. Every comment, every apology, every action, it was all to make YOU look better." She pointed a finger at him. "You can be a great magus Grim, surround yourself with the right people Grim, don't be so silly Grim."

"I did that to help you!"

"Help me? Belittling me was *helping*? Starting arguments, lashing out? Saying I can't make friends, picking and choosing who I should trust…"

"That was to protect you. Protect you from making bad decisions."

She barked out a laugh. "I'm a fucking adult, you prick! You've criticised every decision I made. Insulted my friends-,"

"You insulted my friends too."

"Yes, because George is an *asshole*!"

"At least he was looking out for me while I've been here, something you haven't done."

"Like you needed me? You made yourself look like the perfect student who's helping the sad little magus with no magick. George was right, all this time I've been your best *asset*."

"You are so much more than an asset!" He shouted back, stepping towards her again. His cheeks were bright red. "You are the best thing that has ever happened to me."

"Yes, the best thing, the best thing that *you* could use to your advantage. To show that you could succeed, and WIN." Screw keeping her distance, she stepped closer to him, getting right in his face, and speaking in a low voice. "I am done being your prize."

The two of them didn't speak for a moment. Grim felt the fire of rage burning deep inside of her. Her heart was beating so quickly, and she could hear Lukas' sharp breaths. He then did something unexpected, and leaned in, kissing her on the lips.

And as soon as he did, her fist flew up and knocked into his cheek, sending him reeling backwards.

"*Fuck*!" Lukas exclaimed, holding his cheek.

"Who the *fuck* do you think you are?" Grim forced herself backwards, cradling her fist. "You…why would you do that?"

"Isn't it obvious?!" He stood up straight and brushed down his jacket as if he were about to give a grand speech or give a presentation. "I love you, Grim."

"Excuse me?" Her voice had no emotion. Disbelief was the word to describe it.

"I love you. I have for years. And I need you."

She started shaking her head. "For fuck's sake Lukas!"

"Grim, think about how happy we would be, how happy everyone would be for us, think about your future."

"My future?" She scoffed. "My future involves being as far away from the Order, the Magus, and now *you*."

She stepped back again.

"Stay away from me. Don't try to talk to me, don't send George or any of your little friends after me. I want nothing to do with you."

He didn't move. Didn't try to stop her, but his eyes were pleading, but Grim would see the transparency in their truth. "Raven…please."

She laughed, despite herself. That name. As if using that name gave people power over her anymore. The anger still ate at her. But another feeling replaced it.

Unburdened. Of freedom. Like she had cut the cord on the weights that were drowning her on the ocean floor. Tears, hot from the fires of frustration, ran down her cheeks.

"I am grateful for everything you did for me, Lukas. I had a shitty childhood and you were the saving grace. But I am *done* with trying to justify your behaviour. I am done defending you."

She wiped her face with her sleeve, and Lukas took another step toward her. "Don't leave me."

Grim turned her back to him. Refusing to continue this rampage any more. "Go get some ice on that cheek."

June

A box arrived at Grim's door on the afternoon of the ball. She had dumped it on her bed and opened it up.

On top of a gawky pink ball gown, adorned in sequins and glitter, was a note.

Have an amazing night with Lukas- we will see you soon. Mother and Father x

Something in Grim snapped. She had spent the past couple of weeks managing to distract herself from the carnage with Lukas. She spent her time in the company of Cain, Finn and Anna. Everyone had heard about the argument. It had spread like wildfire. Every five minutes somebody was asking Grim to forgive Lukas. She hadn't spoken to him, hadn't looked at him. She refused to sit near him in classes and sat as far away from him at dinner. She either ate breakfast alone or with her friends. Now that the exams were wrapping up, she was able to hide out wherever suited her. But this was the final thing. She hadn't told her parents. She had to go home like everything was happy and peaceful with her former closest friend.

She grabbed a pillow from her bed and flung it towards the door.

Thwomp.

Then there was a knock on the door.

A bitter voice spat out a response. "*What.*"

"Um, it's Minda? Can I come in?"

She relaxed her shoulders a little. "Yeah, yeah. Come in."

The door opened, and Minda stepped inside, closing the door behind her. "I heard you throw a pillow. What's up?"

Grim put up her hands and pointed to the dress box. Minda walked to it and pulled the dress out, the skirt fell with grace. It was a nice dress. Long sleeves and enough sparkle to shimmer against the chandeliers, and a floating skirt with many layers. It wasn't a dress for Grim though.

"I mean…it's beautiful. What's the matter?"

"I'm not…" Grim was struggling to explain. "A girl. My parents don't accept that."

"Oh…" Minda's eyes widened, and with careful hands put the dress down on the bed. "I'm getting Remi."

"Remi?"

Minda was already out the door, leaving Grim alone and awkward in the middle of the room. Five minutes later, Minda was ushering Remi inside and closing the door.

"Hi…Grim?" Remi looked at Minda. "What's going on?"

Minda pointed to the dress, and Remi walked over to look at it. They stared in disbelief. "Oh my god."

"Yep. Grim is having a dress disaster." Minda explained. "Do you still have that pantsuit from last year? The glitter one." She turned to Grim. "Are you okay if things sparkle?"

Grim shrugged. "I don't care."

Remi nodded. "I still have it. You're thinking about your overskirt, aren't you?"

"Yes!" Minda clapped her hands. "Grim, how are you with black?"

Remi burst out laughing. "This is Grim, we're talking about Minda."

Grim spoke, at last, a stammer in her voice. "Are you sure? I don't want to have you guys run around."

"Oh shush." Minda waved a hand, but she eyed the dress. "If you don't want the dress…can I try it on? I borrowed something from my mother but-,"

Grim smiled. "Minda, it's yours. Try it on."

She picked the dress up from the bed and draped it over her arm. "You're an angel. I will be back with the overskirt."

"Give me five minutes to dig out the pantsuit."

"O-okay!" She replied, a little overwhelmed that the two of them wanted to help her.

They left. Grim dug around under her bed to pull out a pair of black shoes, with a slight heel, that her parents made her pack. Strangely, she was grateful for it. As she managed to find them, the door opened once more, with Remi and Minda coming back. Remi was holding a garment bag, and Minda had a dress box.

"I'm ready!" Minda declared.

Remi rolled their eyes with a chuckle and pulled the pantsuit out of the garment bag, handing it to Grim. "Try this on."

An hour later, Grim was ready. Remi's pantsuit had a high neckline, covering most of Grim's chest, with thin spaghetti straps. It was shimmering, with little spots of glitter in the black fabric. Minda's overskirt was black and see-through, covered with gemstones. Minda had combed Grim's hair and found a small black jewelled clip to hold back her fringe.

Grim looked at herself in the mirror. She looked… beautiful, in its twisted form. None of this was traditional.

But, she could feel herself standing up a little taller and smiling a little more.

"Oh, Grim!" Minda clapped her hands, giddy with excitement. "Oh, you look amazing."

Remi was grinning. "You clean up good."

"I…" Grim was choking back a few tears. "Thank you, to both of you. This night could have been a lot worse."

Minda wiped her eyes. "You're making me cry. I'm going to miss you next year."

That was the other thing. The fact Grim wasn't coming back had also spread around the school.

"I'll miss you too…thanks, Minda. And you too Remi."

Remi patted Grim's shoulder and headed towards the door. "Anytime."

Minda nodded. "I'm heading back. Time to try on that dress."

"You'll look better in it than I ever did," Grim commented, smirking.

"I'll see you in a bit."

It was only Grim and Remi after the door closed. Remi picked up the garment bag, and from the bottom of it, pulled out Grim's journal.

"I never doubted you for a second." They said, handing it back to Grim.

"D-Does this mean you're ready?" She tucked the journal under her bed, hiding it in a pillowcase.

Remi smiled. "Trust Cain. That's all I'll say."

They left. The door closed, and Grim was alone in the silence, staring at herself in the mirror. Her hands brushed across the skirt, and a wave of nerves washed over her. She would be walking in there, *alone*. She hadn't arranged a backup plan without Lukas.

But she realised she wasn't alone. Finn and Anna would be there, and so would Remi and Minda. She had relied on Lukas for so long. Since cutting ties with him, she noticed what a great range of friendships she had. Even if they didn't last forever, or evolved into something different, somebody cared for a while, and that was okay.

Then the lights in her room went out. She reached out, and she touched the wall, trying to steady herself. The room *bloomed*. Bloomed, flowers started appearing on the walls, spreading up the ceiling. The floor turned into shattered stone. It bathed her bedroom in soft purple light.

She smiled. *Cain*.

It was time.

My dear Momma,

I am looking forward to coming home soon. I will admit that as much as I love Elderwall, I've missed you and comforts of home greatly. You'll be happy to know I passed my first year with flying colours, and you should expect the official results shortly.

I know I've been too busy to write to you sometimes, but I promise to tell you everything when I'm home. We can spend the summer catching up and preparing me for my second year. I have so many stories to tell you, and my friend George is considering coming by for a visit! It would be great for you to meet him.

As for Grim...we have not spoken recently. I'm not sure what happened, but I think the pressure was getting to her and she snapped. We had an argument, and she stormed off. She's refusing to speak to me, I am not sure if my actions caused her to become upset. I'm hoping to try and speak to her at the ball.

Keep well Momma, I will see you soon.

Plenty of love and light,

Lukas

The grand hall was dazzling. They decorated the room in gold and white, with soft ballroom music played by a live orchestra. The students looked glamorous, with elegant ballgowns and suits. People were already dancing, spinning each other around the room. There was such an energy in the room. The chandelier sparkled above them with flickering candles. Grim could see her face on the polished marble floor. It seemed like everyone was enjoying themselves. She spotted Oscar speaking with Remi, who was wearing a midnight blue pantsuit. They noticed Grim and waved before continuing to talk with Oscar. Minda was wearing the pink dress, with a matching hijab. She kept pointing to her dress with excitement before talking with her friends again. Grim also saw Finn and Anna. Anna was watching, in a knee-length red dress, and Finn was dancing with Callum. Anna looked proud, which she should have been since she helped him to do this.

Grim couldn't see Cain, so decided to head over to Anna, until *Lukas* stood in front of her.

It hit her in an instant. He was wearing a black suit, with a *pink* bowtie, and was holding a *pink* rose corsage in his hand.

"You look beautiful." He said, breathless.

She said nothing and kept her face straight. He offered her the corsage.

"I bet our parents thought we should match but…"

Grim pushed the corsage back to him. He looked at her, crushed beyond compare. This was it; she had decided that.

"Be well, Lukas."

"Ray-,"

She walked away and headed to Anna. She had styled her black hair into a braid, with several sparkling hair grips. Anna was beaming, having the time of her life.

"Grim!" She exclaimed, and Grim leaned down to hug her. "You look *amazing*."

"Aw, thank you. So do you!" She looked over at Finn and Callum, in their matching tuxedos. Callum was wearing a red corsage on his wrist, which matched Finn's bowtie. "Your scheming worked; it seems."

"They're so cute together," Anna said, beaming.

"They are." Grim agreed, with a nod.

"I'm going to miss you…" Anna put her hands together and looked up to Grim. "You're going to write to us, yeah? About all the cool things you're doing."

"Of course, as often as I can. Once I've…worked out what's happening."

"You'll work it out. I have all the faith in the world."

"Um…Grim?"

Grim looked over to who was calling her, and her eyes met with Cain's. He was wearing a completely black suit, with a black bowtie. He had combed his hair, and he stood with one arm behind his back.

"Hi." Her reply was awkward. He was staring at her like Lukas was. The current dance ended, and the room gave the band light applause.

Cain held out a hand to her. "If it's not too much trouble… may I have this dance?"

Grim looked to Anna, who was beaming and mouthed *yes* to her. Grim let out a breath and took Cain's hand. He led her to the middle of the ballroom floor. They stepped together, and the dance started.

The music swelled, and Grim tried to remember the steps. Cain laughed as the two of them spun around. When they slowed to a gentle sway, Grim took the courage to ask the important question.

"So…are we going to address the garden in my room?"

Cain let out an awkward chuckle. "Can I first say you're reminding me of when we first met?"

She raised an eyebrow. "How so?"

He blushed. "You look like a star, and that's what I first thought when I met your eyes, they were like stars."

Grim looked away, not replying, and Cain pulled her a little closer as they spun again. She spoke again after a moment of silence. "I'm still trying to convince myself that I look beautiful tonight."

"You've always been beautiful." His voice was soft, and Grim had to catch her breath. He kept her close. "You're an abomination of greatness, remember? I've thought that from the moment we became friends."

"I…" Grim didn't know what to say.

"You don't have to reply, it's fine." He continued moving them along the ballroom floor. "So…I should tell you it's time."

"I guessed as much."

Cain spun her around on the spot, then they continued to dance. "I didn't tell you…but the first crystal is here at Elderwall. We're going to destroy it tonight."

"Tonight? But everyone-,"

"Is distracted by the ball, which means we can do it. As far as the faculty are aware, we're leaving early tomorrow morning because of how far away we live."

She realised that they had thought this through. Decades of waiting for this starting point. "Can I help you?"

It all made sense. Everything. She finally realised what was troubling her, about everything. Every expectation, every demand, was never needed. The Order was never needed. Nobody needed magick, nobody needed to be triumphant. The world never asked for silent heroes, martyrs in the dark. This world didn't need the magus. It was fine alone.

The dance finished, and the room applauded. Cain turned around and saw Remi walk towards the door. As if the two of them were having a silent conversation, they nodded. Once.

"Yes. *Yes.* You can come with us." With a casual air, he walked to the hall's double doors, Grim next to him. As they entered the hallway, Remi was standing across from them, waiting. The hallways were empty, and all was silent.

Remi smiled. "Welcome to the Order of Chaos."

They pulled out a small square of paper from their pantsuit pocket and passed it to Grim as the three of them walked. "These are the plans we managed to dig up from when the school was first built. There's a hidden wall that has a pathway to the portal."

Grim unfolded the paper. "This is the art room. I know which wall we need to break."

They barked out a laugh. "I hate to admit it Cain, but you were right."

"I'm always right, you should have more faith in me."

Grim walked a little faster to be ahead of them. "Come on, I know a shortcut there."

As they were about to walk, a familiar voice stopped them.

"Going for a moonlight stroll?"

The three of them turned around to see Finn, a hand pushing up his glasses.

Grim stepped towards him. "Something like that…I thought you were dancing with Callum."

Finn smirked. "I needed some fresh air, and it seems I caught you guys at the right time."

She looked back at Cain and Remi. Remi looked ready for a fight, either physical or a shouting match. Cain waited with patience, looking at his friend, waiting to see what he would say next.

Finn put their hands back in his trouser pockets. "Whatever you're doing while burning the midnight oil…be careful, alright?"

He winked at Grim, and at that moment it was clear Finn wasn't here to stop them. He was here to wish them luck.

Grim smiled at her new friend. One of the many she had made this year. "Give Anna a dance from us, okay?"

"Your wish is my command."

He saluted the trio with two fingers to his forehead and walked back into the grand hall. Remi let out a sigh of pure relief. "Okay…lead the way."

Grim weaved them around the hallways. She avoided the common room and other areas that might be busy with students looking for some quiet. The art room door was open, and as Grim suspected, it was empty. She held up the plans again and then pointed to the eastern wall. "That one!"

The three of them started to move the tables out of the way until the wall was clear. Cain ran his hand along the wall, his fingers tracing the chipped stone until he stopped at a certain point. "Here. I can sense the portal."

"You can…sense it?" Grim put her hand next to Cain's. She felt something, like a little spark of electricity.

Remi put their hand on the wall as well. "He's been trying to track the portal for the whole year. It's here, we need to shatter the wall. We don't have any tools so we'll have to use magick…"

Grim felt that little spark growing stronger. A humming across the palm of her hand, tingling at her fingertips. The feeling she would always get whenever she tried to use her powers. That little trace of whatever lurked inside of her.

"Grim?" Cain knelt next to her. "What is it?"

She tried to concentrate on the feeling. "I can…feel the wall? I'm not powerful enough though-,"

"Oh my god, all this time you had a speck of a Psychic in you," Remi said, laughing in disbelief. They knelt and took Grim's free hand. "Concentrate. Hard. Feel my energy and take it with you."

Cain placed his hand over Grim's. "Feel our energy channelling and push it out onto the wall."

"This isn't the time for a magick lesson guys-,"

"Grim! Concentrate." Remi snapped. "Breathe."

In. Out. Seven. Eleven. Inhale. Exhale.

Breathe.

Feel the energy.

Breathe.

Feel it move through the blood in the veins and release it.

One.

Two.

Three.

Four.

Five.

Six.

Seven.

Right where Grim's hand was, the wall shattered into dust, creating a doorway.

"I can't believe that fucking worked." Remi blurted out in shock, hurrying to their feet.

Cain helped Grim to her feet. She stared at the doorway. "I…I did that?"

"You did." He announced, full of joy.

"Come on then, let's go." Remi ushered them into the doorway, and they entered the tunnel.

Who would have guessed Elderwall was hiding the key to its own meaning underground? The tunnel wasn't lit, so Cain pulled out a lighter from his jacket pocket and they descended with caution. Whoever built this tunnel had kept it clear and straight. Almost as if they wanted to make sure they could check on it. A light was appearing at the end of the tunnel, soft and purple. They stepped into the clearing, and there it was…the portal and the crystal.

The portal was hovering off the ground, tilted at an angle. Light radiated from it, illuminating the walls and the cave ceiling. It glowed, the centre rippling like an ocean. The crystal next to it hummed with energy, a flow coiling between the two entities. Two pieces of string untied.

Cain sighed in relief. "We were right. Let me get ready to destroy it."

"What are you going to do?"

He pulled out a crystal from his pocket. It was a soft golden yellow. "Golden herderite. It has enough energy to break it, but I need a minute."

Cain was walking around the portal. He used his index finger to carve symbols into the rock walls and onto the dirt on the ground.

Grim investigated the portal as she stood next to Remi. "So…how many other worlds are there?

Remi thought for a moment. "An infinite amount, all tied together. So many stories, so many lives, and the magus decided that it was theirs for the taking."

Grim's voice was quiet. "Some of the journals said they saw these worlds in their dreams."

"Perhaps it was the magick as it tied each world to this one," Remi suggested. "We brought them chaos. Their world became disturbed. Shifted ever so slightly. They never asked for that, and I hope, with this, we can help them."

"Minda is going to kill me for ruining her skirt," Grim mentioned, trying to break the tension while Cain got ready.

Remi chuckled. "She'll get over it. You gave her that dress."

"I'm ready." Cain declared, standing back with the crystal in his hand. He looked at them both. "If anyone is having any second thoughts-,"

"No."

"None."

"Okay…step back, both of you. Keep your eyes on the portal for me."

Grim and Remi backed up towards the entrance. Cain stood at the edge of the circle he had drawn, and with a quick movement, crushed the crystal in his hands. His eyes went white, he moved his arms out to his sides and let the crystal particles fall to the floor.

There was a rush of golden light, like the sun burning through. Grim held herself against the wall, as all three of them felt the energy rushing through them. Her eyes were on the portal, and that's when she saw it.

A woman, dressed in black, standing in a graveyard.

A young girl sat in a room of white.

A beauty and a beast.

A flintlock pistol and a silver bullet.

Every world. Every story. Every thread connecting her life and their lives.

And so many more that she could not even see. Stories yet untold.

Then the room went black. Cain pulled out a lighter from his jacket pocket and flicked it open. He sounded breathless. The only noise there for a moment was the sound of their breathing. The portal was gone. The crystal was in shards on the floor, which were dissolving.

Cain seemed like he didn't have the energy to smile, but he tried to. "Come on, let's get outside."

Remi, Cain and Grim stood in the garden of shadows, far away from Elderwall and the liveliness of the Ball. The three of them stood on the path, still in their fancy clothes. The weight of what they did had begun to settle in.

"What now?" She asked, wrapping her arms around herself as the evening air brushed past them.

Remi looked behind them. "Cain and I need to go. Stick to the plan."

"How long do you think it's going to take before someone notices?"

"We blocked the hole with the tables, and you are the only one who goes in there." Remi was pacing back and forth. "The ball should be wrapping up now; I'm going to walk back to my room to get my things. We'll be gone before anyone wakes up."

Cain nodded and looked to Grim. "Are you going to be okay, Grim? They saw us leave together; they might ask you questions."

She shrugged. "I don't think Starching will point the blame on me. He knows I don't have any magick. And Ms. White is arranging everything for me to leave Elderwall. If they ask, I'll say you walked me back to my room after I had an anxiety attack. After that, I went to sleep and didn't see or hear anything."

"Sounds plausible...I should go." Remi said, putting their hands in their pockets. "Don't stay out here too long."

They walked forward and put a hand on Grim's shoulder once more. "We'll meet again Grim, that I can promise you."

"Don't let me down. I want to hear about every adventure when you're done."

Remi smirked. "You'll know about it sooner than you think."

Before Grim could ask what they meant, they had already walked away. Their figure disappeared back into the College. Then it was the two of them, alone in the garden, like they had been many times before.

But this time, it was different.

"This is goodbye then. You need to head back." Grim said, her voice falling into a mutter.

"Yeah…I need to go." Cain didn't move, didn't make any attempt to step away as they watched each other.

"Cain." She turned to him. "It's okay, I'll cover for you. Go. You need to go."

He didn't say anything, kept staring at her, watching her. Watching those starry eyes. "I'm sorry about this-,"

"Wh-,"

He pulled her in and without a moment's hesitation, kissed her on the lips. He held her close, wrapping his arms around her waist. Grim's hands reached up to his face, cradling it. She didn't pull away. It felt like *fire*. Burning energy, like she felt when she shattered that wall, but she felt it with Cain. The safety, the comfort. A warm, crackling fire, filled her heart.

She was the one to break it first. They stood there, breathing in the electricity and the adrenaline of the night. "Wait for me." He whispered. "I'll come back for you."

"Don't make promises you can't keep." She whispered back.

"I promise. Wait for me."

She smiled. "I will."

He kissed her again, and let her go. Without another word muttered between them, he ran off, back to the College building.

Grim waited for another ten minutes before she went back. She breathed in the familiar sounds and smells of the garden, and the feeling of Cain's lips on hers. If she could take anything from her year here, it would be this. This feeling, this warmth. That's what she would take with her, no matter what happened.

The feeling that every secret was now revealed. And it was *all* true.

Cain,

I'm sending this to you without the Order knowing. I'm praying it gets to you or Remi.

It's time. I have the list. Thanks to Grim, I managed to compare the Archive notes to the information I had gathered. I have attached a map of where the crystal is located in Elderwall.

Destroy it. And run.

I will meet you at the train station after the Ball. Everything is in place. Be safe.

Love,

Father

"I thought I would find you here."

Grim looked up from her sketchbook. Ms White stood in the middle of the garden of shadows, looking around at the blooming summer flowers. Grim had been coming here every day since the rest of her friends had left to go home for the summer. Her parents hadn't wanted her home yet. They said they wanted more time to make the proper arrangements, now their *daughter* was leaving Elderwall for good. Grim was not looking forward to finding out what these arrangements meant.

"May I sit with you?" She asked, turning towards the bench. Grim nodded, and Ms. White walked over, heels clinking on the stone, and took a seat with the same level of grace as always. She leaned over and looked at what Grim was sketching. "Wonderful work, you've come along well."

"Thank you," Grim replied, putting down the pencil. "Is there something you need?"

"Always straight to the point aren't you?" She chuckled. "Yes, actually. Your parents are ready for you to come home."

Her heart skipped a beat, irregular from the surprise. "T-they are?"

Ms. White nodded. "They told me that they had gotten what they needed to in order, so you'll be going home this week. It's all arranged."

"Huh."

It was a weird feeling. After the year she had here, it should have been a relief to be able to go home. But that didn't feel like a comfort. There was still the uncertainty, the unknown she would have to face.

"It's going to be very strange not seeing you around, or in my office." Ms. White added.

Grim frowned. "You'll have a new flock of students to contend with. Nobody will miss me, it's not like I did anything spectacular."

"It's funny you say that." Ms. White crossed one of her legs over the other and leaned backwards on the bench. "I found the most *curious* place in the library. A place, as I discovered, which was found by a student with no magick."

She felt her heart racing inside her chest and was ready to make up some excuse or some explanation.

But Ms White was smiling.

"Starching didn't even tell *me* about the Archives."

Grim remained silent as Ms. White continued to talk. "I'm not one to raise speculation or go wild on a conspiracy theory. But it's very clear the wall in the art room didn't collapse due to the poor structural integrity of the college."

Grim attempted to respond, but it came out as a muddle. "The building is very old…"

"That it is. The Order is very old too. We are rigid in our ways, with tradition at the foundation of everything we do.

I have come to realise that they kept many secrets from me. Because people are still upset I stopped being *Mr* White."

She closed her sketchbook as the Headmistress continued looking out across the garden. "The Order masks truth as lies. That's what I've noticed."

"Exactly." Ms. White replied with a slow nod. "And I hold no ill will to the people who decided to command their futures and right an ancient wrong. They have more courage than I ever had."

"And if those people…if they cause the end of the Order, would you still hold your opinion of them?"

Ms. White's smile softened. "Everyone would call them villains. I could call them a hero, but the world isn't so simple. But in my eyes, they would have done the right thing."

She stood up, looking at Grim. She offered a hand to her now-former student. "I wish you all the best that life can offer you, Grim. You will do great things, without needing the Order."

She shook Ms White's hand. As the headmistress turned to walk away, she called out one more time. "I thought you would like to know-,"

Ms White turned around. Grim smiled. "That I was able to use some magick the other night…with some help from my friends."

She paused for a moment, processing what Grim had told her. She returned the smile. "Well, colour me impressed. Excellent work."

Ms. White left the garden of shadows, and Grim opened her sketchbook once more. She picked up her pencil, and content in the place she had felt most calm, she began drawing again.

July

The place that Grim called home hadn't changed much while she had been gone. Her parents had left her at home while they went shopping. They left her with the task of unpacking her things, something they declared to be difficult for her. Still, as an adult, they commanded her like a child, but that was the typical routine at this point.

Grim's bedroom was more *her* than her room had ever been at Elderwall. The walls were a soft brown, like sugar. She had tacked her drawings and paintings to the wall. The carpet was a darker shade, worn from the years of youth, filled with smudges of oil pastels and chalk dust. Her desk still had her old textbooks on them. A combination of her college work and officially sanctioned Order books. Her old sketchbooks were in a drawer underneath the desk, next to paint tubes and brushes.

Her bed was already made, she guessed by her mother while she had been gone. Her red sheets, with white flowers, her patchwork quilt folded and tucked at the end of the bed. Her mother had arranged the pillows, a touch of the organised genetics that she had not inherited.

Grim's suitcase was open on the floor, and her wardrobe doors were open. Her brain was trying to be cognitive and organise everything. It felt strange to have to reconnect with what had become two different lives. She pulled out the pink dress she was *supposed* to have worn to the Equinox Ball. Minda had kindly returned it to her before she left. Minda had loved wearing it and gushed to Grim about how kind she was to lend it to her.

Grim hadn't talked with her parents yet about what happened, and they didn't know she hadn't worn the dress at all. She hadn't told them about her arguments with Lukas. The timing had never been right. But her parents had promised they were all going to sit down and make a plan and talk everything through. For now, though, awkwardness hung in the air like toxic gas.

She flung the dress onto the bed, thinking she would try and convince her parents to sell it. Then, not a moment later, she heard the doorbell ring. Grim climbed over her suitcase and went downstairs. Her footsteps stomped up to the front door. She kicked a few pairs of shoes out of the way, grabbed the pair of keys on the side table, and used them to open the door.

Lukas stood there, a small bouquet of yellow tulips in his hand.

Grim's blood went cold.

"Hey…"

He hadn't changed in the month she had last seen him, but that wasn't surprising. He was still perfect Lukas, with neat hair and an ironed shirt.

Her hands were shaking, and Grim gripped the side of the door, ready to close it. "I thought I made it clear I didn't want to see you."

"Can I come in? So, we can talk, at least."

"It's not unreasonable if we talk out here."

"I don't think it is. I *need* to talk to you, about Elderwall, and the Order…"

She hesitated. Lukas frowned, sighing. "Please, let me come in and talk to you. I can explain."

Grim stepped aside, holding the door open for him. Against her better judgement. Her willingness to give her oldest friend one final chance was strong. Straight away, Lukas walked into the living room. She locked the door and followed him.

"Wow, this room hasn't changed." He said, turning around and handing her the bouquet of tulips.

Her parents had designed this living room. A beautiful sky blue covered the walls. A rectangle blue rug covered the wooden floors in front of the ornate fireplace. The leather sofas had square pillows covering them. Family photos lined the walls, all posed in a studio. There was an open archway into the next room, which had become the kitchen. The fireplace was cold, not needed this time of year. Her parents entertained everyone here. On a small table near the door, next to a vase of flowers, the landline phone sat with a small red light flashing. Grim took the bouquet and put them on the arm of one of the sofas.

"What do you want Lukas?" She asked, refusing to indulge his attempts at idle conversation.

"I know we left things on a bad note before-,"

"I made it *very* clear at the ball that I didn't want to speak to you anymore. Say what you want to say, and then leave."

Lukas huffed. "Fine, I'll say it. What did you do that night when you left with Cain?"

Grim crossed her arms. "If this is some dumb jealousy thing you're leading to…"

"It's *not*." He replied, lying to himself. "Tell me what happened."

"Why do you want to know?"

He spoke through bitter teeth. "Because something *happened* that night. Everyone's hearing about it. A wall collapsed in the art room, and rumours are flying around."

"You think *I'm* involved?"

"No, Cain is involved, and he's dragged you into it." Lukas pointed at her with an accusatory finger. "I never trusted him, or any of his friends. Any of the people you chose to hang out with."

"Lukas, I am not doing this again."

Grim went to walk back to the front door, but Lukas grabbed her arm, holding it in a tight grip. He spun her back around. She stumbled, letting out a cry. "Let go!"

"You need to tell me what happened that night Grim. What they did, what…what *you* did."

She tried wrestling her way out of his grip, pulling away from him, but he held on.

"I don't have to tell you anything."

Lukas pulled her arm, trying to bring her closer. She tried to move at the same time and stumbled again. He took the chance and pushed her against the wall, his other hand pushing into her shoulder. She gasped, breathless as she banged the back of her head against the wall, denting the paint. Her arm was going numb. "Lukas, let me go!"

"NO! You need to listen to me!" As he shouted, he spat across Grim's face.

"What has gotten into you?!" She shouted, desperate. "Lukas, you're hurting me…"

As she said that, he relaxed his grip, but only a little. His eyes were burning with a rage Grim had never seen before. "I can protect you. Whatever happened, you can tell me. I still love you, in spite of everything."

"Nothing happened!" She was losing her breath; black edges were creeping into her vision. "And I don't love you! I made that very clear."

Lukas' hand moved to her neck, and he gripped her face. If the situation had been different, it would have been an almost romantic gesture. "We could have been the perfect team. But you had to choose *him*. Of all people." His tone changed; he was begging her. "You can change your mind."

His words confused her and she spoke in a panic. "I don't understand."

He simply shook his head. "Choose me. Please.

Her face was burning. Grim realised why. It was not from the pressure of the moment. She remembered Lukas was an Elemental. There was *fire* on his palm, smouldering flames that he was burning into her neck.

"Lukas! *Let go!*"

Then the phone rang.

Both of them froze. The piercing tones of the landline filled the silence. Lukas lowered his hands and stepped back, the realisation of what he did to her setting in. His face went white. Grim slumped against the wall, pushing herself onto her knees. She ignored the agonising pain she was in from the full burn Lukas had given her. She reached for the phone.

"Hello?"

A familiar voice crackled on the other end of the line.

"Oh, Grim dear, hello." Evelyn Lightchild's voice came through. "It's good to hear your voice. I'm sorry to disturb you sweetheart but…is Lukas with you?"

Lukas could hear what was being said and had a quizzical look on his face.

Grim took a deep breath. "Y-yes Lukas is with me."

She heard Evelyn's sigh in her ear. "I'm so sorry but, could you pass the phone to him?"

She met Lukas' eyes. The eyes she once trusted. She held the phone up to him. "It's for you."

Lukas took the phone off her and held it to his ear. His mother's tone changed in an instant.

"Lukas, you're at Grim's house?"

"Yes, I had to talk to her Momma, she-"

"Come home now."

"W-what?"

"You heard me. Lukas Lightchild, come home now. I raised you better than this. I've called the Order, get home NOW."

He froze in place. Grim heard everything and backed herself against the wall. "Now," Evelyn continued. "Give the phone back to Grim. I will see you at home."

Lukas put the phone back in Grim's hands. Without another word, he stormed out of the house, the door slamming behind him. Grim sat on the floor, phone in hand, shaking like an earthquake.

"Grim?" The phone crackled again. "Grim are you still there?"

She put the phone to her ear. "I-I'm h-here."

"I will deal with this. I am *sorry*. So, so unbelievably sorry."

"It's not your fault."

"No, it is. He heard about the collapsing wall, and I...I shared something about my past he didn't take well. But, between me and you Grim it was finally time he knew the truth."

"Evelyn I don't understand what-,"

"You don't have to say anything. Now, are you hurt; do you need me to call someone?"

Grim dared to touch her neck. She winced.

"Grim?" She heard Evelyn's voice again.

Her vision was blurring, the shock of everything catching up with her. She choked out a voice that didn't sound like her own. "He burned me."

"Oh my god." Evelyn's voice sounded tearful. "Go find cold water, now. Stay on the phone, I'm getting you some help."

My dearest Grim,

I think we have passed the point of pleasantries, don't you? The Equinox Ball proved that to me. When we first met, I thought you were just another blind yet unsatisfied devotee, who would follow the Order simply because you thought you had to. Over time, you changed, and you became somebody that I greatly admire. That I still admire, even as I write this.

I am writing to you discreetly for one reason only. I want you to come with us. You know all the secrets we do now, and I know you have always wanted to do the right thing. I like to think throughout this year, we have become friends. Maybe something more, but always friends. I feel a kinship to you I cannot ignore, and I pray somehow you feel it too.

It's not long now until we leave to destroy the other portals. It's going to be a wild adventure. I know we made a promise that night, but I will not be upset if you change your mind. I won't force you to be a part of this, but if you still want to be, then reply to this letter, and I will meet you wherever you need me to.

Find your own freedom, my dearest friend. Find courage in your own heart and do not allow it to be twisted. I trust you.

And no matter what, we will meet again.

Yours,

Cain

To Grim's surprise, within a few days, two Magus straight from the Order came by to take her statement on what had happened with Lukas. Ms White had joined them as well. They talked more to her parents than they did to her. She realised that was because they had already come to their conclusions.

"It's his first offence." The first Magus explained to her parents, while she sat on the sofa next to Ms White. "So, he's getting a strict warning, and orders to not approach you, or he will face the consequences."

"We will be keeping an eye on him over the summer." The second Magus continued. "And if *Ms* White is satisfied, he can return to Elderwall in September."

"Thank you so much for your help." Her father said, cheerful as ever as he led them to the door.

Once they had gone, both her parents sat down on the other sofa, looking at Ms. White and Grim. Grim, on pure instinct, touched the bandages around her neck. Lukas' palm had left a lot of tender skin, and a nasty scar. Despite the power they boasted, the Order didn't have anything magickal for healing. As such Grim dealt with the stress of a day at the hospital.

"Audrey…" Her mother began. "I don't know what to do."

Ms White gave a warm smile to Grim's mother. "Well, the good news is that this matter with Lukas is closed, and Grim wasn't seriously hurt."

Her father shook his head. "I don't know what you did to make him lash out like that Ray-,"

"Don't blame her Will." Ms White's statement was firm. "It wasn't her fault."

"Audrey is right." Her mother stood up, fussing with the yellow tulips which were now in a vase by the phone. Grim shuddered, looking at them. "We need to look to the future."

"Exactly, the future being what you're going to do now that you've left Elderwall."

Grim's mother sat back down. "Audrey, is there no way you'll have Grim back another year? Maybe she needs more time for her magick to come through."

"I don't think it's right for her. She would have to go through the Baptism again, repeat classes, and I know it's not something she wants." Ms. White turned her head to Grim. "We've talked about it, haven't we?"

Grim took a deep breath and looked at her parents. Their smiles showed patience that was wearing thin. "I don't think I can be a Magus."

It had been an unspoken truth that was at last acknowledged.

"Well…" Her mother sighed. "What are you going to do Grim? You need to do something fulfilling. Even without magick, you can still contribute to the Order."

"We can put in the good word for you, there may be some openings in the records department, or with the researchers." Her father explained, the gears in his head already turning.

"But I don't want that," Grim replied, trying to take charge of the conversation. "I could get a job somewhere else, save up some money."

"No." Her mother frowned. "Absolutely not. I'm not having my daughter become some washed-up *Mortal-*,"

"Delilah!" Ms White exclaimed.

"But it's true Audrey." Her father said, continuing his wife's sentiments. "We are a family who has served the Order for many generations. I do not want that legacy to end."

"Grim is an adult," Ms White replied. She nodded at Grim, which gave her a slight comfort. "Who can make her own decisions, and decide what's best for her. You two need to support that."

"She is an adult, yes." Her mother crossed her arms. "But she is still a Mortem, and there are expectations which come with that name."

Grim stood up from the sofa and walked to the door. Ms White stood up as well.

"Grim, where are you going?"

She knew they had reached a stalemate. There was no getting through to her parents when it came to matters such as this. They had a lot of love for her, but it was love for the person they wanted as their daughter. Not necessarily love for the one they got.

They wanted her to carry on the family name. She couldn't carry that name for them. If Grim had taken one thing from her time at Elderwall, it was choosing when to project her anger, and when to keep her head down and take a quieter approach.

"I need some fresh air." She mumbled.

"I'll come with you." Ms White went to the door with her. Her parents watched, disapproval re-emerging on their faces. "We'll be back in a moment."

A minute later, Ms White and Grim were leaning on the brick wall outside. Grim was focusing on her breaths. Inhale. Exhale. Seven. Eleven. Ms. White watched her for a moment. "It seems like you already have your mind made up."

Grim nodded, her mind thinking back to the letter she received from Cain. "Something like that."

"Penny for your thoughts, Grim?" She asked with a whimsical smile, looking up at the sky.

"Well, some friends have invited me to travel with them. Go on some adventures, see some wild places."

Ms White gave a knowing smile. "You know, that sounds like a wonderful idea. See the world, go somewhere that's green, and experience it with people who care about you."

Grim felt some relief that she had finally told someone. She had thought about it and hadn't replied to Cain's letter yet. She had hidden it inside one of her sketchbooks, knowing her parents wouldn't look. There was a reassurance in knowing that somebody didn't see it as a terrible idea.

"Have you told your parents?" Ms White asked as a moment of silence passed them.

Grim shook her head. "I don't even know how to begin to tell them. They would hate the idea from the outset." She chuckled. "I am half-tempted to make a run for it in the middle of the night."

"If you do, at least leave a note. I'll have to clean up the aftermath otherwise."

The two shared a laugh. Grim sighed. "I'll tell them. Now, I think. Will you back me up?"

"Of course. I'll make them understand as I did before."

August

Mother and Father,

Despite Ms. White's attempts to get us to communicate, I think
we can all agree that some things are better left to heal in
their own time. As I mentioned before, I am going to spend some
time travelling with a few friends I have made.

Please do not worry about me, and do not come after me. I am
old enough now to make this decision, and you no longer have
any control over me.

I know you wanted what was best, but you lost sight of what
was best for me a long time ago. When I come back, we can try
talking this through, but until you accept that I have changed,
and I will not try to become what you want me to be anymore,
we can have no relationship.

Still, I love you both. Look after each other, and I will see you
soon.

Grim.

Grim stood on the train platform of the small station in the next town from her. She had told Cain where she would be, and what train she would be getting off from. The time, the likely platform, all the details she could give him.

She held onto the straps of her bag, her suitcase wheels coming to a stop. The summer wind had grown cold with the evening air. The sun hadn't set yet, but it blasted through the sky on the open-air platform. Grim stood on the train platform and waited.

She couldn't steady her breathing throughout the whole half-hour train ride. Doubts clouded her mind, the worry of whether Cain would be there. This choice decided her future. Her actions were final. Her decision has changed the course of her story. She had left her life behind for the pursuit of truth.

In the hope that she could save the broken.

She heard footsteps coming up onto the platform. Cain emerged onto the platform, out of breath, placing a hand on the wall. He saw her and broke into an exhausted smile. They were the only two on the platform.

He walked up to her, and the two immediately pulled the other into a tight embrace.

"You actually came." He whispered into her ear.

She lifted her head off his shoulder. "What, did you doubt me or something?"

"A little doubt is good for the soul…" He stepped away from her, not letting go of her hand. He noticed the scar on her neck. "What happened?"

She shook her head. "It doesn't matter, I'll explain another time."

Cain's eyes lifted back to hers. "Are you ready? There's still time to change your mind. We're about to change everything."

"I know. I'm done being angry at this world, I want to do right by it for once. Let me help you change fate. I want to help the people we saw in those worlds." She smirked a little. "Plus, you said it would be a wild adventure."

He chuckled, and kissed her quick on the lips, making Grim flush red. Cain's cheeks were pink when they looked back at each other once more. "I promise you; it will be."

Cain grabbed her suitcase from her and continued to hold her hand as they walked to the platform steps. "My father's waiting in the car. Remi's coming over in a few days."

"Then the adventure starts?" She asked, smiling.

Cain nodded. "That's when everything begins again."

To the untrained eye, nothing special had occurred on the train platform. Except, for two people, who were close to each other, reuniting as one got off the train.

Nobody would expect it would be two people ready to take down their entire society. Ready to right an ancient wrong. One person who was so sure of themselves and what they had to do, and the other finally found their path to end it all.

Circumstances, in their fickle nature, brought people together at the point in their lives in which they needed it most.

Even though the Order had declared what their place in life was, that it was their right and their fate, it seems that fate has other plans. Sometimes the seeds of chaos and the attempt to make amends for a lifetime of empty promises meant that fate could change.

And to change fate? Well, that is one wild adventure.

To Finn and Anna.

I hope you don't mind that I'm writing this letter to both of you. but time is short and I'm out of paper. Besides. I know you had plans to spend the summer together.

I'm sorry that I've not been in touch. Things have...changed at home. and my relationship with my parents has hit a new low. I wasn't honest with you about what was going on. But I'm going to be going away for a while, and you won't hear from me. I don't want you to worry. I promise I'm safe and I'm with people you can trust.

I wish I knew what to say. I wish I could tell you but it's better if you don't know. Besides...I think you already know what's going on. don't you?

We'll see each other again soon. Take care of each other.

All the best.

Grim

Five years later

September

The Order were a collective group of individuals called Magus. They had advanced abilities that had helped to shape society and shape humanity.

The Order, and the Magus, had lost their magick overnight three years ago.

The reckoning was dawning upon them, as month after month they lost their abilities until there was nothing left.

Elderwall Boarding College, the prestige institution that trained the future generations of Magus, was now an abandoned building. Though there were government plans to turn it into a university, or some other building to benefit the masses.

The Magus didn't know why their magick had vanished. Everyone was scrambling for an explanation. That is until the Order had to announce that for centuries, they had been stealing magick from other worlds. What came next was a riot, a demand for the restoration of the portals. But the Order said there was nothing they could do. They told everyone they should decide to start planning for their return to a normal life.

This was the end for the Order and the end for Magus.

As for the reason? Nobody knows. The students of Elderwall still have no idea who was behind the Order of Chaos. But, they know that they made a promise to stop the magick. The culprits will fade in time. Every *former* Magus has declared the Order of Chaos the villains and the cause of their demise.

Grim Mortem hadn't thought about this for a while now. It still hit xem that xe were a part of this. It was baffling, to be honest. Purely baffling. Regardless, xe walked down the busy main street. Xe headed toward the library where xe now worked. Xe missed this, how alive the world was when nobody decided to tamper with it. Sure, it was still horrible and shitty sometimes. But it was still a world that was embracing the thrill of living, and xe couldn't fault anyone for that.

When xe had gotten home, xe had tried to sit down with xyr parents. It was an awkward discussion over tea. They spent the entire hour complaining about how difficult their lives would be now, and how Grim *must* get a fulfilling job like they plan to. Xe had stood up, and without another word, walked out the door. Since then, xe had no contact. Remi had kindly offered to let xem stay at their place while they worked everything out. That was when xe found a job at a library, and everything fell into place.

Grim hadn't spoken to Lukas. He had sent one letter to xem, moaning about his struggles. He said he would find it in his heart to forgive xyr if she talked to him again.

She was tempted to burn the letter. But, she didn't. She didn't want to keep being angry.

Evelyn told Grim Lukas still had a hard time accepting the truth. About everything. Even his own mother's involvement in the Order of Chaos. After all this time, she still called Grim every few months to check in.

In her own words. "Lukas is old enough to deal with it."

Xe checked xem phone while standing at the edge of the pavement, waiting to cross the road. That's when xe heard a familiar voice, one that xe hadn't heard in years.

"Grim? Grim is that you?"

Xe turned around and beamed. "Finn?!"

Finn smiled back. "Oh my god, it is you! Come here!"

Xe stepped towards xyr old friend, and they both pulled together for a tight hug. "It's so good to see you!" He exclaimed.

Finn had changed, which I supposed was good. He still projected that joyful personality of his. He had grown his hair out a little more, and there was a small amount of stubble on his chin. He was wearing a shirt and tie, which made his appearance match his age.

"You look…" Grim couldn't stop smiling. "You look well."

"So do you!" Finn laughed. For a moment, his eyes flashed to the now almost faded scar on her neck, but in an instant, he looked back up to her. "What are you doing here? I didn't think you lived around here- I thought you'd gone back home."

"Oh, long story." She rolled her eyes and giggled. "I'm staying with Remi for a bit. What are you here for?"

Finn pointed up the road. "I go to the university here! I'm studying law."

"Oh my god, *a lawyer*?" Xe burst with pride, but the shock was on xyr face.

"Yeah, yeah! It's cool. What about you?"

"I work at the library up the road. I was on my way for my shift."

Finn looked flabbergasted. "I go past there every day! I'm on my way to a lecture, can I walk you to work?"

"Absolutely!"

They shared a laugh, and both started walking up the road to the library. They couldn't stop talking over each other, catching up, and filling in the gaps that five years had left.

"So…Anna is studying chemistry?"

"She is *so* good at it," Finn explained. "Like it's a natural talent."

"Have you heard from everyone else?"

He thought for a moment. "Oscar still thinks we can get it back. There are some Magus who haven't gotten over it. Last I heard Minda was working in an office somewhere and found it more enjoyable than she thought. Starching has retired, and Ms White is working in a high school."

"Wow. That's great to hear."

"Yeah! What about Cain? And his friend Remi? Have you spoken to them?"

Grim smiled, and her cheeks went a little pink when xe thought about Cain. "I'm still close with them. Remi has a job in event management, and Cain is doing a mechanics course."

"To be fair he was good at getting into my locker when I needed him to," Finn replied with a laugh.

They reached the library and stopped by the door. Grim put xyr hands in xyr pockets and sighed. "Listen, Finn…I'm sorry for not reaching out sooner. I-,"

"Hey. *Hey.*" He put a hand on xyr arm. "You don't need to apologise. You had to go work things out. Plus, there was everything with the Order collapsing." He turned his other hand around as if trying to come up with the words. "It was a lot for everyone."

Xe nodded. "You seem happy, though."

"Oh yeah…you know when it first happened, I didn't know what I was going to do. I thought I had nothing going for me, and then I kind of realised…I have a whole new world open to me now. What I could do for myself was endless. We never needed magick. We only used it so we could feel better than everyone else so that we could be mightier than mortals. I appreciate everything I do for myself now. I like the normality. I like my little room in my accommodation. I like cooking, cleaning, and meeting friends after class. Maybe this is what it means to live, to be normal."

Grim swallowed, trying to hold back the tears forming. "I'm so glad Finn, you deserve it."

"And so do you. Everyone hated on you a bit too much for having no magick, I can see the appeal now." He smirked. "And besides…I have my theories about the Order of Chaos."

They looked at each other, and Finn had a sparkle in his eyes like he had connected something together. Grim shook xyr head. "One day, *someone* will tell you the story."

"I'll look forward to it. Also, I'm so glad I didn't have to do the blood pact."

"I freaked out when I saw that." Grim smiled. "I need to get started on my shift then, but we need to catch up again."

"Oh! You have a phone, right? I know the Order never caught onto them but-,"

"Yeah, I have a phone," Xe replied with a laugh.

"Let's exchange numbers."

They hugged one more time. "Wait! Before I forget." Finn exclaimed and pulled out his phone again. After a second of typing, Grim's phone vibrated.

Finn had added her to a group chat. There were three people, and she saw the first message.

Hey, Anna when you get out of your lecture…say hi to Grim :D

Grim grinned and chuckled at the message. Finn put his phone back in his pocket. "Ask Cain if he wants in next time, you see him. There's this amazing Korean BBQ place, Anna and I will take you there when you're next free."

"Sounds amazing. I'll see you soon Finn."

He walked off, and waved at xem, turning back to scream over the crowd of people. "Bye Grim!"

Xe laughed and headed into the library to work. Xe went into the staff room, hanging up xyr coat and bag, and xyr phone pinged one more time. It was from Cain.

Hey- are we still on for tonight? X

Turns out, no matter the passion of a kiss in a garden at midnight, closing portals across the world and dealing with the fallout of a magickal order collapsing means there is little time to talk about your relationship with someone. Cain and Grim agreed to wait. Until all the dust had settled, so they could try and see where their connection took them.

If love is anything, it's knowing that like a flower, it needs time to grow.

Xe tried to stop the fluttering in xyr chest.

It's a date x

Grim walked out into the library, to the familiar shelves. Everything was in its place and arranged so that everyone could find what they were looking for. There was a cart of books waiting for organisation, and with a nod to xyr co-worker, Grim got to work.

As they were sorting a shelf, a young woman came up to xem. This woman was wearing all black. She had dark brown hair and lilac eyes.

Grim stopped for a moment. A memory appeared. Or was it a dream? Xe could not remember. The magick that bound this world to others was fading, but Grim still sometimes had dreams of the other worlds she had saw brief glimpses of.

"Excuse me?" The woman asked, looking at her with a worrying frown.

Grim turned, shaking off her confusion to smile at the woman. "Hi! Can I help you?"

"Do you have any books about magic?"

Xe had to stop xemself from laughing too hard, but luckily it came out small and polite. "Not real magic I hope?"

"No, no!" The woman laughed back in reply. "I think I need a nice fictional story for once."

Grim nodded. "You were at the right end, but you need the next shelf over. They start at 242.5."

"Thank you."

The woman turned around and headed down towards the shelves. Grim shook her head, confounded by the strange encounter. But xe didn't want to worry. After all, there was no magick in this world any more.

The world could exist in the simple consistencies of beautiful normality. That was enough.

Grim went to bed each night with the comfort that those other worlds, and the people xe had seen, were safe. Their stories were not theirs to tell. There would never be a true ending to what grew beyond xyr, and xyr time here.

This was only the beginning.

<u>**Acknowledgements**</u>

To my Dad, who has read more drafts of Grim's story than anyone should legally have to. Thank you for reading every single one. This is the last one you're going to read now, I promise. Please, for the love of everything sacred, burn your copy of the first one.

To my other parental figures, thank you for putting up with your adorable little weirdo. I'm sorry that you must put up with my nonsense.

To Sam, you thought I was but an irrelevant trumpeter, but you will find I am most relevant.

To Morgan and Maisie, thank you for the Twilight movie nights.

To the rest of my family…buy my books.

To the brain worms Dorian and Wynn, thank you for all your encouragement and your constant screaming in support of my chaos. Also, I'm sorry for all the *"it's more likely than you think"* jokes I made in the group chat.

To Ian and Mich, thank you for your help with the final section, and making sure I used neopronouns respectfully. To the rest of the House…the moss connects us all.

To all my theatre friends, thank you for being my weekly joy.

And thank you again, for reading. This is just me living out my silly little dreams, but it means the world that people are enjoying them. See you in the next adventure.

P.S. Yes, my books are now connected in a multiverse. You're welcome.

About the Author

Emma (she/they) is an author, artist, jack of all trades and being of chaos. She is an absolute nerd (and proud of it).

Her published works are all independently produced. Yes, this means they are very tired.

When they're not writing, Emma is either in the theatre (both onstage and backstage) or in a cafe rolling a d20.

She can be found on Instagram, TikTok, Twitch, Twitter and YouTube if you search "PixieStarr"

They are aware that they are talking in the third person, and will stop doing so now.